JESSICA'S HERO

Durango Street Theatre – Book 4

Emily Mims

ALSO BY EMILY MIMS

Durango Street Theatre

Vivi's Leading Man

Maggie's Starring Role

Wade's Dangerous Debut

The Smoky Blues series

Mist

Smoke

Evergreen

Indigo

Emerald

Mistletoe

Violet

Ruby

Amethyst

Noelle

The Texas Hill Country series

Solomon's Choice

After the Heartbreak

A Gift of Trust

Daughter of Valor

Welcome Home

Unexpected Assets

Never and Always

A Gift of Hope

Once, Again

Other Romances

Season of Enchantment

A Dangerous Attraction

For the Thrill of It All

Boroughs
Publishing Group

www.BOROUGHSPUBLISHINGGROUP.com

JESSICA'S HERO
Copyright © 2020 Emily Wright Mims

ISBN 978-1-951055-61-5

To real-life hero, Major Brian Mims, an army officer and physician's assistant by trade, Brian spends much of his free time making prosthetic hands with his 3-D printers. He designs each hand individually to accommodate the recipient's particular needs. The recipients, most of whom are children, get to pick out whatever colors they would like to wear, and Brian always sends a doll or an action figure in a matching color so the children will have something to practice grasping. He's made over fifty hands, and has sent them all over the world. All the hands are donated free of charge (he pays for the supplies out of pocket and always wants more plastic for his birthdays and Christmas), and he says that the smile and wonder on a child's face the first time they pick up something with the new hand is payment enough.

ACKNOWLEDGMENTS

As always, this book was not written in a vacuum. I would like to thank beta readers Edwin Floyd, Sharon Middleton, and Troy Bernhardt for their time and valuable suggestions. Michelle, your input during our conversation early in the writing of this story is much appreciated. As always, my thanks to the Boroughs Art Department for a knock 'em dead cover.

A quick note: You can read Jack and Amanda Vance's story in *For the Thrill of it All*.

JESSICA'S HERO

Chapter One

Jessica sat back in her chair and fought not to roll her eyes. Loretta Fernandez leaned forward, her expression earnest. "I really think Jeremy would make a wonderful Curly, don't you? He has so much talent. Honestly, it takes my breath away."

"He's talented, yes," Jessica conceded to Jeremy's mother. "And I look forward to seeing him in major roles in the future. But he's only been with us for six months. And Curly's a bit of a big role for a six-year-old. Think of all those lines he'd have to memorize. As talented as he is, it would be too much to ask of him. So I don't think we'll be using Jeremy for Curly."

Loretta's face fell. "He's going to be so disappointed."

No, Mama Fernandez was the one who was going to be disappointed. Jeremy wasn't going to care one way or another. "Actually, Jeremy seems excited to be dancing in the ensemble. And of course, he'll be right on the front row. He's an excellent dancer and we'll want to take advantage of that."

Loretta perked right up. "He is, isn't he? So he'll be on the front row. That's good."

"And later, when he has more experience, he'll certainly be in the running for lead roles. He's quite talented."

"Well, if you're sure."

"I'm positive." Jessica smiled encouragingly. She sang Jeremy's praises for a couple more minutes, and with a sigh of relief showed Loretta Fernandez to the door.

There were days when being the Children's Academy director at the Durango Street Theatre sucked, and today was one of those days. Jessica shook her head and counted on her fingers. Loretta was the fifth parent today she'd had to soothe. As much as she appreciated the support the Durango parents offered, too often that support came with a boatload of unrealistic expectations. Like Loretta believing that a six-year-old could carry the lead in a full-length stage play.

Well, almost full length. The elementary productions were shorter than the teenage and adult shows. But most of the time it still took a nine- or ten-year-old to pull off the leads. At least Loretta had been polite. As of late, Letti Aldrete had become the stage parent from hell, and Jessica was sick and tired of the pushy woman.

She left the door to her office open lest she was needed elsewhere and sat down, taking a minute to look around at her brand-new office with gratitude and appreciation. She, along with the rest of the employees and volunteers of the Durango, had despaired last spring when the old theater and accompanying academy were bulldozed. She should've had more faith. Their fairy godfather in the form of businessman Miguel Abonce had purchased the old strip center in the Deco District housing the Oakmont Theater. He'd remodeled the vintage theater into a veritable palace for live community theater as well as converting one side into the Durango Street Theatre Academy, a to-die-for facility with large and small rehearsal rooms, and a huge mirrored dance studio. And the classiest office she'd ever enjoyed.

Thank you, Miguel.

She savored her new digs a couple more minutes before picking up the Academy budget printout she'd been looking at before Loretta's interruption. The Academy also owed a boatload of gratitude for the Harrington Grant and to the Navarro Corporation for their generosity. Between their largesse, and the tuition the more affluent parents paid, the Academy budget was healthy. It was teachers she was short of.

True love had cost her two of her instructors when they moved out of town with their boyfriends. A third lost her day job in San Antonio and had taken another one in Dallas. Her other instructors were covering some of the scheduled classes, and she and Artistic Director Rachel Castillo were covering the rest. But she needed to find new instructors, and soon. The parents were paying for top-of-the-line instruction for their children. Jessica was determined they get the quality they were paying for.

She put the budget printout aside and was going through a bunch of lackluster résumés in her email when she looked up to see one of her favorite people peeking around the corner with a smile on his face. "Wade. You're back." She jumped up and enveloped him in a huge hug. "Are you all better now?" Wade's appendix had burst the week after Thanksgiving, and he'd spent the entire month of December and his Christmas vacation recovering.

Wade hugged her back. "They decided on another damned round of antibiotics, but I finish those in a couple of days. I went back to work yesterday and am dancing well enough to audition for *Oklahoma!*."

"That's super. Is Owen auditioning also?"

"Yes. And I brought someone with me today I hope will also grace us with an audition." He stepped aside to reveal his companion behind him. "Brian, come meet Jessica Clary, our Academy director, and one of our most talented actresses, when we can pry her loose from her Academy responsibilities. And if that isn't enough, she choreographs a lot of the adult productions, including the upcoming *Oklahoma!*."

Jessica's eyes widened as the newcomer came into view. *Oh. Wow.* Six feet and then some of sexy male stood in front of her. Broad shoulders. Muscled chest under the tight t-shirt. Narrow waist. Square jaw. Sexy dimples. Dancing green eyes. And the reddest hair she'd ever seen that hadn't come out of a bottle.

God, what a looker.

And probably gay, if he was a good friend of Wade's. Jessica tamped down her enthusiasm. Still, the man was worth a fantasy or two if nothing else.

"Jessica, this is Brian Howard. He and I did a little theater together at A and M. He's the one who dragged me to my first audition and got me started in the theater in College Station. I'm hoping to return the favor."

"Glad to meet you," she said, smiling as she stuck out her hand.

Brian's eyes widened and he took her hand. "Well, hello there. I'm glad to meet you, too. Wade, you didn't tell me your Academy director was gorgeous. I was thinking more an old schoolmarm." His fingers trailed over hers for a moment as he gave her a once-over. She was glad that she wasn't dressed in her usual yoga pants and loose T-shirt, having opted this morning for figure-hugging skinny jeans and a lacy camisole.

"No. Twenty-five and as beautiful as they come," Wade said. "She works magic on stage with the kids."

"I don't know that I'd call it magic," she protested. "But the kids frequently surprise us with their talent. So you're an old college buddy of Wade's?"

"We had an engineering class together. I said something about doing a show and Wade mentioned that he'd done a production or two in high school. So my girlfriend and I shanghaied him. Wouldn't take no for an answer. He got a part right off the bat and was active in the theater until he graduated."

"And aren't we glad," Jessica said. "So will you be joining us for auditions Sunday?"

"Based on the warm reception I've gotten from everyone this afternoon, that would be most likely." He gave her a sexy smile and another appreciative once-over before disappearing with Wade.

Jessica sat down in her chair with a thump. Well, that was interesting. Brian Howard was one gorgeous tall drink of water. That smile would have every woman at the Durango hyperventilating. He must be talented or Wade wouldn't be trying to recruit him. And from the way he was checking her out and flirting with her, she guessed he wasn't gay, or was bi.

How *very* interesting.

She went back to the résumés and tried to read them over, but Brian Howard kept creeping into her thoughts. His smokin' hot body. His dancing green eyes. His eye-popping red hair. His impossibly sexy smile. In all honesty, she hadn't been this taken with a man in a long time.

Not since good-looking rookie cop Robby Clary had smiled at her for the first time seven years ago.

She forced her thoughts back to the résumés and was about to call one of the applicants when Letti Aldrete stuck her head in the door. "Have a minute?"

Jessica groaned inwardly. *Like I have a choice?* "Sure. Come on in."

Letti walked in and plopped herself down in the chair across from Jessica. "I want Sophie to have the Ado Annie role in the teen production," she said without preamble. "She'll be perfect in the role."

"Ya do, huh?" Jessica steepled her fingers in front of her. "Whatever happened to the process of trying out and earning the role?"

"She's the best mezzo soprano you have in the teenage company and you know it," Letti shot back. "By all means, hold the tryouts. But remember, the Navarros expect quality. And my Sophie can deliver that quality."

Jessica cocked her head. "I'm sure they do. And they will get that level of quality, no matter who is eventually cast in the role," she added tartly. "At the same time, the other parents, especially those paying tuition through the nose, expect a fair audition process. As long as I'm in charge of the Academy, that's what they'll get."

"But Sophie *needs* that role," Letti protested. "She's trying to build her résumé for a college with a strong acting program. Boston University or Carnegie Mellon, or New York Film Academy, or someplace like that. The more leading roles like Ado Annie she plays, the better that résumé is going to be." Letti leaned forward. "She's going to have the chance at Hollywood and stardom that I didn't get, by God."

"And she will have that chance, whether she is cast as Ado Annie or not," Jessica said calmly. "But I still have to be fair to the other kids, Letti. She's not the only one trying to build a résumé."

"*She's* the only one with enough talent to make it professionally. And everybody in the theater knows it." She threw up her hands. "Fine. Whatever. Do what you think you have to do."

"Thank you. I'll do that."

Letti graced Jessica with an "f-you" look and stomped out of the room. Honestly, the woman was impossible these days, and had only gotten worse since her ex-husband had taken up with Wade. Letti's determination to see Sophie in a fancy acting college had become damn near an obsession. Normally, Jessica would dismiss such a confrontation with no further concern. But Letti, a theater professor at the local university, was directing *Oklahoma!*, and as choreographer, Jessica would be working closely with the overbearing woman.

She placed a call to the first potential instructor, only to learn that the woman had already taken an evening job that paid more than Jessica could offer her. She left messages with two more potential faculty members and was about to call her mother and check on Bobby when her phone rang and her sister's name flashed on the screen. Jessica hit the answer button with trepidation. "How ya doing, Heather?"

Her sister paused before answering. "Okay, I guess."

Which wasn't the answer Jessica hoped to hear. "Okay, I guess" was Heather's shorthand for "Not good, but not admitting it."

"Just okay?" Jessica asked softly. "Tell me, sweetie."

Heather was quiet for a minute. "Mike's mad at me again. He found a bottle of pills I hadn't opened. He thinks I should have been taking them."

"I doubt Mike's mad at you," Jessica said soothingly. "But he is probably frustrated, and I know he's worried. Heather, Dr. Kowalski wouldn't give you those pills if you didn't need them."

"But they make my head all thick inside. Like I have cotton stuffed in my brain," Heather complained. "Honestly, I'd rather go back to bed."

"You can't do that," Jessica reminded her older sister. "You have to take care of Kinsey."

"I know that," Heather said defensively. "I'm taking care of her fine."

Yes, but for how much longer? How much longer before the depression became so overwhelming Heather couldn't care for her daughter anymore?

"I know you're caring for her. And doing a good job of it." Jessica paused a minute. "Are you busy this Sunday? Would you and Kinsey like to go somewhere for an early supper with Bobby and me? We can get hamburgers or pizza or something the kids would like."

"I—I guess so. If it's not too cold or raining or something."

"Doesn't matter what the weather's doing. There's plenty of indoor stuff we can take them to. We have tryouts for *Oklahoma!* at one on Sunday but that shouldn't take but a couple of hours. Bobby and I will come by the house and pick you up afterwards. Okay?"

Heather mumbled something Jessica took to be affirmative and hung up. She took a deep breath and reminded herself her sister's depression was biological: a chemical imbalance that Heather had no control over. Part of her still couldn't understand it. Not completely. Her sister had what other women only dreamed of: a loving husband who cherished her, and their beautiful child. Heather lived in a lovely home, she didn't have to work, and she wasn't sleeping by herself every night. She wasn't leaving her child with Grandma every day and scrambling to pay her bills. Heather had nothing to be depressed about.

Damn. When Jessica started to feel like that about her sister it was time to take a break and indulge in some adult company, if there was still any to be had in the offices on the other side of the theater.

The shortest way to the offices was through the Academy. One studio flowed directly into another, with no hall connecting them. She began making her way through the maze of large and small studios. The large dance studio was filled with serious-faced middle schoolers, many wearing workout clothes they'd gotten for Christmas, learning the steps to the *Oklahoma!* dream sequence ballet. Their teacher, college dance major Melody Chasen, invited Jessica to say a few encouraging words about the difficult routine.

The high-school girls in the back studio seemed happy learning "Many a New Day" but she still stopped for a moment to share a word of encouragement with them and their teacher. Then, she cut through the back of the theater before reaching the makeshift suite of offices in the third building comprising the theater complex. Executive Director Josh Goldstein's light was off and his door closed, but she could hear feminine voices coming from Rachel's office, where she found Rachel with Development Director Maggie Gutierrez. Both ladies had their heads bent over what looked like architectural plans and neither of them noticed her. "What are you studying with such intensity this evening that you didn't even hear me walk up?" Jessica teased.

Maggie and Rachel looked up and blinked. "The new office specs," Rachel said. She motioned Jessica to a third chair. "Take a look. Our offices are gonna be almost as swanky as yours. Thank you, El Jefe."

"The Navarros to the rescue yet again? God bless those people." Jessica slid into the chair and ran an eye down the plans. "I know zilch about this. But if you say it's gonna be nice, I'm sure it will be. Is Miguel's company doing the work?"

"Who else? He's even getting paid this time," Maggie quipped. "At least a token payment. I doubt it's what he normally charges."

"That's good of him." Jessica sighed to herself. Miguel Abonce had bought the theater and done the most pressing renovations all to please his actress wife. "I wonder what it would be like to have a man love you that much, and to have the money to act on it."

"Don't know. Never been loved like that," Rachel admitted.

Maggie shrugged. "I imagine Kirby loves me that much. But rookie lawyers don't make that kind of money."

"Robby didn't either," Jessica said. "Cops sure don't make that kind of money. But he probably did love me that much," she said slowly. "In fact, I'm sure he did."

"You still miss him, don't you?" Maggie asked, compassion warm in her eyes.

"Sure I do. But it's not the kind of acute stab-me-in-the-gut pain it was in the beginning," Jessica admitted. "It's more of a *something's missing* every morning. It's been four years now. I guess I've gotten used to him being gone. Although sometimes the hurt comes back, smacking me in the face when I least expect it.

"Bobby asked me again this morning why he doesn't have a daddy like his cousin Kinsey does. I try to tell him that he did have a daddy, but that his daddy's now in heaven. That's not getting anywhere with him. He said if his daddy loved him, his daddy would come home at night like Uncle Mike does."

"Oh, brother," Rachel breathed. "What do you say to something like that?"

"Not much I can say. Maybe when he's older he'll understand."

"Or maybe it's time for Mama to get out and find him a new daddy," Maggie said thoughtfully.

Jessica shrugged. "I've dated some. But most of the guys I'm attracted to take one look at Bobby and run the other direction."

"Then you're not dating the right guys," Rachel said. "There are plenty of good men out there who would be delighted to raise Bobby with you."

"Maybe. But I don't want to kiss any of them."

Rachel patted her hand. "He's out there, Jessica. I promise."

Or maybe he'd come by the theater this afternoon with his good buddy Wade.

It was way too soon to even be thinking about Brian Howard in those terms, she reminded herself later as she walked to her truck, the cold January wind whipping her ponytail back and forth. She'd seen him for less than five minutes. For all she knew, he was an incorrigible flirt and already had a girlfriend. He might not like little kids. He might have a thing against dating women who already had children. Or he might not have a thing in common with her.

Or he might, just might, be the answer to her every prayer.

Jessica got in the truck and started toward her mother's house where she'd find Bobby fed and bathed, and waiting in his pajamas to go with her to the starter home she and Robby purchased a few weeks before his death.

As she sped down the expressway, she went back over what she had learned about Brian during their brief meeting in her office. He was a graduate of Texas A&M. Except for the Corps of Cadets members who went into the military, A&M was known for cranking out farmers, veterinarians, and engineers: people who held nice, safe jobs.

Brian had met Wade in an engineering class and was most likely an engineer. He didn't get up in the morning and strap on a holster with a pistol. He didn't get involved with hostage situations or chase down criminals or defuse bombs. He made his living in a perfectly safe manner, building bridges and the like. His loved ones didn't have to sweat blood every time he left to go to work.

He would be a great boyfriend. A great Mr. Right Now. Maybe even a great Mr. Right somewhere down the line.

She sure hoped he would come on Sunday for an audition.

Maybe, he'd even ask her out on a date.

Chapter Two

Jessica swore out loud as the light turned yellow and the pokey old Oldsmobile in front of her started slowing down. "*Damn*, lady. You could have made that light and so could I. God deliver me from octogenarians going three miles an hour in old tanks."

Four-year-old Bobby let out with a peal of laughter. "Mommy said 'damn.'"

"Mommy sure did." She glanced in the rearview mirror at the laughing child perched in his car seat. "Sorry about that."

"Granny Jean says 'damn' isn't nice."

"Granny Jean's right," she agreed solemnly. Most of the time Jessica agreed with her genteel mother and emulated her mild-mannered ways. But poke-slow drivers brought out the worst in her, and always had.

Especially when she was running late. She pulled to a stop behind the old Cutlass, fuming and drumming her fingers until the light turned green. Thankfully the ancient car turned right a block later, clearing the way for a speedy glide down the Deco artery and into the parking lot of the Durango, already full of everything from pickup trucks to fancy sedans to the econoboxes driven by the young ensemble hopefuls. She parked Robby's old truck on the end and hoisted Bobby onto the gravel parking lot, the damp winter wind cold on their cheeks. "Mommy, look at all the rocks."

He bent down to pick up a rock. "No way, bud," she said as she grabbed his hand and started toward the back door. "You're not going in there dirty this afternoon." Or any other afternoon, if she could help it. Bobby had plenty of opportunities to get as grubby as he wanted to in her father's flowerbeds. Bobby wasn't getting dirty when he would be going into the painstakingly remodeled theater.

He made a token protest but was smiling by the time they reached the back door. They wound through the storage room and backstage areas before taking the stairs leading to the auditorium chairs, where a larger than normal group of hopefuls sat patiently waiting for auditions to start. Josh, Rachel, and Chairman of the Board Cameron Heiser sat conferring on the front row with clipboards in front of them. Letti, minus her usual snarky expression, sat with them, and Wade and his lover, Owen Aldrete sat toward the front, holding hands with the look of a couple who'd made love for most of the night. Jessica turned away, hoping her wince didn't show. The guilt that swamped her every time she looked at Owen, her husband's old partner, was unreasonable. She hadn't been the one who'd taken a reckless chance and gotten Owen blown up and scarred for life.

It was ridiculous to feel responsible for what her dead husband had done.

She looked around the auditorium again. The one face she'd hoped to see this afternoon was not anywhere in the room.

Brian had decided not to audition after all.

Beating back her disappointment, she waved at Wade, and he and Owen motioned her over. "How's my man?" Wade said, reaching for Bobby.

Bobby jumped into Wade's lap. "I got to come today. Aunt Heather made Granny Jean laugh. They had to go see her."

Wade and Owen looked puzzled. "Actually, Mom said that Heather sounded a little funny over the phone. They wanted to go see if anything was going on. She and I were supposed to take the kids out later this afternoon, but Heather called this morning and cancelled."

"Sorry to hear that," Owen murmured. Neither Wade nor Owen looked surprised. They were familiar with Heather's issues.

Owen looked up with a smile on his face. "How you doin' these days?"

"Fine. You're doin' better," she teased, gesturing toward Wade.

"I am. Why don't you bring Bobby over sometime for dinner with us? We're at Wade's place now."

"I'd love to. We'll pick a night we don't have rehearsal."

The men nodded. She sat down next to Wade. The invitation from Owen was a welcome surprise. After years holed up by himself, apparently he'd decided to join the land of the living again. Maybe they could have more than an email relationship. As comforting as that had been for her during the worst of her grief, it would be nice to visit with him face to face, despite the heartbreaking evidence of Robby's recklessness.

Rachel stood and the room quieted down. She gave her usual welcoming spiel and called up the first group of hopefuls, who sang and danced and strutted their stuff. Jessica smiled to herself when two Academy graduates outshone the others in the group. They would at least make the ensemble, if not a minor role.

Jessica auditioned in the third group. She had put down on her application that she would take any role. But she was hoping to play Laurey. When it was her turn to sing, she sang Laurey's "Out of a Dream," earning applause for her efforts. Then she requested the pianist play some of the dream sequence. Thanks to the ballet lessons her mother had insisted she take along with her other dance training, she could dance the sequence herself, rather than have them bring in a ballerina. They would probably still have to bring in a trained male dancer to dance Curly's part. She went through part of the routine, pirouetting and whirling as best she could with no partner, and earned applause again. As she made her way back to where Bobby sat with Wade and Owen, she spotted the face she'd hoped to see sitting to one side a couple of rows back, a lazy grin on his face as he gave her two thumbs up.

Brian had come.

She returned his grin with a quick smile and sat down beside Wade, but peeked around for another look to find him staring at her with another dose of the masculine appreciation she'd enjoyed when they met. Her face flamed, but she winked and gave him her best come-hither smile before turning back around. The A&M tee stretched across his chest and emphasized the muscles in his upper arms, and she wondered if his ass was as great as his chest. She looked forward to finding out when he went on the stage to audition.

Two more groups of mostly young hopefuls were called up before Wade, Owen and Brian's names were called, along with a couple more. Wade handed the almost sleeping Bobby over and the men trooped to the stage.

Bobby snuggled close and drifted off. Jessica settled in to watch the auditions. They must have decided to put all the hotties up there together, she thought as Wade, Brian, and Owen climbed up the side stairs. Wade and Owen were eye candy of the highest order, with sexy smiles and bodies to die for, and unbelievable talent. And

Brian, with his fantastic body, chiseled features, and lazy smile, had them beat by a country mile.

And he did have a great ass. Even in the shapeless sweatpants.

The pianist asked them what to play. Wade chose "All Er Nuthin'," one of Will Parker's songs. Owen sang Ali Hakim's "It's a Scandal!" and then at Josh's request, Owen sang Jud Fry's "Lonely Room." Then it was Brian's turn. With a voice that filled the theater, he belted out "Oh, What a Beautiful Mornin'" in a rich, velvet baritone that had everyone in the theater sitting up straighter. He finished that number and leaned over and whispered something to the pianist, who then started an instrumental version of the same song, only a bit slower and dreamier.

And he started to dance.

Jessica, and everyone else in the theater, stared in shock as Brian leapt across the stage in a perfectly executed *jeté*. He pirouetted and whirled, oblivious to the stunned audience as he danced with his imaginary partner. Her heart thudded in her throat as she watched. *Brian could do his own dancing in the ballet sequence.* They wouldn't have to bring in someone else to do the dance scene.

He just landed the part of Curly McLain.

He danced a few more steps before motioning for the pianist to stop. Rachel turned around and frantically motioned for Jessica to get up on the stage. Letti jumped up and took Bobby from her arms and Jessica practically ran up the steps, her pulse pounding. She didn't know what in hell Rachel and Letti were thinking. Ballet was always carefully, painstakingly choreographed. She and Brian had never danced together. Hell, they'd barely said twenty words to each other.

Letti and Rachel conferred for a minute. "We realize you have nothing choreographed," Letti said slowly. "We want to see you dance together for a minute. Make it up as you go along."

Yeah, right. She and Brian looked at one another. "I'm game if you are," he said slowly. "We can show them something."

He was right. They could do that. "I'm game," she murmured.

He turned to the pianist. "Play the same sequence you played for her by herself."

The pianist started in and Jessica began moving in time to the music, basically repeating the dance steps she'd done alone. But she wasn't by herself any longer. Brian was dancing right along with her, mirroring some of her moves and contrasting others, adding in an impromptu male accompaniment that worked wonderfully with her dancing.

She felt herself responding to his movements, their steps complementing as they followed each other's rhythms. Spontaneous and far from perfect, she thought if they could dance this well making it up on the fly, she could hardly wait to see what they could accomplish with her choreography.

The pianist finished the passage. Brian grasped her hand and led her to the front of the stage, where he pulled her into a bow for the clapping, stomping auditioners. Letti gave them a surreptitious thumbs-up. Rachel was beaming, and Josh smiled smugly at the two of them. "Thank you," he said to them. He nodded to the rest of the group. "Thanks to all of you."

Rachel stood and called out the next group. Still holding her hand, Brian steered her toward the steps. His hand was warm, his palm and fingertips lightly calloused.

"Nice job," he murmured into her ear.

"Nice job yourself," she said. "Where did you learn to dance like that?"

"That's a story for another time." He let go of her hand, his finger trailing lightly over her palm. "We'll talk later."

She followed Wade and Owen off the stage. Letti looked down at the still sleeping Bobby and shook her head, so Jessica left Bobby in Letti's arms and slid in beside Wade.

"I can't believe he can dance like that," Jessica whispered as the next group of auditioners trooped to the stage.

Wade's eyes danced. "Our Brian is a man of many talents."

Understatement much?

***

Brian fought to hide a yawn as the last group of hopefuls went through their paces. He was beyond tired, having pulled his regular eleven-to-seven shift and then responded to what turned out to be an easily resolved domestic dispute. The one-hour nap he'd given himself had turned into two and he'd almost blown off the audition. With the hours he worked, he had no business trying to do community theater again. But he was going back on a daytime shift in a couple of weeks, and if he landed a role he could stay on the day shift until the production was over.

Besides, it wasn't often that he got to dance with his dream come true.

He'd miss sleep for a month to get to do that.

He gazed across the theater at the back of her head. Jessica Clary. Twenty-five years old, and about five-three or so: shorter than most ballerinas. But she had the gorgeous legs that usually graced dancers, along with a compact, shapely body that spoke of hours at the *barre*.

Her hips, waist, and lovely breasts were in perfect proportion: her arms and neck were slender and graceful. And that face. Oh, that face. Fine-featured and delicate, with big blue eyes framed by long, dark lashes, Jessica was a natural stunner, including her long blonde hair.

He couldn't have dreamt a more perfect woman.

He wondered if she was as beautiful on the inside as she was on the outside.

There was only one way to find out.

He fidgeted impatiently while the artistic director gave her post-tryout spiel, barely noting that he would receive a call or email to tell him of their casting decisions. When Rachel finally finished, he hopped up and made a beeline to Jessica, who was standing with Wade and Owen, only to stop in his tracks when a gorgeous fortyish woman he thought was the director handed a sleepy little boy over to her. His eyes narrowed as he eyed the child, who looked too much like her to be anyone but her son. He felt himself wilt inside.

His dream-come-true girl belonged to someone else.

Or maybe not. She wore a ring on her right hand, a bold diamond-encrusted flower, but her left hand was conspicuously bare. Emboldened, he continued his march toward her and the boy, who was waking up and didn't appear too happy about it. "It's okay, Bobby," she soothed. "You had a good nap. Do you need to go potty?"

"Boy's potty," the child said. "I wanna go to the boy's potty."

Jessica looked helpless as she turned to Wade. "He absolutely, positively refuses to go in the ladies' room these days. Do you mind?"

"Not in the least." Wade scooped up the child and headed up the aisle.

Owen's eyes danced. "With all the bathroom hoo-ha in the news lately—"

"Owen, he's *four*," Jessica protested.

"Never too young to state your preference," Brian said. He offered his hand. "Owen. How are you?"

"I'm good."

The men shook hands. He'd met Owen once before, when he'd run into him and Wade at the big New Year's Eve party downtown. He'd thought he'd heard Owen's name somewhere before, but damned if he knew where. He'd been mildly surprised to learn Wade was gay, but when he thought about it, he probably shouldn't have been. Wade's girlfriends in college had been few and far between, and he'd never dated the same girl for more than a couple of months. Wade was happy and Brian was happy for him.

He turned to Jessica. "You dance beautifully. Wade said you were choreographing the show?"

"What few dance numbers there are, yes. It's not like the work I did on *Anything Goes* last year, or what I'm doing on the teenage production of *Footloose*."

"But you'll be choreographing the ballet," Owen said. "And most likely dancing it." He glanced around. "You know you two are shoe-ins for the parts," he whispered.

"I would never presume to be that confident," Brian said. "I hope I get it, of course."

Owen turned to Jessica and she smiled and nodded once. She clearly thought they'd earned the roles.

Maybe she was right.

Josh Goldstein, the young man Wade had introduced as the executive director approached them with a smile on his face. "Thank you for auditioning." He held out his hand to Brian. "We're always interested in new talent."

"Good to know." Brian shook Josh's hand. "That's not always the case."

"True, unfortunately." Josh turned to Owen and laid his hand on Owen's arm. "I have a hypothetical question for you."

"Okay."

"Would you be willing to play Jud Fry without the concealing makeup?"

"Hypothetical, my ass," Jessica said, wincing a little inside. Owen's injuries left scars that would make the creepy loner Jud Fry character all the more ominous.

"Okay, so it's not hypothetical," Josh said. "It was Letti's idea, but she thought it would be insensitive to ask."

"Letti didn't want me to say 'no' out of hand," Owen said dryly. He touched the cheek that was covered with scarring. "I—I don't know. I'd have to think about it."

"Fair enough. Let us know what you decide." Josh excused himself and wandered away.

Jessica hesitated a moment before speaking up. "I'd be self-conscious too about not wearing that great makeup you have, but if it wouldn't make you feel awkward, it would be perfect."

Owen nodded. "It would, wouldn't it? You know, I might do it."

They spotted Wade and Bobby coming down the aisle together, holding hands and smiling. "He's always loved kids," Brian murmured.

"And thank God for that. He's the closest thing Bobby has to a father figure," Jessica said. "My father's good with him, but he's Granddaddy, not Daddy."

A-ha. So Bobby didn't have a father. Which meant that Jessica was single.

This was getting better and better.

Wade handed Bobby over to Jessica, who then turned with the child. "Brian, this is my son, Bobby. Bobby, this is Mr. Brian. He's a friend of Mr. Wade and Mr. Owen."

Bobby held out a small hand. "Glad to meet you, Mr. Brian."

Wow. Somebody had taught this child some manners.

Brian squatted down so he was on Bobby's level. He took the child's tiny hand and shook gently. "I'm delighted to meet you, Mr. Bobby."

"I'm just Bobby. You're Mr. Brian. You're all grown up and old. Like Mommy and Mr. Wade."

Jessica winced. "Thanks, kid," Wade murmured, his eyes twinkling.

"I see." Brian fought a smile as he rose. "I don't know about you, but I could use an ice cream cone about now. Anybody else interested?"

Wade and Owen shook their heads. "My son has a basketball game at the church in thirty minutes," Owen said. "We're going to have to scramble as it is."

Brian turned to Jessica. "How about you and Bobby? You two up for some ice cream?"

Jessica looked down at her son. "You up for an ice cream cone?"

"Ice cream? Yay!"

She smiled at Brian. "Ice cream it is."

Chapter Three

"Is there any place close, or do we need to drive somewhere?"

"There is a lovely Fruteria down the block that does ice cream too. Bobby loves it there."

"The Fruteria it is, then." He motioned for her to lead the way.

She took her son's hand and together the three of them walked up the aisle. The lobby was deserted but for the artistic director having what appeared to be a lively discussion with the beautiful woman who'd held Bobby for Jessica. "I wonder what was that all about?" Brian asked as they left the theater.

"I don't know. At least it was friendly. Sometimes it's not, especially with Letti." She gestured down the sidewalk to the Fruteria. "I'm glad she's directing this time. She won't have an opportunity to get mad about the casting."

"What doesn't she like about the casting?"

"Letti insists on trying out for roles she's aged out of and then gets mad when they won't cast her. You'd think she would learn."

"Maybe she's sensitive about her age," he offered.

"Oh, my God. Your perception of the obvious is outstanding." He laughed a bit at Jessica's feigned amazement. "It's gotten worse since Owen, her ex, took up with Wade." Brian winged up his brow. "Now that I have your full attention, where did you learn to dance like that?"

"My mother owned a dance studio in Fort Worth. There were never enough boys to partner the girls, so guess who was drafted into service at the age of five. I danced for her until I went off to college."

"Hmm. Does that mean you can dance anything?"

"Just about. Got lucky with the singing voice. No formal training in singing or acting, but I did musicals all through high school and college, and learned as I went."

"What about afterward? If you and Wade are old college buddies, why has it taken you so long to make your way to the Durango?"

"I've only been in San Antonio for a year or so. I worked awhile in Fort Worth and spent a year in Austin. My job isn't particularly conducive to the demands of the theater."

"Lots of positions aren't. It took Wade a while to make his way to us. I'm lucky in that regard. I'm already at the theater when it's time to rehearse."

"That would be nice." He glanced down at Jessica, again marveling that she was so close to his idea of perfection. The cold wind wafted around them, teasing his nose with the fragrance of her light, woodsy shampoo. Her stretchy leggings and the polka-dotted tee shirt worn under a pink fleece were casual, but still showcased her dynamite body and delicate femininity. He could only imagine the treasures hidden beneath her unassuming attire, until he saw the real thing.

With the cold, damp wind and heavy clouds making hot cocoa more tempting than cold treats, the Fruteria was almost empty. They stepped up to the counter. The bored-looking clerk put away her phone. "What can I getcha?" she asked.

Brian turned to Bobby. "What would you like this afternoon?"

"That one," Bobby said, pointing to an ice cream concoction covered with strawberries and blueberries.

Brian turned to Jessica. "Believe it or not, he loves the fruit," she said. "A small one will be more than plenty."

"And you?" he asked.

"Caramel ice cream sundae. Unlike my son, I'm not that wild about fruit."

"That sounds good." He turned to the girl. "A small sundae with the berries, and two big ones with caramel." Before Jessica could object, he whipped out a twenty. "Keep the change."

Rather than protest, Jessica smiled gratefully. "Bobby, we need to tell Mr. Brian thank you for the treats."

"Thank you," Bobby said. He smiled up at Brian. "I love ice cream!"

Adorable kid.

It stood to reason. His mother was adorable.

Brian ushered them to a table near the window. They could see the clouds that hung heavy in the sky. "Looks like rain," he observed.

"My yard wishes."

"I wish I had a yard, period. The condo's nice, but it's all about concrete and a pool. The only reason I rented it was the extra room where I can put my printers."

"You need a whole room for your printers? Mine sits on a desk with room to spare."

"Oh, not that kind of printer. I'm talking about my three-D printers. I have four of them."

"You have four three-D printers? What do you do with four of them?"

"I make stuff." He reached in his pocket and fished out a four-inch-tall Marvel action figure. "I'd say this has Bobby's name on it. What do you think, Bobby?" He handed the action figure to the child.

Bobby's face broke into a smile. "Can I have it?"

"Sure."

"Wow, thanks. Do you have another one?" Bobby asked.

"Bobby."

"Jessica, I'll make him all he wants. I share a lot of them. With the young, and the not so young."

She raised her eyebrows. "Great gimmick to pick up women in a bar."

"I might have used it a time or two."

"But really. With four of them, you're printing a lot more than little action figures."

"I've printed a lot of things. I make Mom a new vase every so often. She loves them because they don't break. I made my niece a small ukulele. I didn't know it would really work until she posted a clip of herself playing it on Facebook."

"Vases and ukuleles. How industrious of you," she teased.

"I also make hands. I make a lot of those, actually."

Jessica's head snapped in his direction. "Hands? What are you talking about?"

"I make prosthetic hands. Let me show you." He whipped out his phone and scrolled through the pictures. "Here. I shipped this one off last week." He handed the phone over.

Jessica stared for a minute at the image of the blue and red Captain America hand on the arm of a seven-year-old. "Hot damn. You weren't kidding. You really do make hands. That is so awesome." She started scrolling through the pictures. "Wow. How many have you made?"

He had to think a minute. "Probably upwards of fifty. I'm part of a national organization that matches the kids, and sometimes adults, with a volunteer. They send me a picture of whatever their arm or hand consists of. I use that picture to make a digitized 3-D model of the limb and design a hand and arm specific to whatever they have to work with. The hand straps on either above or below the elbow, and I let the child pick out the colors for their hand. The boys usually want blue and red, something from an action movie. The girls like pink and purple and are more into princess and Barbie themes. I always send along a coordinating action figure they can practice grasping with."

"The arms work?" Jessica took a closer look at one of the pictures.

"They can't play 'Moonlight Sonata,' but they can anchor a peanut butter jar tightly enough to get the lid off. Mostly it's to get the child used to using a prosthesis so they'll have a feel for it when they grow up and get a sophisticated one. And it does wonders for their self-esteem."

"I know what you mean. It's already bothering Kinsey and she's only three."

"Who's Kinsey?"

"My niece. Her arm stops about two inches from where her wrist should be and she has no hand at all."

"I bet I could help her. Got a picture?"

"Oh, hell no. Her mother won't let her be photographed with the bad arm showing. Do you think you could help her? Oh, wait. How much does it cost?"

He held up his hand with his finger and thumb shaped into a zero. "I donate everything. My family knows to get me printer plastic for Christmas and my birthdays."

"Wow. Aren't you something else? Using your engineering talent like that."

"I don't know about that." He didn't know what engineering talent she was talking about. "If you'll have your niece's mother get in touch with me, I'll see about making her something."

"You better believe I will."

The girl brought their sugary concoctions and they spent a few minutes in silence enjoying them. Then Brian steered the conversation back to Jessica while Bobby continued to eat. "You know all about my dancing and my hobby, and I know practically nothing about yours. How did you get started in dancing?"

"Mom put my sister and me in lessons from the time we were little. We did some competition dancing, but Heather tired of the whole thing and I got into singing and performing. I'd planned to go to New York or California to go to a fine arts college. But life intervened." She looked over at Bobby, her expression sweetly wistful. "I ended up a lot closer to home at Texas State for my fine arts degree. I majored in theater and dance. The degree has served me well."

"Is that how you ended up at the Durango?"

"I was doing a show two years ago when the dance school I was managing closed the same month the Durango's Academy director moved to New Orleans. It's been a match made in heaven. Most days, that is. Right now I'm short on instructors, which makes scheduling difficult. And we won't talk about the days when the stage mothers from hell gang up en masse."

"Stage mothers, huh? Challenging."

"You better believe it. But sometimes I look at Bobby and think he's the brightest, most talented kid in the world. Moments like that I understand where they're coming from."

"He's a great kid."

"Thanks."

"So what do you do all day?"

She took a few minutes to describe what sounded like an interesting job, hiring faculty and scheduling classes and recruiting students. "Some of our most talented kids are on partial or full scholarships," she boasted. "It's not a status-symbol academy for the offspring of the affluent. Although we have plenty of those also."

"Are those the parents who give you grief?"

"Mostly. But I have no trouble being firm with them. I'm not above reminding them I make all the decisions regarding Academy casting. That's usually hint enough."

"And your work on the adult productions. Is that also paid?"

"Nope. All the acting, mine included, is volunteer. It's a lot of time for free, but we all believe it's worth it. Once in a while I use a few Academy hours on the choreography." She paused a minute. "With the kind of time we spend together here at the theater, we become friends. Close friends. My best friends in the world are probably Rachel and Josh. And Vivi Abonce. You'll meet her sooner or later if you keep hanging around." She looked him in the eye. "Which I hope you will."

"I hope I will, too. Tell me. Does everyone stay in the friend zone, or does Cupid ever shoot his arrow?"

"Oh, heaven's yes. Cupid's arrow flies all the time. Sometimes in a direction it shouldn't." Her eyes danced. "A couple of years ago, one of my married daddies took up with one of the married mommies. You want to talk about awkward." She laughed. "But then, sometimes Cupid gets it right. Like with Wade and Owen."

"They seem happy," Brian said.

"They are," she concurred. "And I'm so happy for both of them." He didn't miss the wistful expression that flitted across her face.

"So it wouldn't be inappropriate for, say, a couple of co-stars to go out on a date sometime?" he asked, meeting her eyes boldly.

"No, it wouldn't," she replied. Her eyes widened and he held his breath. "I... I... Are you asking me for a date?"

"That would be exactly what I'm doing. My dear Miss Jessica, would you be so kind as to accompany me some evening for dinner and a movie?"

"Yes. Sure."

Hell, yes. "Super. I'll have to check my work schedule and see when they have me working. I'll give you a call later and we'll set a time. Text me so I have your number."

She got out her phone and he rattled off his number. In a moment his phone pinged. "There. I'll call or text you when I know something."

"Works for me." She turned to her son. "Bobby, are you about finished?"

"About." He popped the last berry into his mouth and scrunched up his nose as he chewed it. He threw up his hands and laughed. "All gone."

Jessica looked at Bobby with an indecipherable expression. "Robby did exactly the same thing," she murmured. "Sometimes it's spooky, how many of Robby's mannerisms he has."

"Mommy says I'm just like my daddy," Bobby boasted.

"Not so strange if he learned them from his dad," Brian observed.

"He didn't learn them from his dad. Robby died three months before Bobby was born."

"Mommy says Daddy's in heaven," the child told him solemnly. "She shows me pictures sometimes. I wish Daddy would come see me. The other daddies do."

"He thinks it's like being divorced," Jessica said under her breath. She turned to Bobby. "Sweetie, we've talked about this. Daddy misses you as much as you miss him. If he could come see you, I promise you he would."

"That's what Grandaddy Eddie says. Daddy was a hero. He died saving people."

Jessica turned to Brian. "Sorry. I guess it got a little heavy for ice cream."

"That's quite all right." He turned to Bobby. "Your daddy was a hero. That's good." He leaned over. "Sometimes I get to be a hero, too."

"You do?" Bobby asked.

"I do." He looked from Bobby to Jessica, who was staring at him. "I'm a policeman. I'm on the SWAT team. That means we save people sometimes."

"Like Daddy?"

"I guess so."

"Robby was on the bomb squad," Jessica said, her tone flat. "He was killed in the same explosion that injured Owen Aldrete." She looked at Brian with eyes that were shuttered. "So you're a policeman."

"Sure am. And proud of it." Brian felt the little punch of pride he always felt when telling people his profession. He enjoyed the looks of admiration and the occasional "Thank you for your service" that was usually forthcoming. And it was a great pick-up line in a bar when he wanted to impress a woman.

But to his puzzlement, Jessica was looking at him with, if he didn't know better, disappointment. "I see," she said quietly. She looked at her watch. "Wow. I didn't realize it had gotten so late. Bobby and I need to get home so I can put something on for dinner." She stood and practically jerked Bobby out of the chair. "Thank you for the ice cream. We enjoyed it." She hustled Bobby toward the door.

What the hell? Within the space of a minute, something had happened, but he'd be damned if he knew what. Brian jumped up and beat her to the door. "I'll walk you back to your car."

"Okay."

They started down the sidewalk. He asked a question about the usual rehearsal schedule and her reply was brisk, making him think she really did need to get home. After she settled Bobby into his car seat, she turned around with what looked like sincere regret. "Maybe us going out on a date isn't such a good idea," she said slowly. "My sister usually keeps him for me, but she's been having some issues lately and I don't want to bother her."

No way, dream girl. Brian knew a brush-off when he heard one, and she wasn't getting away with it. "I bet his grandmother wouldn't mind keeping him for an evening," he said smoothly. "Sounds like she keeps him a lot for you already."

"Which is why I hate to impose on her for a date. Dating's different when you're a mom."

"Then we'll adapt to whatever that difference is. You promised me a date and I'm holding you to it. If we have Bobby in tow, that's fine. We can do McDonald's and a Disney movie. But you and I are going on that date, one way or another."

He leaned over and kissed her cheek before she had time to respond. "I'll call you and we'll pick a day. See you soon."

He walked away before she could answer.

He felt her eyes on him as he walked to his truck. His cocky grin faded as he drove out of the parking lot. She had shut down faster than a B-movie with bad reviews. He didn't know why. They'd been getting along like a house on fire. Then her husband had come up in conversation and suddenly all she wanted was to beat a hasty retreat. Something about that conversation had her running for the hills.

Brian put on his blinker and turned the corner. Maybe she was still in love with the poor bastard. Not that he blamed her, especially if the man had died a hero. But that wasn't going to do her much good at this point with him four-plus years in the grave.

Brian was alive with healthy appetites. He wanted to get to know her, spend time with her, hold her hand, kiss her, and so much more. He'd had enough of short-term dating, and was looking for something meaningful. They'd connected, and he knew she felt it, too.

She needed to take that first step. She needed to go out on a date with him and let him show her life could be fun again.

She needed to give him the evening she'd promised him so he could give her a reason to come back for more.

Chapter Four

Jessica pulled out of her parents' driveway and headed down the street toward her sister's home, three exits down the expressway. It was a couple of hours before she was due at the theater, but she'd already dropped Bobby off at her mother's where she'd shared an early lunch with her worried parents. "Please talk to your sister," her mother had asked. "You're the only one she'll listen to."

"We were over there for two hours on Sunday, and she didn't hear a word we said," her father added, his voice shaking. Eddie Herrmann was a retired cop and could face down the toughest of criminals, but Heather's issues reduced him to tears. "She refuses to take her pills. She won't do anything the doctor tells her to do. I'm scared, Jess."

She'd told her parents of the cancelled dinner date with the kids, which alarmed them. So here she was, making an unannounced call on her older sister, who most likely wouldn't welcome the visit. But somebody needed to get through to Heather, and Jessica knew she was the best bet.

She and her sister shared a special bond, born of too many anxious nights when their father had been on the job, working with the gang unit or some other equally dangerous assignment, and their mother had spent the evening drowning her worry in too many mojitos. Thankfully their father had retired from the force and their mother had cleaned up her act, but the sisters' closeness remained. Occasionally, Jessica resented Heather for the anxiety she caused others, but most days, like today, Jessica was worried and wanted to help her sister.

Maybe Heather would perk up when she heard about Brian's offer to make Kinsey a prosthetic hand, which would open up another can of worms—this one for Jessica. How was she going to ask him to make her niece a hand and at the same time turn him down for the date? It had been two days since auditions, two days since she'd gone out for ice cream with the dreamiest man to come her way since Robby, only to find out that he was not only a policeman, but on the SWAT team. Which made him completely, totally, and entirely off limits. She'd honestly thought he was an engineer, having gone to college with Wade, and designing prosthetic hands. It had stunned her to her core to discover that he held an even more dangerous job than her late husband had. Robby defused bombs. Brian rushed toward people who were shooting at him.

Crazy and unacceptable.

She would be crazy to get involved with him.

But it was damned disappointing. She'd actually shed a few tears on the way home that afternoon, quickly wiping them away before Bobby could see them.

This was the second daredevil man she'd been insanely attracted to. She'd wondered more than once if there was something in her makeup that made reckless thrill-seekers her thing. Maybe it was the role model she'd grown up with. Her father wasn't exactly a by-the-book kind of police officer. He'd taken his own share of chances, earning nearly as many reprimands as commendations during his years on the force. Whatever the cause, she was determined not to give in to the attraction she felt for Brian Howard.

She would hold out for a handsome accountant. Or a sexy schoolteacher. Or *anybody* who didn't put his life on the line as his job.

She couldn't risk once again going through what she had when Robby died—having her heart ripped out and back to being a single parent. Robby had died a hero. The department and the mayor's office had played up that Robby had died trying to save a mother and her child. Officially, no one mentioned Robby's recklessness. The only other person who knew for a fact that Robby didn't have to die was Owen, Robby's partner who'd survived, but was seriously scarred. Owen had kept his friendship with Jess alive, but in her heart she knew he blamed Robby for the scars, the loss of his eye, and his career.

She'd heard the comments about "Reckless Robby Clary." *He acted too quickly. He was careless. He should have waited. He should have given Owen a little more time. He always did love to take chances. He earned his nickname this time, didn't he?*

Nonetheless, policemen and other first responders had lined the street in front of the funeral home and for another four blocks, their uniforms crisp and their badges gleaming. The funeral procession, with nearly two hundred squad cars and other first-responder vehicles from all over the state, had snaked through the city and down the highway for miles to the Clary family cemetery outside Comfort.

A scholarship fund had been set up for Bobby's education. The department had awarded Robby posthumous medals for bravery and service. He had been given every honor the department and city could bestow on a fallen officer.

But nothing could bring him back. All those well-meaning people had been supportive, but they went on with their lives while she had to go through her first pregnancy alone, and raise a boy who'd never know his father.

The light changed and she pulled onto the artery intersected with the expressway.

Knowing the DNA that made first responders run toward danger was nothing she could change, even if she was so inclined. The best thing she could do was to stay as far away from Brian Howard as she could. No matter how appealing he might be.

She pushed all thoughts of Robby, Owen, and Brian aside as she pulled into Heather's driveway, parking behind her sister's two-year-old crossover. Of late, the once-cheerful house had taken on forlorn air, with a yard that needed mowing, and trim that could use a fresh coat of paint. Kinsey's little pink tricycle sat in the grass and had been there for a while, if the layer of grime and dust that coated it was any indication. Jessica wondered when Kinsey had ridden it last, or if the child and her parents had given up on her learning to steer it with one hand.

Jessica might have to go on that date after all. Kinsey needed Brian's help too badly to risk pissing him off.

She rang the doorbell twice and then knocked as loudly as she could. She was beginning to get alarmed when she saw the front curtains twitch and her niece's face peering through the folds. The little girl smiled and waved through the glass, clearly glad to see her.

There was no sign of Heather.

Jessica pulled out the emergency key to her sister's front door and let herself in. Kinsey launched herself at Jessica, grabbing her around the knees, her grip surprisingly strong for having one hand. "Hi, Aunt Jess."

Jessica leaned down and hugged the pajama-clad child. "I'm glad to see you, little one. Where's Mommy?"

"She's still in bed."

Still in bed? It was noon. "Have you had breakfast?" she asked more sharply than she intended.

"Mommy gave me Cheerios and went back to sleep."

Kinsey led Jessica into the spacious great room where a children's channel played softly on the big TV screen. She pointed to a bowl of dry Cheerios on the floor. Jessica tried not to be appalled. Bobby had eaten dry Cheerios for breakfast more than once. But he hadn't done it in his pajamas in the middle of the floor while his mother slept.

Things had reached critical.

Jessica strode down the hall to the bedroom Heather shared with her husband Michael. Finding that bed empty, she sucked in a breath and started back up the hall, stopping when she heard a soft snore coming from the guest room. Heather was huddled up in the fetal position under the covers, her nose barely visible as it poked out from under the comforter. Jessica stifled a groan. Sound asleep with a three-year-old running around the house unattended.

This was worse than anything she could have imagined.

She shook her sister's shoulder. "Heather. Wake up."

No response. "Heather," she said, more sharply this time.

Her sister blinked and turned groggy gray eyes toward her. "Wha'cha doing here?" Her long, ash-brown hair was tangled around her face and in need of a shampoo.

"I came to check on you. Mom and Dad are worried."

"Shit." Heather turned over and pulled the covers over her head.

"You need to get up, Heather. It's time to make lunch for Kinsey."

"Don't be stupid. I gave her breakfast a few minutes ago."

"Heather, it's noon."

"Noon?" Heather sat up and looked around frantically. "It can't be noon. I laid down for a ten-minute nap."

"Yeah, well it's noon."

"Well, hell." Heather pushed herself out of bed, her movements slower than usual. Jessica looked at her sister's eyes. She didn't appear to have been drinking or indulging in any of the illegals she'd dabbled in during her teenage years. "No, I haven't taken anything," Heather said crossly. "Only those pills Dr. Kowalski thinks are so damned wonderful."

Maybe Heather was right about the pills.

"Don't you have to be at work today?" Heather asked.

"I don't have to be there for a couple of hours. If you'll get a shower and wash your hair, I'll get Kinsey dressed and fix something for you to eat."

Heather shrugged and headed toward the en suite bathroom in the master bedroom. Jessica found Kinsey munching on the last Cheerios and found her a pair of jeans and a pink tee with sequins. The refrigerator had little in the way of staples, but was full of takeout cartons with half-eaten meals inside. She went through the cartons, keeping what still looked edible and tossing the rest.

Jessica finally put her hands on a package of sliced cheese and found a loaf of frozen bread. Heather reappeared a few minutes later, her hair freshly washed, dressed in jeans and a pink tee similar to Kinsey's. As Jessica plated grilled cheese sandwiches for Heather and Kinsey, she said, "Here. Sit and eat." She pushed Heather's plate across the counter and seated Kinsey in her booster chair at the kitchen table.

Heather picked up her plate and sat down next to Kinsey. "What do you want to drink?" Jessica asked Heather as she poured Kinsey a glass of apple juice, the child's favorite.

"Some of the same, I guess."

Jessica emptied the apple juice carton into a glass for Heather and threw the carton in the trash. "From the looks of the fridge, you're due a trip to the grocery store."

"I'll have to do that. Or maybe Mike can do that on his way home from work. *If* he comes home from work. That's all he does lately," she added bitterly.

Jessica didn't answer. Mike did work a lot, putting in hours of private duty directing traffic and providing event security on top of his long hours on the PD. Ostensibly he was doing it to save money for a down payment on a larger home, but Heather thought he did it to get out of the house, and sometimes Jessica agreed with her. But she wasn't about to sympathize and fan the flames of an already bitter dispute in the Werner household. Part of Jessica understood all too well. She wouldn't want to live with Heather, either.

It was time to do something productive. "Do you want to make a grocery list for whoever does the shopping?" Jessica asked.

"I guess I better."

Jessica handed Heather a notepad and pencil. She stood at the open refrigerator and named off the items Heather was out of. Her sister nibbled at her sandwich and listed the items Jessica suggested. They did the same for the dwindling pantry items. "That's quite a list," Jessica observed as she sat down at the table. Kinsey had finished eating awhile back and was again parked in front of the television set.

"Sorry I backed out on you Sunday. I wasn't up to facing the world. Mom and Dad came over and did their hand-wringing routine." She laughed bitterly. "I should have gone with you. It would have been a lot less stressful."

"Probably. But I did have an interesting afternoon after the auditions. One of Wade's friends took me and Bobby out for ice cream. Nice guy. It's a shame I won't be going out with him."

"Yeah. Not much point in dating gay dudes."

"Brian is anything but gay."

"So why aren't you going back out with him? He an asshole? What's the problem?"

"He's a cop."

"Oh."

"SWAT and proud of it. He actually bragged to Bobby that he's saved lives."

"Maybe he wasn't bragging. I have no doubt that he does save lives." Heather thought a minute. "If he's on SWAT, he probably knows Mike."

"I hadn't thought of that. I was so damned disappointed when he said he was SWAT that I shut down. He's the best looking, nicest man to come my way since I slipped Robby my phone number, and he's another damned cop."

Heather shrugged. "No law says you can't take up with another cop. Dad's a cop. Mike's a cop. It seems to be a family tradition."

"It's a tradition I will be proud *not* to uphold," Jessica said firmly. "One was enough."

"I hear that," Heather echoed. "I feel the same way and mine's not even dead yet. It scares the shit out of me sometimes, especially when they come on the news about a SWAT thing."

Jessica winced. "But I might have to go out with him at least once, if I want him to make Kinsey a hand."

Heather reared back like she'd been slapped. "What are you talking about, making Kinsey a hand?"

"He makes prosthetic hands and arms on his home printers. He's made a ton of them. Let me see if I can find a picture or two." It took her a couple of minutes, but once she entered the name of the national organization and "San Antonio," Brian's website popped right up. She found the picture of the little boy with the Captain America hand. "What do you think?"

"It doesn't look like a real hand."

Jessica rolled her eyes. "Of course it doesn't. That's not the point. The hands work, Heather. She could hold a tricycle handle and open a jar."

"She could?"

"She could. She could get used to wearing and using a device, so that someday, when she's old enough for a professionally made one, she's already proficient. Or she might continue to use something similar. He's made them for adults, too."

Heather studied the pictures. "It would be worth looking into. How much do they cost?"

"He donates them."

"Sounds like a really super person. Too bad you've sworn off cops."

"Yes, and no."

They both turned as they heard a key in the lock and Mike stepped in. His face was drawn and bags rode under his tired blue eyes. His blond hair was windblown and his uniform and shoes were covered with construction site dust. Heather's eyes narrowed as Kinsey ran toward him. "Daddy! You're home!"

Mike leaned down as Kinsey leapt into his arms. "Missed you, baby." He hugged her and stood with her in his arms. "Mornin', Heather. Jessica, good to see you. Is there anything I can eat for lunch? I need to grab a few hours of sleep before I have to go back to work."

"There would have been if you'd gotten here in time," Heather said snidely. "And it's not morning. It's already afternoon."

Jessica flinched at both Heather's tone and the look that crossed Mike's face. "Maybe if I wasn't out trying to earn the money to buy you that bigger house you think you need, I would have been here." He put Kinsey down.

"Bullshit. You don't want to come home anymore," Heather snapped.

"Mike, there's plenty of bread and cheese. I can make you a couple of sandwiches," Jessica threw in quickly before Mike said something to escalate the quarrel.

Mike looked from her to Heather and quickly sized up the situation. "That would be much appreciated," he said quietly. "Do I have time to take a shower?"

Jessica nodded. Mike trudged toward the bedroom. Heather jerked up the grocery list. "Kinsey and I are going to the store." She grabbed coats out of the entry closet for her and Kinsey. The front door slammed a minute later.

Sighing, Jessica assembled three sandwiches out of the last of the bread and cheese. She put them on to grill when she heard the water go off in the bathroom and had the sandwiches dished up and ready when Mike returned, wearing flannel pajama pants and a baggy tee shirt. "What would you like to drink?" she asked as he devoured half of the first sandwich.

"Something without caffeine. I need to get a little sleep." He looked around. "Where's Heather?"

"She and Kinsey went to the grocery store. I helped her make a list." She peered in the fridge. "Everything in here has either caffeine or alcohol. Ice water do?"

"Ice water's fine." He ate the rest of the first sandwich. "I'm sorry you had to see that. We usually try to keep our squabbles private." He looked at her shrewdly. "So what prompted your impromptu visit?"

"Mom and Dad were worried. They sent me over here to 'talk some sense into her.'" She made air quotes with her fingers. "Heather was asleep when I got here and Kinsey was in her pajamas eating Cheerios on the floor."

"Good God damn. Kinsey could have gotten into anything. Maybe I should have been here."

Jessica shook her head. "I'm not touching that one with a barge pole."

"I appreciate that. I know I'm gone a lot. But she swears she would be better if she had a nicer house. And I'm trying to make that possible."

"She said the pills were making her sleepy."

"They may be." His eyes were troubled as he looked at Jessica. "What do I do? She's getting worse. I'm worried sick about her, and now I'm scared I can't trust her alone with Kinsey."

"I'd say the first thing would be to get in touch with the doctor and get her medication adjusted."

"And after that?"

"Rethink the new house, and cut back on the extra jobs. Be here for Kinsey."

Chapter Five

Brian whistled under his breath as he maneuvered his truck into the police department substation parking lot. The moonless night was dark, but the lot was ablaze with security lights and cameras. One more week and he would be back on day shift. He was more than ready. Never a night owl by nature, he had even more reason to want day shift for a while. Rachel Castillo had called him early this afternoon, waking him out of a light sleep, and told him he'd been chosen to play Curly McLain. And even better, Jessica had been cast opposite him as Laurey.

Brian did a couple of steps of soft-shoe and clicked his heels together. He'd also heard from his mother, who had called with the news that Donna, his favorite sister, was expecting another baby. She and her husband were awesome parents and he couldn't be happier for them. His mind wandered to a certain pretty dancer and her adorable little boy and he wondered briefly what a child of his with her would look like. But it was way too soon for that. First he had to persuade her to go out on a date with him.

He was still wondering what'd happened to prompt her one-eighty. He could've sworn she was into him, and initially, she'd accepted his invitation with no hesitation. And then for no reason he could fathom, she was scrambling backwards as fast as she could.

She was fine until they'd talked about her late husband. Then things had gone south. Two texts later, and she still wouldn't commit to the date. He didn't want to come off stalker-ish, so each excuse was met with an alternative. He didn't push, but he found a way to turn the *probably not* into a *we can do this.*

He pushed open the door and winked at Lydia Menchaca, the officer manning the front desk. "So how's junior?" he teased.

She narrowed her eyes. "I am so sick and damn tired of being pregnant I could scream. I told Jaime last night that he'd be lucky to get laid anytime in the next five years."

"Oh, honey. You wait until you get in that delivery room." Sugar Johnson's deep-throated laugh filled the vestibule. "You're gonna be calling that poor bastard every name in the book and then some. It'll be worse for him than the time he faced down four gang members by himself."

"Couldn't have been that bad. You've done it three times," Brian teased.

"That's what she gets for marrying the second-sexiest cop on the force," Lydia shot back.

"Glad you know who number one is." Brian grinned impudently.

Sugar fake-punched his arm. "Arrogant much?"

"Me?" She shook her head.

Brian was still laughing as he walked into the men's locker room and slipped off his uniform shirt. SAPD officers had the choice of coming to work in uniform or changing into uniform at the station. He liked to split the difference, dressing at home but donning his body armor and equipment belt here. He took his vest from his locker and was hooking it into position when Mike Werner carried in his uniform and kicked off his tennis shoes. The uniform hung from a dry cleaner's hanger and was shrouded in plastic. "Pretty fancy for a washable uniform," Brian said as he put his shirt back on.

Mike shrugged. "It was the only clean one I have left."

Brian glanced over at his co-worker. Mike looked absolutely exhausted. And worried. The man was an open book. If something was bothering him, the world knew it. "Is everything all right?"

"No, but I don't want to talk about it right now. I need to get my mind on the job." He started stripping down.

Brian nodded. The worst thing a cop could do was go to work with his mind elsewhere.

Mike got all the way down to his underwear. "So what's got you grinning like a damned fool?"

"I landed the lead in *Oklahoma!*."

Mike's head popped up. "Over at the Durango?"

"Yeah. How'd you know?"

"Heather's sister works there. I hear about the Durango all the time."

Brian looked at Mike. "Who's your sister-in-law?"

"Jessica Clary. She runs the Academy."

"She's also cast opposite me. Rachel said she's going to play Laurey."

"And she'll be great. She's got talent out the wazoo."

"I didn't realize your wife was Jessica's sister."

Mike shrugged. "No reason why you would. They look nothing alike. Different personalities. Kinsey looks a lot like Jess and Bobby."

"He's a sweet child." Brian tucked in his uniform shirt. "I took them out for ice cream after auditions Sunday. I asked Jessica out. She was more than happy to accept the invitation at first, but then something changed her mind and she's done everything in the world to get out of it. And, yeah, not looking for a one-night stand here."

"At what point in the conversation did she change her mind?"

"When Bobby said his dad died a hero. I told him sometimes I got to be a hero, too, since I'm a cop and on the SWAT team."

"And then it all went south." Mike pulled on his uniform pants.

"How'd you know? She still carrying a torch for the late husband?"

"She holds him in high regard, but that's not the problem. You admitted to being a SWAT cop."

"Admitted to it? I'm proud of it." Brian's eyes narrowed. "She been in trouble? Or does she have a hard-on about cops?"

"No trouble. She does have a hard-on about cops, but not the way you're thinking. You ever hear anybody talking about Robby Clary?"

"'Reckless Robby?'" The puzzle pieces snapped together. "She's his widow."

Mike nodded. "She was the young hottie who managed to catch the department's risk-loving playboy. He gave up his womanizing for her, but she couldn't do a damn thing about the reckless streak. She might not have even wanted to, if she was into risk-takers. Robby loved nothing more than taking chances. Unfortunately, the place he loved to take them the most was on the job. It finally caught up with him. He was killed, and his partner Owen was badly injured trying to defuse a bomb. It cost Owen his looks, his eye, his career, and his acting. And his marriage, if the rumors got it right."

"Owen's back at the Durango. He's taken up with my old college buddy Wade."

Mike shrugged and finished getting dressed. "Guess the marriage breakup gossip got it wrong."

"And Jessica?"

Mike gave him a half grin. "She doesn't want anyone who puts his life on the line. Her words, not mine. No first responders. No military. You're the worst: SWAT team."

"Not cool to paint us all with the same brush, especially if her husband took a lot of chances."

"Agreed, but her call. She tried to talk Heather out of marrying me. Might've succeeded if Heather hadn't been pregnant with Kinsey. But Jess doesn't—and maybe after what happened, can't—distinguish between putting our lives on the line because of the job and taking foolish chances like Robby did. She's convinced all first responders are risk-takers like him." Mike shook his head. "Listen, bro, better look elsewhere, less aggravation for you and her."

"Whatever," Brian muttered.

Mike tied his boots, and Brian checked his equipment belt then said, "Good shift." Mike locked his backpack in his locker then went down the hall to roll call.

Challenge accepted. The lady was attracted to him, and God knew Brian was attracted to her. That kind of attraction was too rare and special to walk away from. So plan B. He'd take down the walls she'd built around herself one brick at a time. This would be a slow dance, and Brian loved a sultry build up.

***

Jessica shut the restroom door and headed to her office, hoping to get a little paperwork done before she had to teach the teenage voice class. Preparations for the youth productions of *Oklahoma!* and *Footloose* were in full swing, and she had a room full of Curly McLains, Will Parkers, and Jud Frys needing to learn the men's songs. Teaching voice wasn't her favorite thing, and she had an email full of résumés she had to go through before she left. She needed to replace her missing instructors, pronto. So far the parents had been patient with the pinch-hitting, but another week or two and there would be complaints.

And then there was the date she was expected to go on this evening. She'd tried once again to cancel, explaining that she had to work, but he said he'd be there and to please be ready. He wasn't pushy, but persistent in a sweet way. His texts teased, and somehow she hadn't been able to come out with a flat *no* to shut him down—and it wasn't entirely for Kinsey's prosthetic, But tonight she'd had no choice but to postpone. She had to work.

She sat down at her desk and was about to open the first résumé when she heard raised voices in the hall. "Sophie, Sophie, Sophie. I am so sick of that girl I could scream. I'm tired of your kid getting all the good parts because you work here."

"I can't help it if your kid's got no talent. They want quality. Cindy's not that good. And I don't work here. I give freely of my time, unlike some parents."

Oh, hell. Letti was at it again, although it sounded like Patsy Faulkner had started this one. Jess needed to defuse things, and fast. She jumped up out of her chair and jerked open the door before either of them could knock. Letti wore her usual snark and Patsy looked fit to be tied. "I want to know why the hell Sophie was cast, *yet again*, in a lead role," Patsy demanded. "It was Cindy's turn."

"Sophie got the part because she's better," Letti snapped.

"Ladies, please. You're making a scene in front of the kids." Jessica gestured to the circle of wide-eyed tweens behind them. "The last thing we want is for your daughters to be embarrassed. Girls are so sensitive at this age."

They both backed down. She turned to Letti. "Wade and Owen were looking for you a few minutes ago. They said something about rehearsing a couple of scenes with you tonight." To everyone's surprise, Owen had agreed to play bad guy Jud Fry without the makeup that concealed his facial scarring.

"Happy to go help. Since I 'work' here and all." Letti tossed a final smirk over her shoulder as she walked away.

"I want to talk to you," Patsy insisted.

"I'm sure you do," Jessica said mildly. She shut her office door and sat down at her desk with Patsy seated across from her. "I'm sorry you're upset Cindy wasn't cast."

"It's not fair," Patsy ground out. "Sophie gets all the good roles."

"Sophie also gets here for every scheduled rehearsal. She and her mother make her commitment a priority." Jessica reached into her desk and pulled out an old-fashioned attendance book. She flipped it open and spent a few minutes looking through it. "Cindy was in the ensemble of *How to Succeed in Business without Really Trying* last fall. According to the attendance records, she missed a third of the rehearsals."

"She couldn't help that," Patsy huffed. "Her father won't get her here when she's at his house. He says the theater's a pile of crap. He wants her in sports."

"That's too bad," Jessica said.

"Yes, it is. You can't penalize Cindy because her father's an ass."

"I'm sorry her father's difficult. That's unfair to her, but I still can't cast her in a major role if she doesn't come to all the practices. Cindy is talented, but without the commitment..." Jessica threw up her hands and shrugged. "I'm sorry, Mrs. Faulkner. It wouldn't be fair to the kids who do show up to all the rehearsals."

"That's *it*. I'm suing that son of a bitch for full custody. Don't be surprised if you get a subpoena from my attorney. You can tell the judge what you told me." Patsy yanked open the door and stomped out of the office, slamming the door so hard it bounced back open.

Well, hell. She hadn't meant to start a war between Patsy and her ex. And she sure hadn't meant to get herself mixed up in their skirmish.

Jessica rubbed her temples and hoped her small headache didn't morph into a big one. She reminded herself that at the Durango Street Theatre Academy not all the drama was on the stage. But that was the nature of the Academy kids, and the parents who spawned them. They cared with a passion. That was what made them so good.

The rising noise level outside her office was her clue that the seven o'clock classes were finishing up. It was time to go work with the boys. She was heading for the door when it flew open and Brian stood there, a satisfied smile on his face. "Aah." His gaze swept her from head to toe. "You're ready. You look good. Shall we head out?"

"You have to be kidding me." She rolled her eyes. "I sent you a text two hours ago that I had to work tonight. Why are you here?"

"I thought you were making me work for it." He grinned. "I'm here to prove I'm willing."

She wanted to be angry with him, she really did, but he was doing the adorable thing, and she didn't have it in her to be mean. "Really, I'm three instructors short. I have to be the voice coach right now until I find someone to do the job. Please, go home and let me teach the boys before their parents start bitching."

Brian looked abashed. "Sorry."

"We'll go out another night. I gotta go teach them to sing 'Oh, What a Beautiful Mornin'' before I sit down to another hour of paperwork."

She started to walk around him, but Brian put his hand on her arm. "I know every song in *Oklahoma!*. Let me teach that class for you while you do your paperwork. We can go out for a hamburger afterward. Let me help," he urged when she hesitated. "Singing's my forte."

Singing wasn't her forte and teaching it sure wasn't. If he took the class, she could get her paperwork done, have a decent meal, fulfill her obligation to go out with him, and maybe ask him to help Kinsey. "Okay. Let me show you to the studio."

She led him to the small studio in the back filled with every boy cast in the two teenage productions. Brian introduced himself and the boys seemed happy to have a man teaching them. He sat down at the piano and gave her a *go do your thing* wave.

Breathing a sigh of relief, Jessica fled to her office. Suddenly energized, she flew through the emailed résumés and scheduled four interviews for the next two days. She had a few minutes before the class ended, so she ducked in the restroom and combed her hair and applied the lip-gloss she hadn't bothered with earlier.

The Durango polo shirt and jeans she had on weren't really date clothes, but she hadn't been expecting to go out when she dressed this afternoon. Besides, Brian said hamburgers. Jeans and a polo shirt would be fine for a burger.

Brian's class was still going on, so she slipped down the hall and stood outside the door where she could hear but not be seen. The longer she listened, the more impressed she became. He was good. Really good. Good enough for her to see if he would be interested in teaching at the Academy.

As badly as she wanted to avoid him, that was saying something.

The boys filed out at nine on the dot. Brian followed them out, looking cheerful. "That was fun."

"I'm glad you enjoyed it."

"So get your purse or whatever it is you carry and we'll go find us that burger."

They returned to her office. She fished her handbag out of the desk drawer and he ushered her to a brand-new truck. "Nice wheels," she commented. "Maybe in my next life."

"Why would you say that? Yours is a classic. A crew cab dually."

"That's what everybody says. To me it's reliable wheels and no payment. Robby was fixing it up when he died and Daddy and Mike finished it for me. I think you know my brother-in-law. Mike Werner. He's married to my sister."

"I know him." He nodded. "Does a burger still suit?"

"A burger would hit the spot."

He opened the door to the passenger side and helped her in, the touch of his hand warm on her waist. "You need running boards," she teased.

"You need about four more inches on those legs of yours," he shot back, his eyes twinkling.

"My legs are fine. They reach the ground just right."

"Yes, they do. And they're gorgeous. But you know that."

She did, but it was nice to know he'd noticed. She was being ridiculous. It didn't matter what he thought of her legs or any other part of her anatomy. She wouldn't be going out with him after tonight.

Which was a shame. She glanced over at his profile and a shiver ran down her spine. He was good-looking, talented, and fun. And as nice a man as she'd ever met, in some ways even nicer than Robby. If only he weren't a SWAT member. For the hundredth time she wondered why he couldn't have been a teacher or a lawyer, or a plumber. Somebody who did something safe: somebody who didn't put his life on the line every damn day.

The hamburger bar he took her to had recently re-opened after a devastating fire. "I am *so* glad this place is back," she enthused as she hopped out of the truck. "I've missed it."

"So have I." He took her hand in his, his much larger fingers wrapping around hers in a silky caress. Her first instinct was to pull away. But her hand felt so good inside his.

She let it stay.

The dinner crowd had mostly thinned out, leaving a few late diners and two groups of boisterous patrons with empty burger baskets and beer bottles littering their tables. They placed their order at the counter and found a booth away from the noise. Brian looked across at her and sipped his beer. "Thanks for coming out with me tonight."

"Thanks for covering that class."

"It was my pleasure. Are all the kids that talented?"

"Pretty much. But gotta say, you seem to have a knack for getting the best out of them. Have you taught singing before?"

"Yes and no. I worked some with the new singers in college. Wade is one of my proudest protégés."

"I can see why. He sings beautifully. Letti was working with him and Owen tonight on a scene with Curly and Jud. I know it's a little gossipy, but I wish I could have been a fly on the wall. Owen, his ex, and his future."

"I haven't been around the two of them that often, but I can see Wade and Owen having real chemistry together on stage."

"They do. They did a few performances of *How to Succeed* together before Wade's appendicitis took him out of the last production. Wade also had fantastic chemistry with Sandra before she went home to her husband. Long story for later," she said when he looked puzzled.

"Speaking of chemistry…" He motioned between them, his gaze hot enough to melt a glacier.

She didn't know what to say.

Their number was called and Brian hopped up to get their tray from the counter. Jessica breathed a sigh of relief. He was right. With the kind of attraction they felt off the stage, on stage they were going to be dynamite. But that chemistry was going to have to remain on the stage. She couldn't and wouldn't get involved with him.

Brian brought the burgers to the table and they spent the next few minutes wolfing them down. "Damn, that was good," she said. "I didn't realize how hungry I was. I thought I would be handing you half. Not that you needed it." He'd ordered the half-pound patty and killed the entire burger, along with a large basket of fries.

He grinned and winked. "I'm a growing boy."

"No, those kids you were working with this evening are growing boys. I never cease to be amazed how much food they consume at a cast party."

"Good kids with lots of talent."

Jessica bit her lip. "If I offered you a job teaching at the Academy, would you be interested?"

"Interested? Sure. Able to take it? No. Between my rotating shifts and the fact that SWAT can be called out any time twenty-four-seven, you couldn't depend on me."

"I was afraid of that. What are you going to do if you get a SWAT call some night an hour before the show?"

"I'm going to call Wade, who is then going to call somebody named Harry who's done the part before."

"Harry Bell. He's done several shows for us. He's a little old to be a believable Curly, but he would do fine in a pinch."

He looked at her thoughtfully. "But back to the Academy. I hope you'll be able to fill your empty positions quickly, but if you don't, give me a call. I'd be happy to do some pinch hitting until you do."

"Thanks. I may have to take you up on that."

She stole the last fry out of his basket and swallowed the rest of her beer. The place had emptied while they ate, leaving them the only two patrons left in an atmosphere that was surprisingly intimate. He looked at her with an expression that made her sizzle.

He wanted her and made no secret of it.

She was going to have to brush him off.

Sometimes life sucked.

They rose in unison and walked silently to his truck. The tension was like a wound-up spring as they drove silently back to the theater. She glanced across the cab at his face. Even in the shadowed light, she could see the tenseness of his jaw and the way he gripped the steering wheel more tightly than necessary. She caught him glancing at her, the desire on his face making her suck in her breath. He wasn't going to let her go without at least one smoking-hot kiss.

That was all right. Selfishly, she wanted one of those smoking-hot kisses before she had to let him go.

Just one, and she'd send him on his way.

He pulled up next to her truck. "I'll get the door," he said gruffly. She sat until he opened the door before turning and sliding off the seat straight into his arms. "Right where I want you," he said softly. "I know it's a first date, but I have to kiss you."

A first date and a last.

Jessica tipped her head back and smiled. "I'll make an exception."

He bent his head as she rose on her tiptoes. Slowly their lips came together, gently at first, as they tenderly explored one another. Brian tasted of hamburger and beer, and this close she could smell his woodsy shampoo and his warm, male essence. But as their sweet exploration became more passionate, their lips ground together and he drew her closer to his hard warmth, his arms like steel bands lifting her a couple inches off the ground. Her hands roamed the solid strength of his muscled back and waist, his body strong beneath her fingers.

His chest was rock-hard against hers. Her breath was ragged and her heart pounded loudly in her ears. Desire swelled her nipples, which poked into his shirt. Moisture pooled between her legs as the evidence of his longing swelled against her thighs. She clung to him as tightly as he clung to her, willing this one and only kiss to go on forever.

His eyes glittered in the dim light as he lifted his head. "Damn, woman."

"Mmmhmmm." He set her on the ground and she took a reluctant step back.

"Uh-uh, now. We don't need to stop with one." He reached for her, frowning when she took another step back.

She looked up at him and wished he were an actuary. "I promised myself I'd stop at one." She took another step back. "Thank you for the hamburger and the company. I'll call you if I need help with the classes."

Brian's eyes narrowed. "So that's it?"

"Ah, yes." She felt rotten as she looked up at him. "I'm sorry."

"So you're going to walk away 'cause you don't like what I do for a living. How disappointing."

Jessica's head snapped back. "You talked to Mike," she accused.

"No, Mike talked to me. Told me I didn't have a snowball's chance in hell with you."

She looked at Brian with regret. "I really am sorry. Sorrier than you can imagine. You're a great guy. I admit it'll be a long time before I get another kiss like that one. But the bottom line is that I can't be with anybody who puts their life on the line for their job. Nobody. That includes you. If you talked to Mike, you know why."

"I understand why you think so. Obviously, I don't agree. I'm hoping you're going to realize we can be good together, and if we go on a second date we can talk about the difference between doing my job and taking unnecessary risks."

She ducked her head, unable to look him in the eye. Her legs trembled as she jumped in the cab and switched on the engine. She reached up and touched her lips with fingers that trembled. She could still taste him on her lips. She could still feel his arms around her, his chest hard against hers, the evidence of his desire poking into her. She'd been as turned on as he was. And he knew it.

She turned the corner and headed toward the expressway. She shouldn't have kissed him. She shouldn't have done that to herself. Now she knew what she'd be missing by turning him away. But... The stakes were too high for her if she didn't. She wouldn't give in.

But she wished with all her heart that she could.

Chapter Six

Jessica made her way through the maze of Academy studios. She stopped a minute in the big rehearsal room, her face breaking into a smile at the sight of her youngest students carefully mimicking Rachel's steps as they practiced the ballet skills they would need for the sequence in *Oklahoma!*. Their dance was rudimentary compared to the one she and Brian were working on, but it was sophisticated for six-year-olds with no formal ballet training. The sight of young children learning to dance always made her smile. Bobby would be old enough to start next year. She hoped he took after her. Robby had possessed two left feet and swore that it simply wasn't in jocks' DNA to dance.

On the other hand, Brian was every bit the jock Robby had been. And he could dance up a storm.

She tried to push away thoughts of Brian Howard, but it was hard, since he was teaching the class in the next studio. So much for her attempt to walk away from him after a single date. She hadn't been able to get away from the man. She'd only found one new instructor for the Academy, which left her two short, and with her choreographing and rehearsals for *Oklahoma!,* she couldn't cover as many classes as she had been. So she'd bitten the bullet and called him, and he'd been teaching two classes a week for the last two weeks.

Like clockwork, he stopped by her office before each class to say hi and give her his visual appraisal. She wished she was a better person, but she preened under his hot gaze, and his lips twitched when he caught her enjoying it. His last visit, she asked him about making a prosthetic for Kinsey. He agreed to do it without a moment's hesitation.

On top of seeing him twice a week for his class, their rehearsals had started, and she was with him in a rehearsal room at least twice a week as they practiced their scenes together and worked on the ballet routine.

To make matters worse, he was making it crystal clear that he had every intention of overcoming her objections to see him again. He was never without the sexy smile he reserved only for her. He made no attempt to disguise his interest. For the most part he was subtle, but his flirting during rehearsal had earned him more than one zinger from Letti, who ran a tight ship. He was doing everything in his power to remind Jess of how good it felt to be in his arms and how much he would like to have her there again.

She spent a couple more minutes with the little ones and wandered next door, listening through the open door to Brian's class. Tonight he was working with the middle-school cast, which presented a challenge since some of the boys' voices had dropped and others hadn't. Brian sat at the piano patiently taking them through one of the group numbers. It was in a different key than the number in the adult score, and he was struggling to reach the high notes with the kids. She had to give him full marks for helping her, even if he had an ulterior motive. It was a shame his day job prevented him from taking one of the teaching positions full time.

It was a shame about his job, period. But he was no different from Robby, she reminded herself. She would have to resist the powerful, almost magnetic pull she felt for Brian.

She listened for a few minutes before finding her new instructor in the last studio. Jason Arredondo taught in a middle school in one of the roughest neighborhoods in San Antonio. He'd been acutely uncomfortable during his interview to the point that she wondered if he was hiding something. But his principal had written him a glowing recommendation, and in the room with his students, away from her and the other adults, his discomfort dissolved, and he was both at ease with the kids and an effective instructor.

Again she stood outside the door where she could see and hear. He was working with the girls in the high-school production, his smile and his praise genuine. She'd be willing to bet her next paycheck that more than one of the girls would develop a crush on the good-looking young man, especially if Josh was able to persuade him to accept an acting role in their summer production.

Satisfied that all was well with her newest hire, she paid quick visits to the rest of the classes, finishing her last visit as the class was wrapping up. Her phone buzzed with a text from Letti. *We need to rehearse the first scene. See you in studio 3 in 5 minutes.*

That meant two or more hours with Brian.

She ignored the traitorous part of her that was thrilled at the thought.

At least they would have Letti and Nelda Thompson, who was playing Aunt Eller, as buffers between them. She made a quick stop in the ladies' room and was waiting in the studio when Brian sauntered in, a knowing smile on his face as her gaze was drawn to him. "Ready to make the sparks fly?" he asked as he gave her an appreciative once-over.

"Knock it off, Mr. Howard," Letti snapped as she strode in. "Make your conquests on your own time. Not mine."

"You don't want sparks flying between Curly and Laurey?" Nelda teased as she followed Letti in. "I thought that was every director's dream."

"It is, until it becomes a distraction during rehearsal." Letti looked at him pointedly.

He held up his hands. "Right. I can in no way, shape, or form let on how utterly beautiful I think Jess is or how much I would love to take her into my arms and kiss the living daylights out of her." Brian's eyes danced and Nelda laughed out loud.

"Enough, Brian," Jessica said softly. "Letti's right. We're here to work."

"Oh, for God's sake." Letti rolled her eyes. "Do any of you know your lines yet?"

The three of them had their lines down pat. Brian gave Jess a couple more appreciative once-overs before settling down to rehearse. As they rehearsed Curly and Laurey's snappy dialogue, sparks flew. This wasn't Jessica's first time creating magic with a co-star. She and Wade had rocked the ingénue roles of Hope and Billy last year in *Anything Goes,* and she and Vivienne Abonce had played off each other wonderfully as the witches in *The Wizard of Oz.*

But something about working with Brian was different than she'd ever experienced with another actor. Maybe it was because their attraction was real. Maybe it was because Curly's and Laurey's relationship was in some ways like their own. Whatever it was, it was working for them, big time. And from the looks on Letti and Nelda's faces, she wasn't the only one who felt that way.

Letti knocked off after an hour, declaring the scene "damn good." Nelda left, and Jess and Brian commandeered the smallest dance studio. She changed into her dancing shoes and he did the same after removing his ankle holster, and stowing it inside the closed piano lid. They had worked a couple of times on the dance sequence, but she hadn't brought in Owen or the rest of the cast yet. They had a long way to go before they could do that.

She hooked up her phone to a small speaker and called up the music in the dream sequence. "Let's go over what we have so far," she suggested. "We can pick up where Curly and Laurey start dancing together."

They listened to the fifteen-second lead-in she'd included. When it was time to begin, she nodded and Brian entered from what would be stage left. She pivoted toward him and ran across the room and made a nimble leap into his waiting arms. He held her up as she threw out her arms and together they slowly made a circle as the music swelled to a crescendo. He put her down and offered her his arm, and they began a graceful waltz to the tune of "Oh, What a Beautiful Mornin'."

Jessica kept one eye on the large mirrors as he spun her around the room. The sequence ended and they looked at one another. "Wooden," they said in unison.

"Is it wooden because of the steps, or because we're going through the motions?" Brian asked.

"The steps are fine. It's the execution. We're trying so hard to remember the steps we're losing the pizzazz."

Brian grinned. "Okay. One order of pizzazz comin' right up."

"Let's take it from the top." She knew exactly what she needed to do to generate the feeling that hadn't been there before, but it meant opening herself to Brian, letting herself be aware of his masculinity and admitting the desire she felt for him. Dangerous emotions, especially with her determination to nip their relationship in the bud. But necessary emotions, if she wanted the dance sequence to work.

She let out the breath she was holding and started the music. They repeated the waltz sequence. This time she let her feelings loose as she ran toward Brian and leapt into his arms. His hands were warm and strong as he held her for the lift, and his arms powerful and welcoming as they danced across the room. She opened herself to his warmth and gave her attraction to him free rein as their bodies moved together to the joyous tune. She glanced in the mirror as Brian spun her to the music. *Better. Much better.* The steps were the same. But it was a different dance altogether.

Opening herself to him. That was all it took.

God help her.

The music shifted to "People Will Say We're in Love" and she nodded for them to continue. They circled the floor, combining the intricacies and footwork of ballet with the broad, sweeping steps of the waltz. The music swelled and he hoisted her up on his broad shoulder, spinning her as she held her arms out, a blissful smile on her face.

As choreographed, he threw her into the air and caught her in his arms, then leaned forward, his eyes sparkling with devilment and desire as he pressed his lips against hers. Her arms already around him, she tightened them as he deepened the kiss, the dance forgotten as his tongue caressed her lips. Her mouth fell open, as much from surprise as anything else, and his arms wound around her. *Crazy. This is crazy.* But she was powerless to stop his sensual invasion, as he loosened his hold to let her feet slide to the ground but keeping her next to him, his arms warm and hard as they encircled her body. The score played on as they clung to one another, plastered together as her nipples pebbled and he swelled against her.

Jessica had replayed their one and only kiss hundreds of times in her mind. Now she had another to go along with it.

Her head was beginning to spin by the time he finally lifted his head. "That's better," he breathed.

Jessica took a deep breath and stepped back. "Better for who?" She moved across the room and turned off the music.

"Better for both of us," he said gently. "Look, I get that you don't like what I do for a living. And there's damn little I can do about that. But honestly, Jess. Have you ever felt what you felt in my arms?"

Jessica blinked back the sudden sting of tears. "I have. With Robby. And we know how that turned out."

"Then you know exactly what you're missing." He tried to take her hand but she pulled it away. "Unlike you, I've never felt like that in any other woman's arms."

"You're a virgin?"

He laughed. "Hardly. But it's never been like that for me until you." Again he reached for her hand, not letting her pull away this time. "Are you honestly going to let me being a cop get in the way of us going out?"

She looked at him with her heart in her eyes. "I am."

"Even after that kiss?"

"You can kiss me every damned time we practice the sequence and it won't change anything."

"I'm not going to let you get away with that, you know." His grip on her hand tightened. "I *will* kiss you every damned time we dance if that's what it takes to make you change your mind."

She shrugged. "Whatever."

He shook his head. "We'd talked about me making Kinsey a hand. Why don't we go ahead and set up something with your sister so I can get your niece measured? I'm off Monday and Tuesday. Does your sister work?"

"No. Let me text her now." She shot a text to Heather and her phone pinged a moment later. "She's going to be home both Monday and Tuesday. She suggested late Monday morning before I go to work. She said she'd feed us lunch. Does that work for you?"

"Like a charm. Now, are we going to go over this again or are you going to run out of here like a scared rabbit?"

"I don't know. Are you going to take advantage of the situation again?"

"Nah. One kiss like that's about all I can handle in one evening. Unless and until I have a chance for more." He waggled his eyebrows.

She shook her head, but inside she smiled. His tenacity was admirable. "You are positively incorrigible. So let's take it from the top."

They went through the waltz scene three more times before she called it a night. Despite the sparks flying between them, he was a perfect gentleman and made no move to kiss her again. Instead, he walked her to her truck and waited until she was locked in with the engine running before leaving her.

But his seduction had been effective. With every look, every touch, every dance step he took with her, she was reminded of his determination that she—that they—not turn away from something he thought would be wonderful.

The problem was that she thought it would be wonderful, too.

***

Jessica pulled into Heather's driveway and parked in her usual spot behind her sister's car. A norther had blown in yesterday afternoon bringing a bone-chilling rain that lasted most of the night, but the rain had stopped a couple of hours ago and the clouds were beginning to break up. Brian had texted that he was on his way, and she debated waiting for him to arrive before ringing the doorbell. But Bobby was squirming in his car seat. "Mommy, I need to go potty."

"Got it, buddy."

Cold wind slapped her cheeks and ruffled her hair as she unhooked Bobby's car seat. They were almost to the front door when Brian's truck pulled up in front of the house. He hopped out and got a backpack before joining them on the front steps. Bobby threw his arms around Brian's legs. "Mr. Brian. Can we go for ice cream again?"

Brian's grin was devilish as he glanced up at Jessica. "Don't know. That would be up to your mom."

That's right. Put the onus on me. Her own grin was full of devilment as she looked down at the two of them. "Bobby, doesn't your Aunt Heather always serve ice cream when we come for lunch?"

"It's more fun with Mr. Brian."

Jessica smiled faintly. "Let's not tell Aunt Heather that, all right?"

They rang the doorbell twice. Jessica was starting to get worried, then Heather threw open the door. For once, her sister looked put together. Her hair was combed, she was dressed in jeans and a long-sleeved tee, and she even had on a little makeup. Heather smiled hesitantly and unlatched the screen door. "Come on in." She turned toward the living room. "Kinsey. Bobby's here."

Kinsey came running and threw her arms around Bobby. "I'm getting a hand. Mommy said." She held up her arm. "Just like you!"

"She is? Like mine?"

"Maybe not exactly like yours, but it will be a good one." She turned to her son. "Can you manage the potty by yourself?"

Bobby nodded and took off running. Jessica scooped Kinsey up and turned toward Brian. "Kinsey, this is Mr. Brian. He's going to make you a pretty new hand. Brian, this is Miss Kinsey Werner. And her mother, Heather."

"Actually, your sister and I have met. Good to see you again, Heather." He shook Heather's hand and turned to Kinsey. "So this is the beautiful Miss Kinsey Werner. Your daddy talks about you all the time. He says you're really something special." He made a production of shaking her good hand.

Kinsey smiled sweetly. "Hi, Mr. Bwian."

"So are we going to measure first and then eat, or the other way around?" Brian asked.

"The casserole won't be ready for nearly an hour. So measure first, I guess." Heather motioned for them to follow her. "Will the kitchen table work?"

"That will be fine." Brian took off his backpack and set it on the table. He fished out a big plastic sheet marked off in one-inch squares. He spread it out on the table and unrolled a plastic tape measure, which he stretched out alongside the grid. Next he got out a camera. "I can use a cell phone photo if I have to, but this works better," he said when Heather looked puzzled. "Now, can we have the lady of the hour over here?"

Kinsey was on the floor showing Bobby her Barbie doll, but she came quickly when Heather called her. "If you could sit her in her booster seat and have her lay both of her arms out flat. That's right," he said when Kinsey was seated. "Kinsey, put both of your arms out and spread your fingers for me." Gently, he positioned the child's arms so that they were side by side. Heather turned away, but Jessica watched in fascination as Brian snapped pictures of both her good arm and hand and the arm that stopped about two inches from where her wrist should be, with only the vestigial tips of two fingers poking about a half inch from the end. It took him only a few moments. "All done," he said cheerfully. "You want to look at a few hands and tell me what color you want?"

Heather turned back around. "You can't make it to match her skin?"

Brian shrugged. "I could. But kids love the colored ones."

"Heather, it's not going to look like a real hand anyway. Why not let her have a little fun with it?" Jessica asked.

"I—I guess that would be all right."

Brian got out his phone. "Kinsey, I'm gonna show you some hands I've made for other boys and girls. I want you to tell me which ones you'd like your hand to look like."

"Okay." He sat down and helped her climb into his lap. He flipped through his pictures. "Here's one I made for a little girl in Washington State. She loves Ariel the Mermaid so I made hers the same color as Ariel's tail." He showed her a photo of a blue-green hand trimmed in purple. The hand clutched an Ariel doll. "Here's one I made for a little girl in New Zealand. She loves pink so I made hers pink." The image showed a hand with a totally different design from the first one holding a pink Barbie. "Here's a Captain America in red, white, and blue." Again, the design was different from the other two.

"Are all your hands different?" Jessica asked.

"Yes, they are. I specially design them to work with whatever the child is born with."

Kinsey looked at a few more hands before pointing to a green and yellow hand done in the colors of Disney princess Tiana's gown. "That one."

Brian turned questioning eyes to Heather, who nodded faintly. "Tiana it is. You can go finish showing your doll to Bobby."

Kinsey scrambled down. Brian started folding the tape measure. "Now what do you do?" Heather asked tentatively.

"I go home and use my computer to design and make a 3-D model of her arm. Then I design a piece unique to her that fits over it. Since she has no wrist, I'll fit the arm to above her elbow and she will use the bending and flexing of her elbow to make the fingers open and close. Like I told Jessica, she won't be playing piano concertos with it, but she will be able to hold a doll or a tricycle handle. I have older kids riding bikes with them, and one real badass biker rides his Harley."

"That's amazing. And it's all done on printers," Jessica said.

"However you do it, thank you. My daughter compensates well, but there are some things that absolutely require two hands." Heather smiled tremulously.

"My pleasure. Let me get this stuff off your table so we can eat some of whatever I'm smelling."

He cleared the table and sat down in the family room with the kids. Jessica followed Heather into the kitchen. "I like him," Heather said quietly.

"So do I," Jessica admitted. "But I wish he wasn't a cop."

"Is that your only objection to him?"

"Yeah. He's damned wonderful otherwise."

Heather's only answer was a shrug.

Jessica set the table while Heather made a fruit salad to go with the egg and sausage casserole. They rounded up Brian and the kids. Kinsey and Bobby both wanted to sit next to Brian. He agreed to sit between them and they put him at one end with a child seated on either side. He was good with them, patiently answering Bobby's questions and making sure Kinsey didn't feel left out of the discussion. Heather shot Jessica more than one meaningful glance, which she chose to ignore.

Her sister was Team Brian all the way. Which, considering Heather's own unhappy marriage to a cop, surprised Jessica no end.

They were almost finished when Mike strode in the front door. He glanced at the crowd at his table, his surprise morphing into something else when he spotted Brian seated between the two children. He greeted Heather and Jessica and kissed each of the kids before nodding curtly in Brian's direction. "To what do we owe the pleasure?"

If Brian was taken aback by Mike's reaction, it didn't show. "I measured Kinsey for a hand this morning. Heather was kind enough to thank me with lunch. A delicious lunch, I might add. I enjoyed it, Heather."

Mike looked sheepish. "Uh, well, thanks."

"Why didn't you tell me about his hands?" Heather pinned Mike with a glare. "She could have had one a long time ago."

"I did once, but you said you weren't interested," Mike said less than patiently.

"You could have–"

"Mike, sit down and I'll get you a plate," Jessica broke in. "Heather, I promised Bobby ice cream if you have any. And Brian might be interested also."

Mike sat down across the table from Brian. Jessica kept up a stream of small talk while she dished up a generous serving of casserole for Mike. Heather spooned up two small bowls and one big bowl of ice cream. Mike wolfed down his casserole while Bobby, Kinsey, and Brian polished off their ice cream. "Again, Heather, the meal was delicious. I hate to eat and run, but my fridge is empty and I have a hot date with a grocery cart." Brian rose from the table.

"Glad it hit the spot. And it's me who should be thanking you. I appreciate what you're doing for my daughter."

"Likewise," Mike mumbled around a mouthful of food.

Heather scooped up Kinsey and over the child's protests took her down the hall for a nap. Bobby curled up on the sofa in front of the children's channel to wait for Jessica, who was cleaning up in the kitchen. Brian headed out the front door. After a minute Mike jumped up and followed him outside. Puzzled, Jessica grabbed up a sack of garbage and headed to the garage. Mike had worn a determined expression on his face and she'd bet her next paycheck he had something to say to Brian about her.

She pushed open the door from the house to the garage, blessing Mike for leaving the garage door open. Brian was halfway down the sidewalk when Mike caught up with him. "I thought I told you to leave her alone," he snapped.

Brian's look was scathing. "Jesus, man. I came over here to measure your daughter for a hand. Not to seduce your wife's sister on your sofa. Do you want me to make Kinsey a hand or don't you?"

Mike ran his fingers through his hair. "Of course I want you to make Kinsey a hand. But you have an ulterior motive and you know it."

Brian raised one eyebrow. "Actually, I don't. I would gladly make your daughter a hand even if your sister-in-law never spoke to me again. I would have happily made her one before now if you'd given a big enough damn about her to ask."

"Heather said she didn't want one. But that's not the point. I saw the looks you were giving Jess over the French vanilla."

"That's between me and her."

"I told you to leave her alone, and I told you why."

"She's as into me as I am her and I'm gonna wear down her objections sooner or later. She's the best challenge I've had in a long time."

He turned on his heel and sauntered down the sidewalk before Mike could reply.

Jessica trembled as she dumped the garbage in the trashcan. *Arrogant pricks.* She didn't know what Mike thought he was doing warning Brian off. And Brian. She opened her mouth in a silent scream. She was a *challenge.* That's what this was about. That's all she was to him. A damn challenge he had to win.

Pffft. He had no idea who he was dealing with.

But first she had a few home truths for Mike.

She marched back in the house and met Mike in the entry. "Are you through sticking your nose in my business?" she snapped.

Mike grimaced. "You heard."

"Every damned word of it out of both of your mouths. I'm not sure which of you I'm strangling first."

"Damn it, I was trying to look out for you, Jess. You told Heather you didn't want to date him. My wife said he's chasing after you like a dog in heat. I thought maybe if he heard it from me, he might back off."

"How would you feel if I went behind your back and said to someone what you said to Brian? If I didn't trust you to take care of yourself?"

"I wouldn't like it."

"Well, I don't either. I can and will handle Brian without your heavy-handed brotherly routine." She laid her hand on his arm. "You have your own problems, hon. You don't need to shoulder mine, too."

"If you say so."

He wandered down the hall and she gathered up Bobby and started toward her mother's. She had taken care of Mike's interference. Now she had to deal with Brian. She considered chewing his ass out as she had Mike's. But that would roll of Brian like water off a duck's back. He would ignore a butt-chewing like he'd ignored everything else she'd said to him. No, she had to do something that would get through to him and make her point. Something that would leave him without a doubt how she felt about being a *challenge.*

By the time she reached the theater, she was grinning like a fool. She knew exactly what she was going to do. Once she was through with him, he would think long and hard before doing to another woman what he was doing her.

And the beauty of her plan? It was going to be a hell of a lot of fun.

Chapter Seven

Brian whistled cheerfully as he got out of the shower. He ran a towel over his body and blotted the water out of his freshly shampooed hair. His face felt smooth to the touch, but he leaned into the mirror and checked to see if he'd left any stragglers. Nope. Nary a one. The last thing he wanted to do tonight was give Jessica whisker burn when he kissed her. Which he had every intention of doing at least once, and he hoped more than that. He didn't expect to get much further. It was only a second date and she wasn't the type to jump into bed with a man. But surely she wouldn't be averse to sharing a few more mind-blowing kisses that had worn down her resistance to going out with him again.

Underwear, a shirt and a pair of slacks waited for him on the bed. He studied his naked body in the mirror for a moment before pulling on the clothes. Nothing had changed since the last time he'd looked at himself. His musculature was good, but his skin was freckled where the sun hit it and pale where it didn't, with a chest and groin full of red hair that stood out like a beacon against his white skin. His last girlfriend said he reminded her of her mother's Howdy Doody puppet, and she didn't mean it as a compliment. He wondered how Jessica would feel about his body when she eventually saw him naked. Not that she would see him tonight. But if this date went as planned, there would be more dates, and at some point they'd be naked. He hoped she didn't have a thing for tall, dark, and handsome. Tall, pale, and handsome? Tall, freckled, and handsome?

On the other hand, if the way she kissed him was any indication, she found him plenty appealing.

He put on the rest of his clothes, including a paddle holster for the pistol on his hip, and pulled on the dressiest footwear he owned: a pair of black cowhide boots. He flipped through a row of concealing coats and jackets before deciding on a leather bomber jacket. Not for the first time, he marveled at how quickly he'd been able to change Jessica's mind about going out with him. It puzzled him a little. He'd expected to have to work a lot harder, especially given how determined she'd been to keep him at arm's length. Then they'd gone to her sister's and measured Kinsey for the hand. After that, her attitude had begun to soften, and she hadn't protested the stolen kiss the next time they'd practiced the ballet routine. It had taken two more rehearsals and two more stolen kisses before she'd capitulated, her smile enigmatic. "All right. I'll go out with you. Only this time we'll dress up and no Academy lessons or hamburgers will be involved."

He had no idea what had prompted her change of heart. Maybe Mike or Heather had made her see that her concerns had no merit. Or maybe her mother or father had said something but he didn't care what had done it. She was going out with him. That was all that mattered.

"No kids and no burgers," he'd promised. She said she liked most foods and admitted to being particularly fond of Italian, so he'd made reservations at an Italian restaurant on the Riverwalk. Another norther had blown in and there would be no riverside dining tonight, but a fireplace in the indoor dining room would add a soft romantic glow, as would candles and the arias playing quietly in the background. It might be a little over the top for a second date, but she'd agreed to go out, and he was pulling out all the stops.

He slapped on a little aftershave and turned out the bathroom light. The soft whir that was his constant companion these days grew louder as he stepped into the hall. More out of habit than for any other reason, he stepped into the second bedroom, where two tall printers moved back and forth, spinning a thin layer of melted plastic onto the growing hand parts. The red and black plastic quickly hardened into place, forming what would be the finger parts for the hand of a would-be basketball player at a local high school, who had requested the artificial appendage in his school colors and was hoping it would enable him to go out for the game. Brian ran his finger over the touch pad and the computer woke from sleep mode to display the photograph of Kinsey's arm and vestigial fingers. Green and yellow plastic were already on order, and as soon as the basketball player's hand was finished, he would print a 3-D model of Kinsey's arm and begin the process of designing her a hand to fit over the limb she had. A week or ten days to print and assemble the parts, and Kinsey's hand would be good to go. He hoped by the time he had it finished, he and Jessica were already lovers. He wouldn't want her to ever feel like his gift to her niece had anything to do with the way he felt about her.

The air was cold, but the sky was clear and the full moon sat on the eastern horizon. He programmed in the address she had given him and twenty minutes later pulled into a newish community in the far northeast corner of town, almost all the way to the city limits. It was too dark to see much detail tonight, but he'd driven through often enough while on duty to know that it was mostly small bungalows with young couples living in them, the kind of neighborhood that started out nice, but didn't always stay that way. If her husband hadn't been killed, they probably would have already moved somewhere bigger and better.

He pulled into the driveway at her address. The front light was on, and even in the dark, the little home was warm and inviting. He rang the bell. He could hear footsteps and smiled and waved at the peephole. She was laughing as she pulled open the door. "Why didn't you do a soft-shoe while you were at it?" she teased.

In response he hummed a little and did a few dance steps across the porch. "Better?"

"Much. Come on in. I'm not quite ready."

He followed her into the house. She was dressed and her face made up, but her legs and feet were bare, exposing her shapely ankles and pretty toes done in sparkly pink polish. Without her shoes, she was nearly a foot shorter than he was, and again he was struck by her delicate beauty. She ushered him to a small living room littered with an intriguing combination of stuffed animals and little toy trucks and cars. "Can I get you anything? Beer? Soda? Water?"

"A soda."

"Have a seat and I'll get you one."

The oversized sofa dwarfed the room but was super comfortable. He sank down in the cushions and looked around the warm, welcoming space. Another chair, this one more in line with the dimensions of the house, flanked the sofa and a big flat screen graced one wall. The family photos, including a portrait of a very young Jessica in a wedding dress clinging to the arm of a good-looking man in an SAPD dress uniform who was every bit as fair and freckled as he was graced another wall. In his mid to late twenties, the man's eyes danced with devilment and his face wore a cat that ate-the-canary expression. Brian peeked in a small decorative mirror. There was a definite resemblance. He wasn't sure how he felt about that.

On the other hand, if she liked men with freckles, she wasn't going to think he looked like a nineteen fifties puppet.

He was finishing the last of his soda when she returned, wearing sheer leggings and high-heeled ankle boots. His eyes traveled the length of her, taking in the muted plaid jumper and the green knit shirt beneath it. Her hair was loose and curled on the ends and the lightest touch of makeup enhanced her already considerable beauty. He reached out and ran his hand down the side of her face. "You are so damn beautiful it takes my breath away."

She smiled softly. "You ain't bad yourself."

He looked down at her footwear. "Are you okay walking a couple of blocks in those boots?"

"They're great unless I'm running a marathon. I can even chase Bobby across the mall in them."

"Speaking of." He looked around the room. "Where is he?"

She grinned. "On his first sleepover with cousin Kinsey. He's spent plenty of nights with Granny Jean and Granddaddy Eddie, but this is the first time at Heather's. She was going to order a pizza and download some little kid stuff they haven't seen yet."

"He'll have fun." Brian blinked as the implications sank in. *Bobby was gone for the entire night. Jessica didn't have to pick up her child until morning.* She was free to spend the night with him if she wanted to.

He would do his best to make sure she said yes.

He helped her into her coat and held the door of his truck. "So where are we going that I might have to do a little walking?" she asked as he shut the door on the driver's side.

"Downtown. I made reservations for that Italian place on the Riverwalk."

"The pizza place?"

"Nah. The nice one. Nothing's too good for my lady tonight."

He wondered at the strange expression on her face before it morphed into a smile. "I love that place. Thanks."

They chatted about this and that as they drove downtown. The Christmas lights and decorations were long gone, but the Riverwalk still sparkled with colorful neon signs, streetlamps, and the rapidly rising full moon. The crowd appeared to be the usual mix of tourists and locals, all warmly dressed for a midwinter stroll. He took her hand and they made their way down the flagstone sidewalk until they reached steps leading up to an outdoor patio. A few brave diners sat near big outdoor heaters, but most were going inside. "We'll come back when it's warmer and eat outside," he murmured as he pulled open the heavy door for her.

Brian slipped the hostess a twenty and she escorted them to a window table overlooking the river, which made the candle-and-fireplace atmosphere inside more romantic. They opened the menus waiting for them at the table. "Everything in here is so good," she enthused. "It's hard to pick."

"Pick your second favorite tonight and next time we come you can get your favorite. I'm getting chicken piccata."

"I don't order that. I can make it myself at home." She glanced down the menu. "Aha. Here's one I don't do well at all. Veal parmesan."

He looked at her curiously. "You do a lot of cooking?"

"Only on days I'm not working. Otherwise, Mom feeds Bobby and sends me home with a plate, God bless her. She's a fabulous cook. You?"

"I'm great on a grill, mediocre otherwise. What are your favorite things to cook?"

She named off a few dishes and the discussion went from there. Conversation was light but lively through salad and the main course, like any friends would share. At the same time, there was an undercurrent of desire Jessica did nothing to discourage. Her eyes sparkled as she met his gaze boldly. Her lips curved in a special smile. There was nothing blatant or overtly seductive in her manner.

There didn't need to be. He knew exactly what Jessica was thinking.

He was thinking the same thing.

The waiter cleared their dishes and brought them the dessert menu, a mixture of classic Italian and traditional American treats. She perused the menu for a moment. "Cannoli. You?"

"Strawberry cheesecake."

"Hmm. I love that one too."

"I can always share a bit with you."

"I'd like that."

I'd like to share more than dessert with you.

They sat quietly, looking at one another across the table while they waited for dessert. Brian's heart thumped as he looked across the table at the come-hither look in her eyes. It was hard to believe, as hard as she'd tried to put him off. If he wasn't mistaken, and he knew damned well he wasn't, an invitation was there.

He wasn't about to say no.

But he wasn't rushing things, either. The waiter brought their desserts and he cut off a small bite of cheesecake. "You want to try it?" He held the fork across the table.

She leaned forward and captured the bite between her lips. "Mmm. Damn, that's good. You need to eat the next bite."

He slid a bite into his mouth. "It is good." He held her eyes a moment. "Now you try yours."

She cut a piece with the side of her fork. "Ohmygod, it's wonderful." She cut off another bite. "Here. You try it."

She held out her fork. He put his hand over hers and steered the fork to his lips. "Oh, yes. That hits the spot." He grinned wolfishly. "You need some more cheesecake."

He cut her another bite and she in turned shared her cannoli. Damn, she knew how to seduce a man. With her eyes, with her lips, the invitation now was clear and unmistakable. He would be welcome in her bed tonight.

He'd won the jackpot.

He paid for the meal and together they strolled down the sidewalk. By now the full moon was high in the sky, its reflection silver in the rippling river water. They climbed the graceful staircase to street level and held hands as they crossed the street. A chilly gust caught them as they entered the parking garage. Jessica shivered. "Let's get you to the truck," he murmured.

He paid at the machine and the elevator whisked them to the third floor. He unlocked his truck from across the garage. She clung tightly to his hand and turned to face him at the passenger door: the longing in her eyes unmistakable. "Brian, I—"

He needed no further invitation. His lips came down on hers, firm and demanding. There was nothing tentative or hesitant in his touch. His need for her, the desire to possess her, and the longing he'd felt since that afternoon in her office …she was every dream, every fantasy he'd had of his ideal woman, and she was right here in his arms. He shivered as her hands crept around his waist, her hand hesitating only momentarily at the pistol on his hip before snaking them all the way around to his back and digging her fingers into his waist. Her breathing was ragged and he could feel her heart pounding as they clung together. His cock swelled and his thighs tensed. He hadn't lied to her. No other woman had ever turned him on the way she did. He felt momentary jealousy that Robby Clary had touched her first. But it was ridiculous to envy a dead man. Robby was gone and would never kiss her or touch her again.

It was Brian's turn now.

He anchored her head with his palm as he plundered her lips, branding her with his touch. She whimpered a little as his tongue caressed hers, then boldly met his strokes with her own. But it wasn't enough. Far from it. They were in a public place wearing two layers of clothing. They needed to be naked, skin to skin, with nothing but desire between them.

They needed to get to her house.

Her eyes were dazed when he finally raised his head. "I saw an invitation in your eyes earlier. Did you mean it? Tell me now if you didn't."

"Oh, yes, I mean it. I have fresh sheets on the bed and champagne in the refrigerator. Come home with me, Brian. Make love to me."

He didn't have to be asked twice. He lifted her into the passenger seat and hopped in on the driver's side. The expressway was still crowded as they headed for her subdivision. He said nothing and neither did she. But he felt her eyes on him in the dark pickup, eyes that made no secret of her desire. He gripped the steering wheel tightly, willing the cars in front of him to part and cursing to himself when they didn't. Finally they reached the exit that would take them to her house. The subdivision streets were clear and he wasted no time snaking through the deserted streets to her home. They practically ran to the front door and Jessica's fingers trembled as she inserted the key into the lock.

The door finally swung open. Jessica slammed it behind them and quickly twisted the deadbolt. His smile was feral as he turned to her. "Do I take you to your bedroom or take you up against the door?"

She looked at the door and shook her head. "That kind of sex is better on paper than for real." Grabbing his hand, she half-pulled him through the living room and down a hallway to the room on the end, where a king-sized bed was already turned down. She pointed to the bed. "*That* kind of sex is good for real. Sofas work too. But I draw the line at kitchen counters."

"Aw, you're no fun." Brian unzipped her coat and pushed it off her shoulders. "I was hoping for shower sex at the least."

She kicked off her boots and looked up at him. "Only with a stool, Romeo."

The little woman had a point. "Another fantasy bites the dust. You wound me."

She ran a seductive hand up his chest and pushed his jacket off his shoulders. "You wait and see. The reality is going to have the fantasy beat hands-down."

He tipped up her face and placed the gentlest of kisses on her lips. "I suspect you're right about that. Let's find out for sure."

He sat down on the side of the bed and pulled off his boots. He undid his belt and dropped his pistol in his left boot. Neither was shy about removing their clothing, his falling in a messy heap on the floor and hers carelessly tossed across an armchair.

She turned to face him and he sucked in his breath as his eyes traveled the length of her body, from her delicate neck and shoulders to her small but gorgeous breasts tipped with pink nipples. Her waist nipped in and her stomach was flat and smooth with no evidence that she'd carried a child. Her hips were rounded and the juncture of her thighs was capped with a neatly trimmed triangle of blonde curls. Her legs were shapely and muscular, as a dancer's would be. Her skin was fair, but had a healthy glow. "You're right. The reality definitely beats out the fantasy. I know you're beautiful." He reached out and touched a nipple with the tip of his finger. "I just didn't know how beautiful."

She gave him an appreciative once-over, running her fingers through the hair on his chest. "Yum." Her eyes traveled down his body to his already straining, erect cock. "Oh, my. This right here is exceptional." She ran her finger from the base to the tip, dampening her fingertip with the pearl of moisture clinging to the slit. Her eyes widened. "Shit. I forgot condoms. Did you bring any?"

He grinned sheepishly and got a handful out of his jacket pocket. "I'm ever the optimist. I really didn't expect to get to use these tonight."

A look he couldn't decipher crossed her face before her seductive smile returned. "So let's get busy using them."

He didn't have to be asked twice. He swung her into his arms and walked the three steps to the bed, where he laid her on the turned-down sheets. Her arms came around him as he slid in beside her, surprisingly strong as she wrapped them around his neck. They lay side by side as their lips came together. Despite their haste in undressing, neither was in a hurry now. Brian enjoyed a slow buildup on any occasion, but tonight it seemed particularly important to savor every kiss and touch. They kissed and nibbled as their fingers explored. His chest. Her breasts. His stomach. Her navel. His erect cock. Her dewy folds. They touched for long minutes, becoming intimately acquainted with hard and soft, moist and velvety.

Eventually their lips traveled lower. He nibbled his way from her lips to her breasts, teasing the tip with the end of his tongue and watching it pebble up with desire. She in turn explored every inch of his chest and shoulders, her lips hot on his skin as his cock grew even harder. Her touch was surprisingly bold as she continued her path down his body, nibbling her way along the trail of hair until she reached his groin. She buried her fingers in the hair surrounding his cock. "It's as delicious down here as it is up on your head."

She bent her head and put her lips around the tip of his cock.

Brian groaned. "Jess, I don't have that much control tonight." He eased himself out of her mouth.

"Now who's the spoilsport?"

"My turn." He oh-so gently pushed her down on her back and leaned over her. "I hear that ladies can have four orgasms to every one of ours. Want to see if that's true?"

"We're gonna experiment?"

"Just sayin'." His lips traveled down her body much as hers had explored his, teasing her breasts into tight knots before drifting lower, stopping to kiss every inch or so until reaching the juncture of her thighs. He pushed her legs open, exposing her inner folds to his gaze. He bent his head and touched her clit with the tip of his tongue, smiling with satisfaction when she came up off the mattress.

A throaty moan encouraged him to continue his sensual onslaught, drawing her up to the breaking point as she climbed to the apex and tumbled as tremors rocked her body. Her eyes were dazed as she looked at him. "I—I..."

He raised his head and kissed her, the taste of her still on his lips as he caressed hers tenderly. "One down, three to go."

She laughed softly. "After that, do you really think I'm good for three more?"

"Why wouldn't you be?" His hand crept down to where her legs were still parted. His fingers sought out her warmth, but when he would have plunged inside of her she flinched and shook her head. "Only cocks get to go in there."

Emboldened by her willingness to share what turned her on, his fingers found and stroked her sensitive nub, and it wasn't long until she was screaming out a second orgasm, her sensual response wanton.

She collapsed back against the pillows as he rubbed a circle on her bare stomach. "Ready to go for round three?" he breathed against her lips.

"I'm not sure I can." She reached out and stroked her hand down his cock. "When do I get to feel you inside of me?"

"All in good time." He kissed her lips. "I still think you're good for more." He grinned devilishly. "But I'll take my turn if you insist."

"I insist."

He fished a foil packet off the nightstand and suited up. But his lips and his fingers preceded him, with touches and caresses that had her coming off the bed for the third time, shaking and quivering and calling out his name. "Told ya," he said as he parted her legs and rose above her. He wasn't sure how tight she was and eased in slowly, marveling at the snugness with which her body gripped his. "Jesus, you feel good," he breathed as her internal muscles tightened around him. "Are you okay?"

"More than," she assured him as she thrust her hips upward. He plunged even further into her and they established a rhythm, her body deliciously tight around him as they moved together. He gritted his teeth. He was determined to give her the fourth orgasm he'd promised before he took his own pleasure. When he finally felt her start to come apart, he let himself go, and their bodies shook and trembled together as wave after wave of sensual delight washed over them.

He gripped her hips and, without breaking contact, they rolled over on their sides. "I don't want to crush you," he said as he ran his hand down her side.

She nestled her head next to his on the pillow. "I'm not fragile. I'm not going to break."

"I know that. But I probably weigh twice what you do, and that would get heavy." He kissed her, long and lingering. "Thank you for making me welcome in your bed."

Another odd expression flitted across her face before she smiled. "You are most welcome." She kissed the tip of his nose. "Are you interested in the champagne?"

"Do I have to put on my clothes? More importantly, do you have to put on yours?"

"You can wander around buck naked if you want. I have a robe hanging in the bathroom. I don't like to be cold."

"Okay. Naked for me. Robe for you." He went to the bathroom to remove the condom, cleaned up, and returned with her robe.

They popped the cork on the champagne and to his delight there was cheesecake-flavored ice cream. They stood in the kitchen, leaning against the island, drinking champagne and eating ice cream.

When they returned to bed the moon had sunk in the sky, but the sight of her naked body had his cock twitching again, and they indulged in a second round that had them both gasping. He disposed of the second condom and curled up next to her, his nose buried in her hair and her butt snuggling into his groin. She quickly drifted off into a deep sleep, her breathing even with the tiniest bit of a feminine snore.

He laid awake and stared into the darkness, the only light in the room that of the low silvery moon filtering between the drawn blinds. He'd conquered his challenge. He was in Jessica's bed and had been buried deep within her body. He'd vowed to make her his and he had, at least in her bed.

He'd thought it would be enough. Normally it would have. But having kissed her intimately and explored her sensual secrets, he came to the stunning realization that it wasn't enough. Taking her to bed wasn't going to be nearly enough. He needed more. He wanted to talk to her and share more dinners with her like they had tonight. He wanted more ice cream dates with Bobby. He wanted to meet her parents and cook hamburgers with her brother-in-law and sister. He wanted to get to know her better and find out if they had a basis for building a real relationship.

Tonight had been a beginning, and it had been a good one. But it was only the beginning.

The best was yet to come.

Chapter Eight

Kicking him out of her house this morning was going to be difficult.

Last night had been the best sex she'd had in her entire life, and that was saying something—Robby was no slouch.

Jessica lay next to Brian and stared at the dim morning light filtering through the window shades. Her arms and legs felt like jelly and her body was more relaxed than it had been since the last time she'd made love to Robby. But even with her late husband, the sex hadn't been as spectacular as it had been last night with Brian. He'd been the perfect lover. Giving and at the same time demanding. She knew she liked sex. But she'd had no idea she was capable of the responses he'd elicited from her last night. Four orgasms in one session. Amazing. But with him she had done it. And then to go for another round after the champagne and cheesecake that was equally wonderful? Unbelievable.

If the kind of sex they shared last night was all that mattered, she wouldn't care what he did for a living. She'd be all in. Unfortunately, the sex wasn't all there was to dating him or having a relationship. So she would adhere to the original plan and after she shared what she had to say, she'd send him on his merry way.

As his arm pulled her close and cupped her breast possessively, she thought one more round of spectacular sex wouldn't hurt a thing.

She turned over in bed to face a sleepy-eyed Brian with a lazy smile on his face. "What is this sexy softness I'm feeling?" He thumbed her nipple as it swelled into a tight peak.

"I believe that's what's known as a boob." She reached out and mirrored his motions, raking her thumb across his flat male nipple.

To her surprise he flinched and pulled away. "Ow. Not my cup of tea."

She jerked her hand back. "Sorry."

"S'okay. I hear some guys like that, but I'm not one of them."

She put her hand flat on his chest. "So show me what you do like."

He leaned forward. "I thought we established that last night." He scooted over the few inches separating them and wrapped his arms around her. "More of this. Lots more of this." He cradled her face between his big hands and took her lips in a searing kiss.

They kissed and touched one another for long moments. Side by side, leisurely exploring one another's bodies as they lay face to face. Jessica pushed the doubt and regret from her mind. She would savor this last time they would be together. She would hold on to the memory and treasure these stolen moments with another reckless hero, as she'd treasured her memories of Robby. Moments the likes of which she doubted she'd have if she settled down with the kind of man she wanted this time around.

They touched one another slowly and deliberately. He caressed her breasts. She kissed his stomach. He found the sweet spot beneath her triangle of curls. She caressed his swelling cock. When the moment was right, she rolled on the condom and straddled him, her cries soft as she rose and fell above him, his hands steadying on her hips as she took him up and over the edge, her hoarse cry triggering his powerful orgasm as his cock shook inside her body.

Breathless, she rolled off him and stared up at the ceiling. He curled up beside her and nuzzled her neck as his arm circled her waist. "Damn. What a way to start the morning," he breathed as he kissed her cheek.

Hell. Now it was really going to be hard to kick him out.

But she had to do it. If she let him stay and then tried to break it off later, she'd be right back where she started, with a persistent lover who wouldn't take no for an answer. She had to make sure he got it through his head how she felt about him.

She unwound his arm and slid across the bed, ignoring his indignant protest. "Where are you going?"

She shrugged into the robe she found on the floor. "I'm going to make a cup of coffee. And you're going home. Now." She picked up his pile of clothes and dumped them in his lap.

"Why now?" He didn't bother to hide his confusion. "I mean, I know I have to be out of here before Bobby gets home, but you want me to leave now?"

"Yeah, I do. Now that you've met your challenge."

"What the hell are you talking about?" He sat up, fighting off the pile of clothes on his chest.

"Just what I said. I was the best challenge you've had in a long time. Congratulations, Brian. Challenge met. Goal reached. Jessica fucked. Now go home." She sailed out of the room and headed to the kitchen.

She turned on the light and was putting a pod in the coffeemaker when he stomped in, wearing only his boxer-briefs. "What the hell do you mean, I met my challenge?"

She slammed down the lid of the coffeemaker and pushed the button. "Don't play stupid with me. You told my bossy-assed brother-in-law, whom I have already taken down a peg or two, I was the best challenge you'd had in a long time. I was a *challenge* to you. I heard you tell him. I was a fucking goal you were bound and determined to reach. So fine. I made it easy for you. I got you out of my system, and hopefully you got me out of yours."

"Like hell you're out of my system." His eyes narrowed. "Is that all you think last night meant to me? That I was winning some damned challenge? Do you really think I could have made love to you like that if all you were to me is a challenge?"

She looked at him, not trying to hide her exasperation. "How the hell do I know? I hardly know you. All I know about you is when you get something in your mind you won't give up. You were bound and determined I would go out with you. You were bound and determined I'd go back out with you. Your next goal would have been sex. So I gave you that too." She turned away and picked up the coffee cup. "Here. Take this one. I'll make another."

"Keep your damned coffee."

"Fine." With trembling fingers, she raised the cup to her lips and sipped the too-hot brew. "If you don't want the coffee, get your clothes on and skedaddle. You met your challenge and there's nothing more for you here."

"What do you mean, there's nothing more? You can say that to me with a straight face, after the night, and morning we shared?"

She raised her chin and hoped her voice didn't tremble. "I can. I take no pleasure in sending you on your way. But I told you. I refuse to get involved with another man who puts his life on the line for his job. Besides, I don't appreciate being a fucking challenge you felt you had to meet."

"You were more than a challenge and you know it." He didn't try to hide his bitterness. "There was a hell of a lot more than that going on last night, even if you won't admit it." He took a deep breath. "And about the other. Yes, I put my life on the line. That's who I am, and that's what I do."

"And that's exactly why you need to get your clothes on and walk out the door. One risk-taker in my life was enough."

His jaw muscle jumped, his hands fisted and unfisted before he stomped to the bedroom and emerged a few minutes later with his clothes and boots on. He carried his jacket across his arm and his sidearm was clearly visible.

His hair was mussed and bright-red scruff dusted his cheeks and chin. Even angry, his appeal reached out to her and it was all she could do not to touch him. She stood rooted to the spot, her fingers trembling as she clutched the coffee cup. They stared at each other for a long moment. "You could have just said no," he near growled.

"Would you have accepted it? Or would you have kept after me, night after night after night? You refused to take no for an answer. I had to make my point somehow."

"Fine. Point taken. But will you be able to turn your back on what we shared? Because I sure as hell won't."

He slammed the front door so hard the house shook. She gave him time to get out of the driveway before locking the door. Her hands were trembling as she collapsed onto the sofa. She'd made her point. But at what cost? Brian hadn't only been pissed at being played. There had been hurt in his eyes. And she wasn't feeling unscathed. *Great plan, Jess.*

Not the best scenario when they were costarring in a play.

***

Brian trudged tiredly into the substation, yawning in the early morning darkness. He'd laid awake most of the night and had drifted off moments before his 4:45 alarm sounded. The waning moon shone brightly in the western sky and a cold wind plastered his jacket to his body. His head ached despite the two cups of coffee he'd already downed, and he promised himself another before getting into the cruiser.

He hoped there would be no crises to deal with today, because he wasn't anywhere near the top of his game. He could manage a normal workday, and still have the strength to face Jessica at tonight's rehearsal. Steam was still coming out of his ears over the way she'd treated him, and it would be all he could do to remain civil in front of everyone at the Durango.

Sugar Johnson sat at the dispatch desk. "Mornin', sweetcakes. You look like you got run over by a Mac truck."

He shrugged. "Where's Lydia? Is the baby coming?"

"Got here last night about eleven. Jaime texted everybody a picture. You didn't see it?"

"Haven't checked my phone. I'll take a peek in the locker room."

The coffee was still dripping, so he went in the locker room and was zipping up his vest when Mike Werner came in, looking like thunder. He planted himself in front of Brian. "I thought I told you to stay away from Jessica. Instead, you spent the night at her place."

"And I told you to stay out of my fucking business," Brian shot back. "As did Jessica, I understand. 'Bossy-assed brother-in-law' were her exact words."

"Damn it, man. You expect me to stand by and do nothing when you're gonna hurt her?"

"She's a big girl, and knows her mind." *Did she ever.* "You want to take this up with her, be my guest. I've got a shift to do and I need my head in the game." He walked out and didn't look back.

He drank a third cup of coffee during the sergeant's briefing. The day was long and boring as he dealt with the usual fender benders, neighborhood altercations, and a couple of break-ins. He went home and showered before nuking an oversized packaged dinner and heading to the theater.

Jessica was teaching a dancing class when he arrived. He stood at the back of the mirrored studio for a moment, watching her graceful body bend, arch, and skip across the dance floor, and imagined that same body riding his as she had the other morning. His lips firmed and his eyes narrowed. If she thought she'd run him off with her little stunt, she had another think coming.

She caught him staring at her. Her lips tightened and shot daggers. He raised his eyebrow and crossed his arms in front of him. He'd be damned if she would run him off with a glare. But his phone buzzed with a terse text from Letti that he was expected in the rehearsal room across from the offices, so he uncrossed his arms and, as nonchalantly as he could, left Jessica teaching the class.

Letti and Owen were waiting for him in the big mirrored rehearsal room. "We're rehearsing the scene with Curly and Jud in the smokehouse," she announced without preamble. "Afterwards, Jessica's going through the first of the ballet sequence with the ensemble."

"Okay." He shook hands with Owen. "Are we doing the song also?"

Letti held up her phone. "Got the music right here."

They got to work. Owen proved to be a pleasure to work with, bringing the menacing Jud Fry to life under Letti's expert direction. Brian forced himself to concentrate on the scene as he sang the sarcastically funny "Pore Jud is Daid" and they traded lines. They were still ironing out the scene when the ensemble members began to show up, milling around outside the door with the occasional curious peek in through the small pane.

When they finally nailed the scene to Letti's satisfaction, she motioned the ensemble to enter. The mostly young performers trooped in, followed by an unsmiling Jessica. Owen eyed her curiously and leaned over to Brian. "She looks like somebody shit in her oatmeal."

Brian shrugged.

Letti ducked out and Jessica stepped to the front of the room. In thorough detail, she talked the ensemble through what the long dance scene would consist of before breaking it down into manageable sequences. "We aren't dancing it exactly as it was done in the movie. Laurey will dance with the girls first, and then with Curly before the wedding scene. I doubt we'll get to Owen and Brian's sequences this evening, so you're free to go if you like."

Owen gave her a friendly salute and walked out. Brian shook his head and sat down on a bench along the wall. She ignored him and spent the next hour taking the ensemble through the first sequence in which Laurey dances with the girls. Her patience was infinite as she demonstrated the handful of simple ballet steps the scene required. Despite his aggravation with her for the weekend fiasco, Brian found himself admiring her skill as a choreographer. She had put together a series of simple steps that, when put to the lilting score of the old musical, looked like so much more.

She finally called a halt about ten. The ensemble was in no particular hurry to call it a night, and was quick to invite him to go down the street to Thirties, their favorite watering hole. "No can do," he said lightly as he rose from the bench. "I need to go home and get some rest." *Especially since I didn't get any last night.* "Gotta strap on that gun tomorrow and protect the people of our fair city."

Some people smiled, others chuckled, and the group made their way out of the practice room. When everyone had left, Jessica dropped down on the bench and untied a ballet slipper. "If you were all that damned tired, you could have gone home an hour ago," she said caustically.

"I want to talk to you."

"I gather you're still pissed."

"You're damned right."

"To borrow your favorite phrase, tough shit. I don't know why you're so bent out of shape. Unless I didn't make it hard enough for you. Is that it? Were you looking for a Mount Everest challenge and got a hill out north of town instead?"

"For the last damned time, it's not about a challenge. It's about what you and I shared and what we could keep on sharing, if you weren't so fixated on what I do for a living."

"Huh, let me see what that is. Huh. Maybe because what you do for a living could get you *killed.*"

"I'm not gonna get killed. I'm trained to within an inch of my life. And I'm damned careful."

"There is no such thing as 'careful' when you do what you do. Robby thought he was careful, too."

Brian opened his mouth and then shut it. Criticizing her late husband would only make her dig her heels in further.

Jessica jammed her feet in a pair of Crocs. "You got what you wanted," she said tiredly. "I went back with you. I took you to my bed. Now leave me alone."

"No, I didn't get what I wanted. I want to see you again. I want to date you and I want to make love to you again. Damn it, Jessica, I want to see where we can take whatever this is between us."

"I can tell you exactly where it will go. We will date. We will fall in love. We might even marry. And then you'll go out some morning and get your ass killed. Been there, done that, have the folded flag to prove it." She shoved her ballet slippers in her duffel. "So. Not only no, but fuck no. I am not going there. Why should I?"

"Because of this." He reached for her and held her by the shoulders, gently enough so that she could get away if she wanted, and slowly drew her to him. "Because of what we shared before and could share again. Because you and your little boy are my dream come true, and I'm not going to walk away because you're scared. Because...because..." He slid his arms around her and lowered his head, capturing her lips and nudging them open with his tongue.

Rigid at first, he felt her body slowly relax in his arms as he continued his gentle assault on her senses, each touch and caress designed to remind her of the passion they'd shared in her bed.

Slowly but surely he coaxed a response from her, as she went from passively accepting his embrace to actively participating, her arms slowly snaking around his waist and her nipples growing firm against his chest. His cock swelled, as much from the memory of their shared passion as from having her in his arms again. They clung together for long moments, reliving the desire they'd shared and that he so wanted them to share again.

The blood was pounding in his ears when he finally raised his head. "That's why we should go there."

She stepped out of his arms. "Because we have great chemistry?" She sighed. "Brian, if it was only about sex, I'd say yes so fast it would make your head swim. It's everything else that's holding me back."

"'Everything else? What's holding you back is your fear." He leaned forward and dropped another kiss on her lips, this one barely a touch. "You're going to realize fear is keeping you from being happy. Sooner or later, you're gonna be mine, and I hope to God it's sooner, Jess."

He left before she could come up with a reply.

Chapter Nine

Jessica pulled into Heather's driveway. The early February sun shone brightly and the air was almost warm on her cheeks. San Antonio was enjoying one of its respites from the cold of winter, and the forecasters predicted a few more days before another blast of arctic air swooped in from the north. If the weather held until Sunday, Bobby would get a trip to the zoo. Otherwise, they'd be back at the DoSeum. They were regulars at the new, cleverly thought-out children's museum close to downtown. No matter how often they went, Bobby seemed to have a wonderful time. Jess wondered if Heather would take Kinsey when the child would have her prosthetic hand. Her sister shied away from taking Kinsey around other children for fear of stares and ridicule. Maybe the hand would make a difference. Jessica hoped so. It was time for Kinsey to experience the things like the DoSeum that other children her age enjoyed.

Jess knocked on the door twice and was about to let herself in with her emergency key when Heather yanked open the door. She was dressed, but her hair was mussed and one side of her face had pillow creases. "Were you—"

"No, I wasn't asleep," Heather said crossly. "I was laying on the couch watching a show with Kinsey." She opened the door wider. "Come on in. Is Brian here yet?"

"No. He said eleven. I'm early."

Jessica stepped in and closed the door behind her. "Is Mike off today?"

"He's working a funeral. He'll be home in time for lunch."

Kinsey was parked in front of the television. She spotted Jessica and ran across the room. "Mommy said I get my hand today. I can hug you better."

Jessica picked the child up for a big hug. "You will, won't you? That'll be so special. You'll be able to do other things, too. Like ride your trike. And hold your dolly in either hand. That will be so much fun."

"I hope it will help her fit in with other children a little better." Heather wrung her hands.

"How would we know if she fits in with other children? She never gets to be around any."

Heather's eyes rounded at the tartness in Jessica's tone. "She's around Bobby," she said defensively.

"She needs to be around more than Bobby."

"But they—"

Jessica breathed a sigh of relief when the doorbell rang. The last thing she wanted was to get into it with Heather this morning. "I'll get it."

She sprinted toward the door and threw it open to be met by a smiling Brian. "Mornin' beautiful." He looked around. "Where's your good-looking little wingman?"

"Bobby? I took him over to Mom's already."

"Oh. I was hoping to see him." He leaned over and kissed her cheek as he walked in. "I dreamt about you last night," he said softly. "You were naked and riding me again. I've had a hard-on all morning."

"Your problem. Not mine." She shut the door and gestured toward the living room. "Kinsey's in there." Brian smiled knowingly and headed toward the living room.

She wasn't about to admit it, but she'd had almost the same dream last night, and had woken damp between her legs. She'd taken care of the physical need with a sexy fantasy and her fingers, but the longing for Brian had not gone away.

It hadn't gone away in the two weeks since he'd spent the night in her bed. If anything, it had grown stronger the more she was around him. He hadn't kissed her again, and his touches had been limited to their dancing together, but he'd not let up with the sexy smiles, the winks and the verbal innuendos reminding her how good they had been together.

God help her, she was beginning to weaken. Late at night, when Bobby was asleep and the house was quiet, she wondered if it would be so bad to see him. Not to have a relationship with him, and never to fall in love with him, but the occasional date and inevitable booty call that would accompany it. She could have the best of both worlds. She could have him in her life and in her bed, and her heart could remain unscathed.

In her saner moments she knew it was lunacy. But the possibilities were tantalizing.

She followed him to the living room. He knelt and took Kinsey's good hand in his. "And how is Princess Kinsey this morning?"

"My hand. Did you bring my hand?"

"I do believe I did. Let's try it on and see if it fits." He turned to Heather. "Put her in her booster chair and we'll try it out."

While Heather sat Kinsey in her chair, Brian rummaged around in his backpack and withdrew a small green and yellow hand in the exact colors as Princess Tiana's dress. He held the hand in front of Kinsey. "What do you think, sweetheart?"

She reached out with her good hand and touched the prosthetic with her finger. "It's pretty." She smiled brightly at all of them.

"It's awesome." Jessica reached out and touched it also. The small hand didn't look like a real one, and didn't pretend to. It was shaped like a hand with an opposable thumb and fingers that were jointed and had narrow cords attached to a mechanism that would go above the elbow. "When she bends and flexes her elbow, the fingers open and close, right?"

"That's right." He bent the tiny arm piece back and forth and the fingers opened and closed.

Heather stared at the hand. "She's really going to be able to pick something up." Her lips trembled and her eyes filled with tears.

Brian's eyes were warm. "Yes, Mama. She's going to be able to pick up a doll and hold her tricycle handle. Here, let's put it on." His fingers were gentle as he fitted the hand over Kinsey's forearm and elbow and attached it with the Velcro straps. "Good. It fits well."

Kinsey held up the hand. "Lookee, Mommy. I have a hand."

"It's beautiful, Kinsey." Heather's eyes overflowed and she let out with a sob. "Aw, hell. I didn't mean to cry. But look at her. My baby has two hands."

Heather sobbed and Jessica took her into her arms. "Yeah, I know. I'm happy, too." Tears ran down her own cheeks as Heather cried.

Kinsey looked at Brian with puzzlement. "Why are they crying?"

"Because they're happy." Brian gave Jessica a thumbs-up. "So let's let Mommy and Aunt Jessica cry while I show you how to make your fingers bend." He fished out a box containing a Barbie-sized Tiana doll from his backpack. "Let's practice on Tiana."

Jessica and Heather both laughed. They watched as Brian showed Kinsey how to bend her elbow so the fingers would flex, and then handed her the doll. It wasn't long before Kinsey could grasp the doll in the plastic hand, which prompted another round of sobbing from Heather.

Jessica's eyes were damp as she turned to Brian. "I guess it's like this every time."

"Actually, I wouldn't know. This is the first time I've delivered an arm in person."

"Really?"

"I ship them all over the world. The only time I've seen this moment is when a family member sends me a video clip. Half the time it's in another language, but I can see the smiles."

"Isn't the language of happiness universal?"

"I guess it is."

Her sister calmed down and they spent a few minutes watching Kinsey play with the doll. Brian was packing up when the front door opened and Mike strode in. Kinsey made a beeline for her father. "Lookee, Daddy. I have a new hand. And it *works*."

Mike scooped Kinsey up and gave her a big kiss. "That's super wonderful, princess. Show me."

Kinsey ran across the room and picked up the Tiana doll. Mike stared in awe. "My God. It does work." He looked up with eyes that were moist. "She can ride her trike now." He reached out and grasped Brian's hand. "I don't know how to thank you."

Brian smiled modestly. "The only thanks I need are the smiles on everyone's faces this morning. Especially Kinsey's."

"Can I at least offer you lunch?" Heather asked.

"I'm working a job fair at a synagogue this afternoon. But thanks."

"Hell of a note when places of worship have to hire security," Mike commented.

"Amen to that." He shook hands with Mike and gave Heather a gentle hug. "I'll see everyone later."

"I'll see you to the door." Jessica ushered him through the house and followed him out onto the front porch. She reached out and grasped his hand. "I don't know how to thank you. I haven't seen Heather that happy in a long time."

"Glad I could put a smile on some faces this morning." He gave Jessica a sexy wink. "See you this evening, beautiful." He planted a swift kiss on her lips and sauntered down the driveway.

Damn. When he looked at her like that, it was hard not to throw herself at him.

Jessica found Heather alone in the kitchen. "Mike's already got Kinsey out on the patio with her tricycle," her sister said. "Can you stay for lunch?"

"Sure. What are we having?"

"Breakfast for lunch. Eggs and bacon. Canned biscuits. Work for you?"

"Like a charm."

They worked together to assemble the simple meal. Heather kept glancing knowingly at Jessica. "You're only fooling yourself, you know," she said finally. "You're falling for him."

"No. Yes. Maybe. Hell, I don't know."

"It would be hard not to fall for him," Heather said quietly.

"I don't know if falling is the word. But I am weakening, and this morning's part of the reason why. He's not only sexy, good-looking, and dynamite between the sheets, he's a good person. He's a genuinely decent human being. He makes hands on his own time and his own dime, he's helping me out in the Academy until I can get another couple of teachers on board, and he won't let me pay him. He's everything I could ever hope for. And then he puts on a SAPD uniform and straps on a gun."

"And sometimes he puts on tactical gear and carries an assault rifle."

"Who could forget that." She looked at Heather. "Why am I doomed to want that kind of man? Why couldn't I get turned on by an accountant?"

Heather shrugged. "There's something about them. Daddy, Robby, Mike, and now Brian. I can't put my finger on what it is exactly, but they are different. More alpha, I guess. Damn if a lot of women aren't turned on by that. And then, if they're lucky, they spend the rest of their lives worrying about the SOBs."

"And if they're not lucky, they put on a black dress and stand beside a casket."

"Like I'm scared I'll have to someday." Heather took a deep breath. "It's really starting to get to me, Jess. I thought I could do it when I married him. But it's getting harder. And then there's the other." She gestured toward her head. "That's getting worse, too."

"That blows." She stepped to the sliding glass doors. "Heather, come look. She's holding onto both handles and pedaling across the patio." She motioned for Heather to come over. "You watch. I'll scramble the eggs."

Jessica found fresh tortillas and salsa in the refrigerator. She put the biscuit package back in the fridge, and the eggs and bacon turned into tasty breakfast tacos. For once Heather and Mike weren't sniping at one another, and Kinsey glowed with happiness. This was the way it should be, Jessica thought as she and Heather cleared the table and loaded the dishwasher. Happy. Relaxed. Comfortable.

Brought to you this morning by the kindness of Brian Howard.

Heather took Kinsey down the hall for her nap. A commotion broke out a couple of minutes later. "No, Mommy. I want it. Leave it on."

Jessica and Mike looked at one another and started laughing. "I think the arm's a success," she said.

"I owe him big, don't I?" Mike asked.

"That's not why he made it. He meant what he said this morning. Your smiles were enough reward for him. Damn. I wish…"

"I know what you wish, and I'm sorry, Jess."

"Me, too." She bit her lip. "Heather said something this morning about it starting to get to her, too. You and the danger. Has she said anything to you?"

"She doesn't have to. I can see it. She's getting worse. She's losing ground right in front of me. But with her, the question becomes if the problems are because she's worried about me, or if it's the chemical imbalance causing the anxiety."

"So she is worse. It's not my imagination."

"No, it's not your imagination. Damn. If I had anything else I could do for a living, I'd do it. But I've been a cop since I got out of college. I don't know anything else."

"And it might not make a bit of difference if you did change jobs. The chemical imbalance might be causing most of the problem."

"It's a fucked-up mess, isn't it?" She didn't answer. She didn't have to. Heather had to go back to the doctor and find another way to treat her condition. Mike sighed. "You know, I have nothing against him. If anything, I think he's a great guy. But if it's going to drive you around the bend, falling for him and then worrying about him every day when he goes to work, maybe you'd be better off keeping him at arm's length. Not because of him. But because of you and how his job makes you feel."

"It sounds kind of ridiculous when you put it that way."

"Don't think that. It's not ridiculous at all. What you went through losing Robby the way you did was about as traumatic as it comes. You're entitled to your insecurities. You've earned them. And you're right to want to protect yourself from any further hurt." He glanced down the hall. "Maybe that's what Heather should have done. She should have listened to you and not married me."

"Aw, Mike. That was my fear talking. You're good for her and Kinsey. The last thing I should do is put my problems on Heather. She's got enough to deal with." She shook her head. "He's such a good guy and I'm turning my back on him."

"You're doing what you have to do. Even if it sucks."

And it did suck.

***

Jessica watched as the ensemble dancers walked in and took their places as the guests at a wedding. She danced between the line of them, her steps light and a smile on her lips as Laurey danced toward her love. The wedding sequence had to be just right, the joy and anticipation palpable as Laurey danced down the aisle toward Curly so when she finds herself facing Jud instead, the audience would feel the girl's horror.

They'd practiced the sequence several times, and the last run-through was spot on. She motioned for the ensemble to stay in place and called Owen over. "The lighting will allow you and Brian to switch places without the audience noticing. When Laurey opens her eyes and sees Jud, she will be shocked and so will they. Let's take it from where Laurey dances down the aisle."

Letti ran the music back and Jessica practiced shutting her eyes and waiting for a moment in anticipation before opening them to see

Jud. Owen and Brian had exchanged places and Jessica opened her eyes to find Owen standing in front of her with menace on his face. She took the requisite step back as the music shifted to a minor key and he grabbed her hands, putting one on his shoulder and holding the other one in waltz position.

He waltzed her around the rehearsal room, his steps deliberately ungainly, before Jessica pulled back and tried to get away. But Owen picked her up in a fireman's carry and twirled her a bit before walking toward where the bar scene portion would pick up. Letti cut the music and Owen put her down to the applause of the ensemble. "Nice job," Jess told Owen. "I hope I don't give you a hernia."

"Nah, you're not that heavy." He turned to Letti. "What did you think?"

Letti handed them her phone and they watched the clip of the dance. Jessica winced at the horror on her face upon facing Owen's character for the first time. Some of the horror was feigned, but a certain amount of it was real. It still killed her to see Owen's damaged face knowing Robby's recklessness had put those scars there. Owen was playing the part for all it was worth, bringing the troubled yet frightening ranch hand to life. "The dancing is good," she said as she watched herself and Owen dancing in the clip. "Not perfect yet. But we're off to a good start."

They ran through the sequence three more times before Jessica called it a day. Letti shared a few suggestions for the emotional aspects of the ballet, and everyone was dismissed. Brian caught up to her when she was about halfway to her car. "I dreamt about you again last night," he said quietly. "You were riding me and calling out my name."

"Maybe you need a stronger sleeping pill," she said dryly.

"Or maybe I need for a certain sexy dancer to give me a chance," he returned. "Seriously, Jess. I'm as sorry as I can be that you thought you were nothing but a challenge to me. What can I do to convince you that you're so much more?" He put his hand on her arm. "Please. Is there anything I can say or do to make things right?"

Jessica stared up at Brian's face, shadowed in the light of a lone streetlamp. He thought it was his fault. And, sure, she'd thought she'd teach him a lesson, only to learn she got it wrong. Ultimately, it didn't make a difference. Well, it did. Now more than ever, she felt the rightness of them, which made her inability to get past her fear that much worse.

She'd never talked to him about her marriage. About the wounds losing Robby had left on her soul. Maybe if she told him more about what she'd been through, Brian would understand that her refusal had nothing to do with him and everything to do with her loss. If he understood maybe he would respect her decision and abandon his pursuit.

"Let's go get a beer. We can talk and maybe I can make you understand."

"You can try, sweetheart. Not saying I'm gonna agree with you."

"But you'll at least listen. Right?"

"Yeah, I'll listen."

Chapter Ten

Brian escorted her to the sidewalk and they walked down the block. Thirties, the deco bar frequented by the Durango crowd, was mostly empty this late on a weeknight. The hostess showed them to an out of the way booth that was relatively quiet and took their order for a couple of craft beers.

Be brave. "First off, you have no reason to need to get back in my good graces. I know you don't—didn't—think of me as a challenge. I got that wrong." He nodded. "You're helping me in the Academy, and you made my niece a hand. Changed her life. Both are much appreciated."

"Thanks, but it's not your gratitude I'm after."

"I know," she whispered. Geez, she hated this. "I think you understand this isn't about you as a person. It's about my loss, and my marriage with Robby."

Brian sat back. "Go on."

The waitress brought their beers and Jessica took a sip of hers. "I met Robby when he came to the high school to do an anti-drug presentation. I was a senior. He was already out of college and working on the force. I slipped him my phone number and he called me up a week later."

Brian's eyes widened. "Definitely reckless. He didn't know if you were jailbait."

"Oh, I was. They didn't call him 'Reckless Robby' for nothing. But in all fairness, his partner recognized me and told him I was Eddie Herrmann's daughter and that he better be damned careful. Robby got Daddy's blessing before he called me." She snickered. "That really took balls."

"Your dad's a cop, too?"

"He was. He retired three years ago. Daddy admired Robby's chutzpah. Actually, he admired everything about him, and gave him the go-ahead. We started dating. I fell for him hard. Robby was exactly what I thought I wanted. Good-looking, a little older, wiser in the ways of the world than the boys my age. Interesting to talk to. He was charming, brave, daring, and yes, reckless, the quintessential ladies' man, and everybody in the department knew it. But I figured I would be 'the one' and I could handle him. Everybody thought I was a naïve kid who didn't know what she was getting into." She chuckled. "I knew exactly what I was getting into and I relished every bit of it."

Brian looked at her thoughtfully. "So you married him."

"A year out of high school. I was crazy about him. He was crazy about me, and gave up his wicked ways. What I couldn't do was curb the recklessness. Not that I ever really tried. I figured it wouldn't do any good. Robby got off on taking chances. It was in his nature. Like it's in the nature of everyone who holds a job like that."

Brian's eyes narrowed. "A job like what?"

"First responders. Military. The people who run toward danger instead of away from it."

"What makes you think recklessness is in our nature?"

"It would have to be or you couldn't do the job."

"Where did he take his chances? Were they all on the job, or was he into other things like extreme sports?"

"He was into rock climbing and motorcycle racing, but he was more into taking chances on the job. One time he stepped between two rival gang members with guns drawn and grabbed the guns out of their hands. He was forever getting between a shooter and their target. Drove his supervisors crazy."

"Well, yeah. Not following department protocol was unsafe for him, his partner, and the civilians."

She knew that. "After a couple of years, we bought the house and I commuted to San Marcos for school. I got pregnant and things were wonderful. Too wonderful. I should have known it wouldn't last." She felt tears gathering in her eyes. "Something that beautiful never does, I guess." She stopped and took a breath. "He got up one morning and strapped on his gun. He gave me a big smacking kiss and walked out the door to go to work. I never saw him alive again."

Brian sat silently, waiting for her to continue.

"I was on my way home from San Marcos. Daddy called me and I could tell from his voice that something was really wrong. I went straight to the hospital. Owen was in surgery and clinging to life by a thread, and Robby was DOA. Daddy tried to stop me, but I made them let me see him. I wanted to kiss him goodbye. But most of his face was gone." She tossed back a gulp of beer. "At least I knew he was dead. None of that 'they have the wrong guy' shit. He had a hero's funeral and every posthumous accolade they could think of. Trying to quash the gossip, I guess."

"What gossip?"

"That he acted recklessly. That he didn't give Owen time to trace out the right wires: that he guessed at which one to cut, and he guessed wrong. Knowing Robby, he'd thought Owen was taking too long and got impatient. That's what heroes are like."

"Do tell," Brian murmured.

"I was six months pregnant, a widow at twenty-one, and the love of my life was in the ground. It did me in. Just about destroyed me. I sunk into a depression like you wouldn't believe. Didn't eat, didn't sleep, didn't get out of bed for days. I considered suicide. And might have done it if I hadn't been pregnant."

"You wouldn't have killed yourself."

"Don't be too sure. You have no idea what I went through. The pain and despair...until you go through it, you have no idea how tempting it is to end it all." She looked at the dregs, and the thought of drinking them turned her stomach.

"I had Bobby and he gave me a reason to go on. But it was slow going. I didn't go out on a date until he was two years old. I have yet to date anyone seriously. You're the first man I've been attracted to. But I'm not about to risk caring about another cop, and I'm sure as hell not falling for a SWAT team member. The ultimate risk-taker."

Brian put his beer bottle down and looked her in the eye. "This is the second time in one conversation you've intimated that all first responders are risk-takers. That we like taking risks. Did it ever occur to you that we take risks because we have to and not because we want to?"

"No. Of course not. Brian, I'm not stupid. You would have to get off on it to even do it. Nobody makes you be a cop or a firefighter, or a soldier. People go into those kinds of jobs because they want to. Nobody put a gun to Robby's head and nobody put a gun to yours. You chose the department and the SWAT team because you like taking chances. You all do. It's the nature of the beast."

"Really? It's not in my nature and it's not in the nature of most of the SWAT team. We train hard to eliminate risk. To save lives, including ours."

"Whether I believe that is irrelevant. Please believe me. I'd give my eye teeth if you did something different. But you don't. Even Mike says I need to stay away from you."

"What does he have to do with it?"

"He watched me fall apart when I lost Robby. He knows me and knows how your job makes me feel."

"Are you finished spouting bullshit?"

Jessica's lips tightened. "I'm not spouting bullshit."

"I don't know what you'd call it, then. Darlin', face it, your beloved Robby was reckless, and a damned fool. I don't appreciate being compared to him."

"That's a shitty thing to say. Robby was a hero."

"No, Robby was an idiot. He took foolish chances for the hell of it, even with a pregnant wife at home. You said it yourself. And I've heard the gossip. I've seen Owen's face. And for the record, I don't get off running toward danger. I do it because I have to, and because when I do, I make the world a safer place. I don't do it because it gives me a hard-on."

Jessica's jaw tightened painfully. "I don't care why you do it. The point is that you do run toward danger. Want to, have to. Not much difference when you're dead."

"The difference is that I'm not out there trying to get myself killed. He was. Talk to Owen. My guess? You didn't know Robby as well you thought you did." He leaned across the table. "We're not all like him. It's about time you realize that."

He threw a twenty on the table, and motioned for her to get up.

They walked in silence, but he made sure he saw her get in her truck and drive off.

***

Jessica pulled into Wade's driveway and parked behind Owen's car. When she'd emailed Owen and asked if they could talk, his immediate response had been a dinner invitation for her and Bobby.

The tantalizing aroma of something on an outdoor grill tickled her nose as she got Bobby out of his car seat. The air was chilly but not freezing, perfect weather for enjoying meat smoked for most of the afternoon. The flowerbed in front of the house had been recently tended, and the planter on the front porch held freshly planted greenery. Good for somebody, she thought as she rang the doorbell. The forlorn air that had cloaked the house since Sandra left was gone. Wade's house was a home again.

Owen answered the door dressed in a long-sleeved tee with a towel slung over his shoulder. He was smiling, and for some reason, tonight the scars didn't bother her so much. "Come in you two. I guess you already smelled the brisket."

"It's probably driving the neighbors crazy knowing they don't get any." She stepped in. Owen engulfed her in a hug before turning to Bobby. "And how's my man tonight?" He scooped Bobby up in his arms.

Bobby gave Owen a big hug. He reached out and touched Owen's face with a gentle finger. "Mommy said you have a big boo-boo. But not to say anything."

Jessica could feel her face turn red. "Sorry about that."

"It's okay." He let Bobby touch the scarring. "I got hurt because a bad man put a bomb in a store. But I'm okay now. And guess what? I found some toys this afternoon that used to belong to Noelle. I bet you'd have fun playing with them too." He looked up. "Does he remember Noelle?"

"Yep. We Skype often. They've asked us to come to Tennessee for a visit, but I couldn't get away last summer. Maybe this year."

Wade came to the door carrying a grilling fork. "Owen and I are going in July. I had a ball last year."

"Lucky you."

"Where's the toys?" Bobby asked.

"In there." Owen put him down and pointed toward the family room.

Bobby took off running. They followed more slowly. Jessica looked around at the redecorated family room. "Wow. What an improvement. It's even prettier than when Sandra lived here."

"It's my stuff," Owen said. "I gave up my apartment in January."

"We fixed up Noelle's old bedroom some for when his kids stay over, and set up a home office for Owen in the bedroom next to the master," Wade added.

"What are you gonna do when your kids and Wade's family all show up on the same weekend?" she teased.

"It's already happened." Owen shut his eyes and shook his head. "Oscar put the moves on Sophie. It was all I could do not to strangle the kid."

Jessica laughed. "What did she do?"

"Told him to come back in five years and three inches. Cheeky little bastard told her he had plenty of inches where it counted. Mom swatted his ass for that one." Wade grinned.

Jessica laughed even louder. "It's so much easier when they're four. What can I do to help you get dinner on the table?"

They left Bobby in the family room with Noelle's Legos. Wade went back out to baste the brisket one last time. Owen put together a salad, and she set the table and sliced the French bread. "What are we having to drink?" she asked.

"Beer if you want it. Or there's a fresh pitcher of tea in the door."

"Tea it is."

She poured everyone a glass of tea over ice. Wade came in bearing a beautifully smoked brisket and in a few minutes the four of them were sitting at the table. Perhaps sensing that what she wanted to discuss wasn't dinner table conversation, Owen and Wade initiated a lively round of theater gossip. Wade confided that Jenna Salazar, the young teacher playing Ado Annie, was pregnant and worried about how her costumes would fit by the end of the show. "She's afraid to tell Letti how far along she is already."

"Tell the girl she has nothing to worry about. Letti played Maria in *The Sound of Music* when she was seven months along with Marco. She'll understand." Owen smiled at the memory.

"A pregnant nun. That must have been something," Jessica mused.

"So how goes the War of the Faulkners?" Wade teased.

"You heard?" she asked.

"Everybody in the theater's heard."

"It's been interesting. Cindy hasn't missed a practice. It's always Mrs. Faulkner who brings her. Mr. Faulkner hasn't shown his face, but at least he's letting her come. And my promised subpoena has yet to arrive."

"So they worked it out amicably," Wade said.

Jessica tilted her head. "Amicably? Probably not. But they must've come to some kind of consensus."

They finished the delicious meal and the three adults made quick work of the kitchen. Wade spirited Bobby to the far side of the family room and sat down with the Legos. "You had something you wanted to talk to me about," Owen said as he loaded the last plate in the dishwasher. He pulled out a chair at the kitchen table and sat in the one next to it.

Suddenly shy, Jessica sat. "I don't quite know how to talk to you. After...you know." She gestured toward his face. "It kills me. Looking at those scars knowing Robby put them there."

"So I've gathered, since every time you see me you flinch."

"I'm sorry. I guess that makes you feel that much worse about them."

"No. Not anymore." He reached out and took her hand. "You don't need to feel badly about the scars. You didn't put them there." He glanced across the room at Wade. "He's managed to convince me they're not all that awful. Not so awful that I need to hide."

"You don't need to hide. You need to do exactly what you're doing: singing and acting, and making our man over there happy. I've known Wade a long time. This is the happiest I've ever seen him. God bless you for that."

She took a deep breath and steeled herself. "Brian and I had an argument. A fight, really. I was trying to explain to him why I don't want to get involved with him, and tried to tell him how it tore me up to lose Robby. How I wasn't going to take a chance on another risk-taker like Robby was. Brian was pretty pissed off and said he wasn't like Robby and that most first responders weren't either. He called Robby an idiot and a reckless fool and said not to speak about him in the same breath as him, and that I needed to talk to you."

"What did you say to that?"

"Nothing. He walked me to my truck, and I went home."

Owen winced. "Did he say why he was so mad at being equated with Robby?"

"I said something about first responders getting off on the danger, and that first responders tend to be reckless."

Owen thought a minute. "That has been your experience. First with your dad, and then with Robby."

"You think Daddy was reckless?"

"Oh, hell, yes. Not as bad as Robby, but Eddie took his share of chances and couldn't understand why everyone else didn't. I've always thought half the reason he gave Robby the green light was because he was flattered that you'd want a man like dear old Dad. But Jessica, recklessness is absolutely, positively not part of the makeup of most first responders. If anything, they are more cautious going into a dicey situation than most people because they know they're going into danger and want to do everything they can to minimize the risk to themselves and others. They're trained to within an inch of their lives, and the vast majority put that training to good use."

"Then why do people go into those jobs in the first place? Why did you?"

Owen held up his thumb and fingers and rubbed them together. "I had a wife and children to support. I went onto the bomb squad to earn the bump that came with it. That's a lot of people's motivation. The soldier who goes to war is looking to pay for an education. The firefighter with a family to feed."

"Are there other reasons?"

Owen smiled wickedly. "It's a great asset in a single's bar." He snickered. "Listen, I'm not going to lie to you and tell you there aren't people who join the force because they want the adulation. But there are the true heroes who do the job to make the world a safer place. I promise you, Jess, almost all of them out there do *not* get off on putting their lives on the line. Every one of us wants to go home whole at the end of shift."

"But Robby did get off on putting his life on the line."

"He did. He took dumb-shit chances and got himself killed. And me hurt."

"He did you wrong."

"He did you a lot worse leaving you to raise Bobby by yourself."

"And you think Brian's different."

"In all fairness, I don't know the man other than what I've seen at the theater. Isn't your brother-in-law on the SWAT team with him? Talk to Mike. He'd know."

Jessica shook her head. "I don't think so. Mike tried to warn me off Brian. They're not fans of one another."

"Then try to talk to someone who would know. Don't let your past with Robby dictate your future, especially if it costs you a nice guy like Brian."

"You know, I do want something with him. He *is* such a good guy."

"Then you owe it to yourself to find out."

***

Brian locked the squad car and trudged across the parking lot. A cold February rain beat down on him, and his uniform was damp beneath his rain gear. The day had been a nonstop merry-go-round of car accidents, with a nasty domestic violence call thrown near the end of shift.

And the day was far from over. Tonight was the teenage production of *Footloose,* and even though he was wrung out, he wanted to be there. He'd spent several nights working with the singers on both the theme song and "Holding Out for A Hero" and he'd seen the kids rehearsing some of the incredible dance scenes Jessica had choreographed. It promised to be a wonderful production, and he wanted to see the culmination of a lot of hard work.

He waved at Sugar, still on the desk, and dragged himself to the locker room. He ducked into the shower, more to warm up than for any other reason, and was pulling on a pair of jeans when Mike Werner walked in and flopped down on the bench.

Brian's eyes narrowed and he glared at Mike. "I thought I told you to stay out of my business."

Mike threw up his hands. "What the hell brought that on? I haven't said a word to you in days."

"No, but you feel mighty damned free to you run your mouth and tell Jessica to stay away from me. Jesus, don't you have enough to worry about with your own woman?"

Mike jerked back like he'd been slapped. "You leave Heather out of this. No, on second thought, let's talk about Heather. My wife is coming apart at the seams. It's driving her crazy, me walking out of the house every morning with a gun on my hip. Do you think it would be any different for Jess? Especially since she's already lived through the worst. Damn, man, she fell apart when that bastard died. No way in hell does she need to go there again."

"I don't know why everyone is so fuckin' sure I'm going to do something stupid and get myself killed. I'm not like that asshole she was married to."

Mike took a deep breath. "I know that. He spent his off hours climbing rocks without a rope, and you spend yours doing community theater and making hands. But my point is, Jess doesn't know that. At least she doesn't here." He tapped his chest. "I'm afraid it would make her as crazy as it does Heather. And their mother. Heather let it slip one time that their mom did more than her share of drinking when Eddie was out taking chance after chance. It's not that I have a thing against you. I'm not convinced Jessica can, or should, deal with the anxiety of loving a cop a second time."

Brian pulled a polo shirt over his head. "I think you're underestimating her. She's plenty strong. She would have to be to survive what she did." He leaned down and to in Mike's face. "You don't understand. I've never felt the kind of attraction for a woman that I do for her. We have something special, and we owe it to ourselves to give that a chance."

Mike nodded. "You think I don't feel that way about her sister? And look where that got us." He sighed. "All right. No more commentary from me. But if you do take up with Jess and it all goes to shit, don't say I didn't warn you."

Brian turned away. Mike had his reasons for feeling the way he did. But by God, Jessica was stronger than her sister. She would be fine once she got it through her head that Brian wasn't like Robby and didn't take chances for the hell of it.

He finished dressing, combed his hair and brushed his teeth. He was almost to the door when an alarm sounded and his phone went off. *Hostage situation. Report to command center.*

Brian looked down and swore.

Chapter Eleven

Jessica stood with Josh and Rachel at the back of the theater, welcoming the families of the Academy kids as they filled the lobby. The excitement level was higher than usual. *Footloose* was a high-octane musical with plenty of lively songs and fast dance numbers requiring considerable skill. The kids had been practicing since December and were ready to strut their stuff. And at the rate the lobby was filling, their friends and family were ready to see them do it.

She spotted Letti coming in with her mother and grandmother, the birdlike octogenarian leaning on a walker. Owen and Wade were a few feet behind them. The two of them approached the women with big smiles, seemingly unfazed by looks the older women were shooting their way. Wade smiled graciously and offered his hand to Letti's mother. "We oughta film this one. Mom and Grandma meeting the ex-husband's boyfriend," Rachel said dryly.

"It's about to get even more interesting." Jess lifted her chin toward the front door. "Walter Faulkner walked in with arm candy that's a good fifteen years younger than Cindy's mother."

"Bet you twenty bucks Mrs. Faulkner gets really pissed and makes a scene," Josh said.

"Nah. She's got more class." Rachel shook her head.

"You're on."

The lobby continued to fill. Jessica took a minute to remind her volunteer ushers their duties, and then the house doors opened. The crowd in the lobby began to thin as families and couples were seated. Letti and her entourage disappeared into the auditorium. Wade and Owen came up with hugs for everyone. Owen's face beamed with pride. "Is my little girl gonna knock 'em dead, or what?"

"She is. She always does. You know that." Jessica gave his hand a squeeze.

Wade turned to Josh and Rachel. Owen bent his head toward her ear. "Have you thought any more about our talk the other night?"

"That's all I've thought about. I still don't know what to do." She gave him another hug. "Thanks for talking to me. It helped. A lot."

"I'm glad."

Owen and Wade drifted into the theater. Walter Faulkner and his date were about to do the same when the front doors opened and Patsy stepped in, dressed to the nines and on the arm of a distinguished-looking older gentleman. Jessica looked at them and did a double take. Rachel stared and Josh's mouth flew open. "Isn't that—" Jessica gasped.

"It's one of the Navarros. Not *El Jefe* or his brother. A cousin from Mexico, I think," Rachel said. "They did a big spread on him in the business section of the newspaper last week."

"And would you look at that sparkler on her left hand? That sucker cost him more than what the three of us put together made last year," Josh breathed.

Walter stared in disbelief as Patsy approached her ex and his date. Patsy greeted them and made a big production of introducing her companion. Walter's shock morphed into a sickly smile as the arm candy made a fuss over the ring Patsy sported. Jessica bit her lip trying not to laugh as Patsy and her sweetie swept into the auditorium, followed by her stunned ex-husband and his confused date.

Rachel held out her hand and Josh gave her a twenty.

"Gotta say, that was a whole lot more entertaining that a throw down." Josh's eyes sparkled. "Love seems to be in the air tonight. Speaking of, where's your sweetie?"

Jessica didn't pretend to misunderstand. "He's not my sweetie, and I don't know where he is. He told the kids he'd be here."

"You better text him and remind him it's tonight. He might have forgotten."

Jessica took out her phone and shot off a text. She had expected him tonight. But they hadn't communicated since the fight in the bar nearly a week ago. Jessica had taken a break from *Oklahoma!* rehearsals to concentrate on *Footloose*.

Finally, she'd hired two new instructors, relieving Brian and all her volunteer instructors. She didn't know if he'd been in the building for rehearsals. She didn't know if he was still angry. She didn't know if he'd given up his pursuit.

What she did know: she missed him.

And she'd given a lot of thought to her conversation with Owen.

Brian swore he was different from Robby. That he didn't take chances for the fun of it. She could see that in his life away from the department. He wasn't out climbing a rock cliff or racing a motorcycle. He was here at the theater or at home assembling a hand for a child who needed one. The question was whether she could trust that he didn't take chances on the job.

And if she could live with the danger he had to face.

She still had no answer to that question, but she'd really like to explore whatever it was that drew them together. She would like to get to know him better, go out with him, laugh with him, and cook a meal for him.

She'd really like to make love to him again.

She ushered in the last of the crowd and stepped up on the stage with a hand-held mic. "Thank you all so much for coming," she said with a gracious smile. She went on to brag a bit about the accomplishments of the Academy students and made a pitch for the summer program. Josh then took the mic, repeating her praise for the Academy and making a special point of thanking her for her hard work. She nodded across the theater at the sound engineer, the house lights dimmed and the lively prelude to *Footloose* blared from the speakers.

She scurried up a side aisle and perched on a stool next to the sound booth, her favorite spot to watch the Academy productions. The show was flawless from the get-go. Sophie Aldrete did her usual amazing job in bringing Ariel Moore to life. Newby Joey Miller, one of the scholarship kids, was rocking Ren McCormack, and longtime Academy student Hector Hinojosa, wearing expertly applied aging makeup, was doing a bang-up job as Rev. Shaw Moore.

The supporting cast was also superb and the ensemble did themselves proud. A deep sense of satisfaction enveloped her as she observed their performances. It was nights like this that made the long hours of rehearsal, the pushy parents, and the occasional drama worth it. Talent like this deserved to be fostered. It was her honor to be able to foster it.

But others had also been part of the success of the production. Brian in particular. So where was he? Why wasn't he here enjoying the show? She checked her phone. Nothing. She hoped to hell he wasn't so mad at her that he wouldn't come see the kids perform. A sudden chill ran down her back.

Something might have happened at work.

Blood pounded in her ears and her fingers trembled as she shot off another text. *Are you okay? Show is on.*

The phone pinged a moment later. *Tied up at work talk later.*

She breathed a sigh of relief. He was all right. Probably doing the paperwork cops hated.

She settled in on her stool and enjoyed the show. She was shaking hands afterwards along with the cast when her sister's ringtone sounded. She'd barely answered when Heather started screaming in her ear, something about *hurt* and *hospital.*

Oh, hell.

Jessica raced from the lobby to the much quieter front sidewalk. "Calm down, Heather, and tell me what's wrong."

"The SWAT team got called out tonight and bunch of them are hurt. Mike's hurt. I need to get to the ER, and my car's in the shop."

"Coming."

So that was where Brian had been tonight. With the SWAT team on a dangerous call, which resulted in ER-worthy injuries.

Ohmygod, ohmygod, ohmygod.

Was Brian among the injured?

Her fingers trembled as she shoved her phone in her pocket. A quick trip to her office for her coat and handbag and she was out the door. Traffic had died down and she made good time getting to Heather's. Her white-faced sister was standing on the front porch with Kinsey in her arms and a car seat beside her. Jessica took Kinsey and pointed to the car seat. "Leave it. She can ride in Bobby's"

They strapped Kinsey in Bobby's seat and jumped in. "Do you have any idea what happened?" Jessica asked as she slammed the truck in gear.

"No idea. The cop who called me said pretty much the whole team was affected."

"Affected by what?"

"They didn't say."

Jessica's hands started to shake on the steering wheel. The traffic was heavier on the way to the hospital and it was all she could do not to scream in frustration. She finally pulled into the crowded emergency room parking lot.

"Drop me off at the door and bring Kinsey in with you," Heather instructed tersely.

Jessica pulled up under the portico, and Heather jumped out and ran for the door. Jess found an empty space at the far end of the parking lot and carried the now-sleeping Kinsey into the waiting room packed with clusters of anxious-looking families. She started shaking all over as a wave of memories swamped her and it was all she could do not to cry out. She had come running into this same waiting room four years ago. She'd stood at the same intake desk. She'd waited on the same ratty furniture. She'd watched the same swinging doors fly open. She'd stood in that same corner as a tired trauma specialist delivered news that shattered her world into a million pieces.

She pushed back the horrible memories as best she could. She recognized a couple of the wives whom she'd met years earlier. Heather was standing at the desk, shaking so badly she could hardly stand. "What do you mean, go sit down and you'll call me? Tell me something. For God's sake, *tell me what's wrong with Mike*," she screeched.

Jessica could identify. She'd done the same thing. *Tell me what's wrong with Robby,* she'd begged at the ER window.

They hadn't told her anything either.

The room quieted as all eyes turned to stare at Heather. "Come sit down," Jessica said quietly in Heather's ear. "Everyone's in the same boat, hon. They'll call you back as soon as they can." She tugged on her sister's arm but Heather refused to budge. "Please, Heather. We don't want to get kicked out of here."

That seemed to get through to her sister. Jess led Heather across the room to the only pair of empty chairs left. Heather sat and reached for Kinsey, but her eyes were wild and she was hyperventilating. If Heather didn't hold it together, Jessica didn't know what she was going to do. She struggled to hold it together.

She fired off a quick text to her parents explaining the situation and asking if one of them could come get Kinsey. She wanted to ask the nurse at the desk about Brian. What had happened? Was he one of the injured? But even if she did ask, they wouldn't tell her anything. She wasn't family. Hell, she wasn't even his girlfriend. She was a self-created one-night stand.

Her eyes flickered around the noisy room. It had been much quieter the afternoon she'd been here for Robby. There had only been the two of them hurt that day, Robby and Owen. The only others who'd been here had been Letti and her two children.

Jess hadn't had to wait long at all. It had taken less than ten minutes for the doctor to come out and deliver the news that Robby was dead. Tonight the wait was going to be longer. No one had been called back yet. Only one family had even talked to a medical professional, and if the look on the older man and attractive young woman's faces were anything to go by, Jessica would just as soon skip that talk for the time being.

She hoped her parents would get here soon. She didn't know how much longer she could hold it together for her sister and herself.

Her parents came in thirty minutes later, turning heads as they strode through the emergency room to where their daughters sat. Jessica watched them approach, her father nodding to the families he recognized. They were a striking couple. They always had been. Her dad was tall and remarkably fit for a man pushing sixty. Personable and good-looking, he'd turned in his badge and hung up his gun belt three years ago, and spent his days writing and producing a successful blog on personal and home security.

Her mom was blonde and pretty, and she still had the body of a dancer. Thankfully, her drinking had never blossomed into full-blown alcoholism, and now that she was out from under the stress of being a cop's wife, she hardly touched the stuff. She had been a godsend to both her daughters, practically raising Bobby so that Jessica could finish her education and support her son, and recently, relieving Heather when the pressures of parenthood got to be too much.

Their parents were proud of their daughters. Eddie was especially proud that his girls had chosen to marry men like him. Never mind if it hadn't been the best thing for them, Jessica had thought on more than one occasion. But that was her dad: a cop to the core, and proud of it.

Heather spotted them and burst into tears. Jessica vacated her chair for her mom, and her dad swooped down and plucked Kinsey from Heather's arms. "Before you ask, Mrs. Borrego next door's watching Bobby. What's going on?" he asked tersely.

"They won't tell us anything. We know most of the SWAT guys were affected by whatever happened." She felt herself start to shake again. "I hate this place."

"I'm sure you do." Her dad looked at her shrewdly. "You said the whole team. Does that include the cop who's been chasing you?"

"I don't know." Her head snapped up. "How'd you know about Brian?"

"I bought Mike a couple of beers. Mike said the man has the hots for you. Said he made that little hand for Kinsey." He looked around the room. "Some of the bigwigs just came in. I'll see what I can find out." He carried Kinsey across the room toward the newcomers.

Jessica leaned against the wall. It took a few minutes but her mother finally got Heather calmed. Her dad carried Kinsey back and laid her in her grandmother's arms. "I talked to the lieutenant. It was a hostage situation. The asshole was holding a woman at gunpoint and had her kids locked in a bedroom. The SWAT team stormed the house and the perp set off a homemade device that poured bleach into ammonia. Every cop in the house was exposed to the resulting chlorine gas. How bad depends on how close they were when the liquids were combined. Most are gonna be okay. One bastard got it bad. He's critical." He shook his head. "Just when you think you've heard it all."

"Do they know which cop?"

"They didn't say who it was."

It could be Mike or Brian.

They started calling families to come to the back a few minutes later. Heather fidgeted impatiently until they finally called for Mrs. Werner. Mom volunteered to go with Heather. Jess sat down beside her father. She looked down at her trembling fingers. Here she was again, in the same hospital she'd been in four years ago, scared shitless at what she was about to learn.

She was right back where she'd been before. And had vowed never to be again.

Shit. Shit. Shit.

They waited for the better part of an hour as more families were called back and a few of the SWAT team members walked or were wheeled out. Finally her mother emerged. "Well?" Jessica demanded.

"Mike's going to be fine," Mom said quickly. "They're keeping him overnight for observation. Heather wants to stay until they have him up to a room."

"Does she have any business staying as freaked out as she was?" her dad demanded.

"No. But she insisted and was about to cause a scene. Jessica, you can go on home if you like."

A part of her screamed to run for it. But she couldn't leave until she knew Brian was all right. "Actually, there's someone else I'd like to check on before I leave."

Her parents looked at one another. "Let me see if I can find out something," her father said. "What's his last name?"

"Howard."

Her father turned as the ER doors whooshed open and a middle-aged doctor walked out, his shoulders slumped and defeat written all over his face. "Is the Kocurek family here?"

The pretty young woman Jessica had noticed earlier raised her head. "Over here." Her expression was a heartbreaking combination of hope and fear.

Jessica watched as the doctor crossed the room and spoke quietly to her. The woman's face crumpled and she would have collapsed but for the older man standing beside her. "*No*," the woman screamed. "*No, no, no. Don't you dare tell me he's dead. You get back in there and do your job. He can't die. We have a little girl. Please, go back there and do something. Please.*"

Her companion eased the young woman down into a chair. Jessica stared, rooted to the spot as another spate of memories surfaced. Screaming at the doctor to do something, demanding to see Robby: looking down at him with most of his face gone. Then collapsing into her father's arms.

Jessica felt herself start to sway.

Her mother reached out and grabbed her arm. "Easy, Jess. It's okay. It's someone else tonight."

Jessica nodded and swallowed the bile in her throat. The distraught woman continued screaming. The emergency room door opened again and Brian emerged. He looked like hell. His eyes were bloodshot and his pale skin was blistered and his drawn face was marked with red lines from an oxygen mask. His SWAT shirt was gone and he wore only his cargo pants and a rumpled tee. From the look in his eyes she could tell he already knew his teammate was dead.

He was her fondest dream and her worst nightmare all rolled up into one.

She stood rooted to the spot as he crossed the room. "What…how?" He reached toward her.

"I brought Heather." Her heart pounded in her chest as panic swept her and bile rose in her throat. "You…you're okay. That's fine. That's good. I've got to get out of here. *Now.* Mom, Dad, I'll see you in the morning."

Panic gripped her as she turned and ran for the door. She could hear Brian calling her name, but it didn't matter, nothing mattered but getting the hell out of here. Getting away from the death and the grief and the terror. She pushed through the door, almost knocking over an elderly woman clutching a walker, and sprinted toward her car.

She was almost there when she felt a familiar hand grab her and twist her around. Brian stood in front of her, the air wheezing in and out of his lungs as they stared at one another under the streetlamp. "Jess, what's the matter, sweetie? What's going on?"

She shook her head and turned as her stomach clenched and vomit spewed from her mouth, splashing the parking lot, Brian's boots, her shoes, and the tires of a dirty pickup. She retched and gagged for long minutes, puking up everything in her stomach.

Trembling, she stayed bent over until the retching stopped. Slowly she rose, backing away a foot when Brian would have taken her into his arms. "It all came back," she said as tears poured down her cheeks. "It all came back."

"What all came back?"

"When Robby died. Same waiting room. Same nurse's desk. Same everything. They came out to the waiting room and told me he was gone. I screamed just like she did." She knuckled away tears. "Damn it." She looked up at the shock on his face and cried even harder. "I was gonna do it, Brian. I was gonna say to hell with being scared. I was going to say to hell with you being a cop. I was going to get to know you and see where it went with us. But I can't. I can't do it. Nights like tonight. Sitting there not knowing if you were alive or dead. I'm sorry." She held her shaking hands out for him to see. "This is what it does to me. I shake. I puke. I fall apart." She swiped her hand across her mouth. "I can't do it. Not even for you."

She left him standing under the streetlight and ran the rest of the way to her truck.

Chapter Twelve

Brian stood rooted to the spot as Jessica got in the pickup and drove away as though the hounds of hell were after her. The cold winter air burned his sensitive airways and a massive headache from the foul gas throbbed behind his watering eyes. But his physical discomforts were nothing compared to the pain of watching Jessica go to pieces. He glanced down at the vomit splashed across his filthy boots. It was one thing to be driven to tears. It was another entirely to be shattered to the point of throwing up.

He had seriously underestimated the effect of what losing her husband had done to her. She'd tried to talk to him, and instead of listening and acknowledging her trauma, he'd gotten pissed off because she'd equated him with her late husband. He should have listened and at least acknowledged the devastation she'd suffered.

Still, she'd been about to change her mind until tonight, when the reality of being with a SWAT cop was rubbed in her face. He swore out loud. From what she'd said, she'd been close, so close. And now he was back to square one.

He scrubbed his arm across his burning eyes.

Maybe it was hopeless after all.

He took a few more gulps of cold night air, ignoring the way it stung his airways, and slowly walked toward the building. It was too cold to wait for Wade outside, so he went back to the waiting room and sat by himself in the corner and shut his eyes. He'd been there only a minute when he sensed rather than saw someone sit down on either side of him. He opened his eyes and found himself sitting beside the older woman who'd been standing with Jessica and the gray-haired man with cop written all over him holding Kinsey. There was concern and speculation in their eyes. "Are you all right?" the woman asked quietly.

"I'm fine, ma'am. Sir." He sat up a little straighter and offered his hand. "I'm Brian Howard."

The woman shook his hand. "I'm Jean Herrmann and this is my husband Eddie. We're Jessica's parents." She gestured to Kinsey's hand. "I understand you made that for her. Thank you."

"It was my pleasure."

The man shifted Kinsey to his other shoulder so he could shake hands. "We do appreciate it." He looked toward the exit door. "Did Jessica go home?"

"I believe that was where she headed."

Jean bit her lip. "Did she say anything to you?"

Brian hesitated. He didn't know these people and had no idea if they knew about him. But her mother already knew something was wrong. "She was upset. She said the memories of this place really got to her."

"I didn't think she was all that upset earlier," Mr. Herrmann said. "She said something about hating the place, but otherwise she seemed okay."

Mrs. Herrmann rolled her eyes. "That's because you're as clueless as a fence post, Eddie. She was barely holding it together. Think about it a minute. She was standing right over there when the doctor told her Robby was gone. And it was back in that ER that she saw Robby for the last time, all blown to hell. You shouldn't have let her go back there that afternoon. You should have stopped her."

"Damn it, Jean. We've had this argument before. I tried to stop her but she insisted. What finally set her off tonight?"

"Hearing that woman screaming. She was screaming like Jessica did that afternoon. She was about to bolt when Brian came out."

Mr. Herrmann turned to him. "How bad was she out on the parking lot?"

"Pretty bad. Shaking, puking, and crying." He stopped there. Her parents didn't need to know anything else.

"Damn. I'll call her in a few minutes and make sure she gets home okay," Mrs. Herrmann said. "I hope she doesn't turn her phone off." She turned to Brian. "Speaking of getting home, would you like Eddie to run you back to the station to get your car?"

"No, my buddy Wade's coming to get me. But thanks."

Mr. Herrmann leaned back in the chair. "I was hoping she'd started to get over all that shit with her husband," he said, more to himself than to anyone else. "She needs to go on with her life. To get over what happened to Robby and find a good man, and give Bobby brothers and sisters." He glanced over at Brian. "She needs a man with enough balls to knock down the wall she's built around herself."

"She'll move on when she's good and ready. And not before." Jean snapped. She sighed. "I always thought she might fall for Wade. But she never did."

"Maybe that's why," Mr. Herrmann said as Wade and Owen came in together, Wade's hand on Owen's waist.

"Oh. *Oh.* Well. So much for that."

Brian bit his lip to hold back his snicker.

Two hours later he sat on his sofa, freshly showered with a beer on the coffee table and a bag of pretzels next to him. Tonight was about as bad as it got. Every damned one of the SWAT team had been gassed, and Pete Kocurek's wife and little girl had lost a husband and father.

And then there was Jessica. Watching her go to pieces had torn him in half. He'd started to go to her house but seeing him again in his filthy uniform would have only made things worse. He would go by and see her tomorrow when he was thinking more clearly and she'd had time to calm down.

He swallowed the last of the beer and munched on the pretzels while he thought back to his conversation with the Herrmanns. His brain was foggy and his head hurt like a son of a bitch. But if he'd heard right, Eddie Herrmann had given him the green light with Jessica. Had as much as told him he was the man to knock down the walls she'd built. Her old man had given him the go-ahead. Just as he had given her late husband a nod. Coming from a true legend in the San Antonio Police Department, Brian considered it high praise.

He took a deep breath. If Jessica's father thought he could break down that wall she'd built around herself, then maybe he could.

But he'd be damned if he knew how.

***

Brian parked in Jessica's driveway behind her pickup. A small smile played around his lips as he thought of the night he'd spent under this roof. That had been one hell of a night. One which deserved to be repeated.

He gathered up the bouquet of flowers and the sack of fried chicken and walked to her door. He still wasn't sure what he could say to her, but he wasn't leaving here until she had agreed to something, even if it was nothing more than ice cream at the Fruteria. He rang the bell and Bobby threw open the door a minute later. A television played in the background and the unmistakable aroma of pine cleaner tickled his still-sensitive nose. "Mr. Brian! Hi. Did you make me another toy?" He turned around. "Mommy! Mr. Brian's here."

The sound of the television faded. She came to the front door a moment later, dressed in yoga pants and a baggy Durango Street tee. Her hair was up in a messy ponytail and she didn't have on a lick of makeup. Her face was white to the point of being pasty and dark circles rode under her eyes. Her expression was solemn, but she didn't appear to be angry with him. She stared at him a minute before unlatching the screen. "Come on in. Bobby, you can turn the television back up."

He stepped in her tiny foyer. Bobby grabbed him around his knees. "Brian, I missed you. Why haven't you come over? Can we go for ice cream again?"

He looked at Jessica as she tried and failed to hide a wince. "I…I've been working a lot," he stammered. Bobby wouldn't understand the truth. "Here, give me a big hug. I missed you too." He picked up the boy for a huge hug.

"Bobby, Mommy needs to talk to Brian for a few minutes. He'll see you afterwards." She looked at him. "Is that all right?"

He nodded, Brian put him down, and Bobby raced back to the living room. She shut the door behind her and they stood staring at one another. "You look like hell," she said finally, taking in his still-irritated skin and bloodshot eyes.

"You don't look much better."

"Thanks a lot. Really good for a girl's ego."

"If I said you look wonderful, you'd know I was lying. Are you still shaking?"

She held out her hands. "No, I'm not. At least on the outside."

He thrust the flowers at her. "For you. I thought they might make you feel better."

She smiled faintly and took the flowers. "Pretty flowers never hurt. Thanks."

He held up the sack. "I also brought chicken. I thought you might be tired and not want to cook."

"Now that's really being thoughtful." She looked at him sadly. "Why do you have to be so damned wonderful?" She turned around and headed to the back of the house.

He followed her into the kitchen and put the sack on the counter. "So damned wonderful, huh. Would you rather I was an asshole?"

She smiled crookedly. "It would make it a hell of a lot easier. It's damned hard when you're everything I ever wanted otherwise."

"Aha. So you do admit you want me 'otherwise.'" He made air quotes with his fingers.

"You know I do." She filled a mason jar with water and put the flowers inside.

"Last night you said you were about to change your mind. How close were you?"

She pinched her thumb and forefinger together. "This close."

"And now?"

She held her arms out to her sides.

He swore sharply. "Damn."

"You asked," she said defensively. "You saw how it affected me. Or are you as clueless as Daddy? He asked me this morning what the fuss was all about."

Brian winced. "Macho cop. Everybody's supposed to suck it up and go on." He sat down on a barstool. "No, I'm not as clueless as your father. I understand why you freaked last night. Under the circumstances I might've had the same reaction. A lot of people would. I owe you an apology. You were trying to tell me how badly you were hurt by Robby's death, and all I could hear was that you thought I take reckless chances. I should have listened to you more closely."

"Would it have done any good if you had? Or would you have still been bound and determined to be with me?"

Brian raised his eyebrow. "Busted. I would have been as determined. In fact, I still am." Her lips thinned. "No, hear me out. I already know what you're going to say. You're gonna remind me how upset you got last night. That you've gone down that road once before and aren't willing to go down it again. I know it killed you to lose your husband and you're not strong enough to do it again, and you're not willing to love another man who puts his life on the line like I do sometimes. How'm I doing?"

"Pretty good. Now what are you going tell me to counter all that?"

"That you're stronger than you think you are. Getting through Robby's death the way you did is proof of that. Jess, you're not like Heather. You're stronger than your mother. Deep inside, you do have the courage to be with me and see where it might lead."

"Thank you for that. But there's something you failed to mention. I don't *want* to be strong, not like I'd have to be. I want to be able to care without the constant anxiety."

"So you'd rather be nice and safe, and bored out of your mind by Barry the dentist?"

"Who?"

"Barry the dentist. That's what my sister used to call the nice, sweet, but boring as hell guys she used to date. The kind your parents wished you would marry."

"Mom, maybe. Daddy was all for us marrying his clones."

Still is. "But is that what you really want? Nice and safe, but boring? Or worse, a nice and safe asshole who will treat you and Bobby like shit?" He looked her in the eye. "Tell me. Were you ever really attracted to the Barrys you dated?"

"Not really." She lifted her chin. "But I didn't have nights like last night, either."

"I guess it boils down to this. You told me you think I'm wonderful. We're good together. We laugh and we have fun, and the sex is phenomenal. I think Bobby is a great kid, and would like to get to know him and spend time with him. The only problem is my job. So I'm asking you. Am I worth it? You were about to say yes. You were about to take the risk until last night. Am I worth less today than I was this time yesterday?"

"Of course you're worth as much today," she snapped. She bit her lip. "Last night was bad. I need some time to get over it."

"How much time?"

"Damned if I know."

"So let's do this. I'll see you at rehearsal. Maybe we can go out for a beer at Thirties a time or two. Or take Bobby for ice cream. You spend some more time with me and you think about it. Think about whether you'd rather have me, or that nice safe dentist that bores you out of your mind. If you decide I'm worth it, you go with me as my date to the Department's awards banquet next month and we go from there. How's that?"

"And if I say no?"

"You think Rachel would go with me?"

Brian almost laughed out loud at the jealousy she tried and failed to hide. "I'll go with you," she snapped. "Even if that's the only date we have."

He stood up and gave her a smacking kiss on her cheek. "Good. Now that we have that settled, do you want to eat the chicken and fries?"

***

Jessica yawned as she pulled into Heather's driveway. The calendar said March 1, but the cold wind coming out of the north proclaimed that it was still winter in San Antonio. Jess was tired. She hadn't been sleeping well, and a part of her dreaded the next two weeks when the cast and crew of *Oklahoma!* would move rehearsals to the stage and work long hours on Sunday and every evening putting everything together. By the end of the two weeks, everyone would be exhausted, but at the same time on a high as the curtains opened and they brought the characters from *Oklahoma!* to life. She was especially grateful to her parents for their help with Bobby during tech week. If she'd been dependent on paid babysitting, she would never be able to perform.

She rubbed her forehead, willing the fatigue and tension headache to go away. She'd dreamed again last night, waking up in a cold sweat with images of Bobby's mangled face blending with Brian's chemical-blistered skin and eyes. She'd gotten up and switched out her sweat-soaked pajamas for clean ones, but sleep was elusive and she gave in and made a cup of coffee, sitting on the sofa drinking it in the predawn quiet. She wasn't sure which was worse, the horror-filled dreams, or the dreams of making love to Brian, riding him as he helped take her there.

The dreams that were the most unsettling were the ones of them together doing the things a couple would do. Eating dinner. Shopping. Once she dreamed of being pregnant with his child. Those were the dreams that disturbed her the most because she wanted so badly for those dreams to come true. And the only thing preventing that was her fear. She laughed at the irony. She was so afraid of the frightening dreams coming true that she was willing to pass on the wonderful ones.

There had to be an answer somewhere. Damned if she knew what it was.

Her fingers refused to work magic on the headache, so she unbuckled her seat belt and turned around to Bobby, who was absorbed with a game on his Leap Pad. "Do you want to wait here while I go get Aunt Heather and Kinsey?"

He shook his head and she unbuckled him. Knowing Heather, she probably wasn't ready anyway. She'd told Jessica flat-out she wasn't going to Sunday brunch. That she was tired of everybody fretting over her. Jessica had come back with the argument that if she didn't show up, her parents would be on her doorstep an hour later to fret over her anyway, so she may as well get it over with. Besides, Mike would enjoy going.

Heather had called this morning saying Mike wasn't going and asking for a ride. She rang the bell and Heather appeared a moment later. Her sister was dressed, but her hair wasn't combed and she was barefooted. Her face was drawn and her eyes looked like two holes burned in a blanket. She threw open the door. "I'll be ready in a minute," she said dully.

Jessica stepped in. Heather disappeared into the bedroom and Bobby ran through the house in search of Kinsey. She followed him into the living room and stopped in her tracks. Mike's recliner and reading lamp were gone, as was the side table where he kept his e-reader and magazines. She looked around the living room and kitchen with a sinking feeling.

The big-screen TV in the living room was still there, but the smaller one in the dining area was gone as were the fancy copper pot and skillet that Mike had proudly hung from hooks on the wall. Jessica wasn't about to look, but she was certain that if she checked the cabinets and drawers, she would find things missing. The furniture in the guest bedroom was probably AWOL as well.

Shit. Shit. Shit. She took a deep breath. Mike had moved out of the house.

Mike had left Heather and Kinsey.

"Yep, he's gone," Heather said flatly from behind Jessica. "Said he couldn't take any more of the craziness. His brother came yesterday and helped him move."

"Did he say why?"

"He said he couldn't stand it anymore. Never knowing if or when I was going to be off my rocker. I'm not sure I blame him."

I blame him plenty. She looked at Heather. "Anything in particular make him decide to leave?"

Heather sank down onto a kitchen chair. "I embarrassed him at the hospital. That night he was hurt. I had a meltdown and started screaming."

So did I. "What happened?"

"They took forever to get him up to his room. Mom wanted to stay but I told her I was staying the night and to go on home. It got really bad once they got him upstairs. Mike was thirsty but they wouldn't bring him anything to drink. They wouldn't clean him up and they kept ignoring the call button. I couldn't take it anymore and I went out to the nurse's station and I snapped. I yelled at everybody and the security guards took me downstairs and made me call an Uber. Either I had to go home or they were going to call the police and have me arrested." She hung her head. "Mike said he'd never been so embarrassed in his life. Me making a scene in front of all his SWAT buddies. He told me I had to get my head on straight or he wouldn't be back."

"Do Daddy and Mom know?"

"No. He moved out yesterday." She put her head in her hands. "I swear. I don't know why I keep trying. I wish it would all go away."

"You wish all *what* would go away?" Jessica said more sharply than she'd intended.

"Everything. I wish I could go to sleep and not wake up."

Cold fear ran down Jessica's back. "No, you don't. If you went to sleep and never woke up, there wouldn't be anybody to raise Kinsey. Mike's gone all the time."

"I know that," Heather said quietly. "Why do you think I'm still here?"

Jessica swallowed the lump in her throat. "Let's head over to Mom and Dad's."

They trooped out to her truck and installed Kinsey's car seat next to Bobby's. She eyed Heather. Her sister was getting worse. The meltdown in the hospital, the thinly veiled suicide threat. Jess was going to have to tell her parents what Heather said. Her sister needed help, and she needed to be seeing a therapist twice a week, at least. Mike leaving was a shitty thing to do. Who gave a fuck what his SWAT buddies thought? He should've been glad someone loved him enough to make a scene to get him what he needed. And Mike was crazy if he thought leaving Kinsey with Heather would keep her from doing something stupid.

Like that ever made a difference.

She cranked up the truck and pulled out of the driveway. "So how goes it with Brian?" Heather asked. "Mom said you had a meltdown of your own that night."

Jessica shrugged. "I was about to change my mind and give it a whirl with him. That night reminded me of what I have to lose if we get involved. I could have my heart broken a second time if I do fall in love with him and something happens."

"So have your whirl but don't get involved. Don't deep six him totally. Date him a little. Do the booty-call thing. He was hot in bed, wasn't he?"

"Oh, yeah."

"So eat your cake and have it, too. He'll be good with it."

"You think he would?"

"What man in his right mind's gonna turn down hot sex and a little fun?"

Brian might. He'd said she was more than a challenge. That he wanted to explore whatever it was that held them together.

On the other hand, he might be totally up for it. No man in his right mind would refuse smokin' hot sex.

She'd find out next Saturday after the award banquet.

Chapter Thirteen

Jessica stared at herself in the mirror and gave herself a single nod of approval. The ice-white, floor length formal flattered her complexion and fit her curves like a glove. The deco-style dress was cut on the bias, with thin straps over the shoulders and a dramatic sweep of satin to the floor. She'd worn it to a couple of Durango Street galas, and from the comments her friends had made, she knew she looked good in it.

In keeping with the style of the dress, her friend and fellow actress, Vivienne Abonce, had taken time from her all-day battle with morning sickness to twist Jessica's hair up in an elaborate deco-style chignon low on her neck, and she lent her a pair of platinum and diamond filigree earrings that had been in her mother's family for three generations. "Put the earrings in a safe place before you have wild sex tonight," Vivienne teased. "Mom would kill me if anything happened to them."

She would do that. If all went according to plan, she had a small jewelry box waiting for them on her dresser.

She still didn't know if she had any business going with Brian tonight. She didn't know that she had any business going with him, period. But she's done a lot of thinking since he asked her if he was worth the risk. She'd done even more since Heather suggested booty calls. Jess decided that a fling was the answer. Good sex. Good fun. Keep it light. No emotional involvement. Brian should be on board with that. If not, they would at least have tonight.

She used concealer to hide the "theatre" circles beneath her eyes. They had completed the first week of grueling rehearsals before *Oklahoma!* opened, and normally she would be curled up with a book and planning an early night. But she'd agreed to going to the banquet with Brian, and to her surprise was looking forward to it.

She applied a modernized version of deco-styled makeup, with dramatic eye shadow, darkened brows, and ruby-red lips. She was brushing on a touch of blush when the doorbell rang. She ran through the house and threw open the door. Her breath caught in her throat. Brian, in his dress uniform, his dress shirt blindingly white under his navy-blue jacket with brass buttons, his badge on his left and the SAPD insignia on his right shoulder. He carried his dress hat under his arm. He looked handsome. So handsome, and a hell of a lot like Robby.

Funny. She'd never noticed the resemblance before.

But that was physical. Brian and Robby were nothing alike otherwise. She needed to remember that.

She smiled and motioned with her hand. "Come in. I have a pair of old-fashioned shoes to strap myself into, and we can be on our way."

Brian stepped in and took her in his arms. "You look beautiful. I know better than to kiss red lipstick right now. But I intend to kiss every bit of it off later tonight. And dismantle that fancy hairdo."

She hugged him around his middle. "I might let you." She gave him another squeeze, taking a moment to savor the feel of his body against hers. Except for the dance rehearsals, she hadn't touched him since the night they'd spent together. She shut her eyes and let herself feel.

It was good to be back in his arms.

He released her. She went into her bedroom and got out the thirties-style open-toed pumps with a T-strap buckling at her ankle. She sat on the side of the bed and tried to buckle the shoe but gave up after a minute and carried the shoes and her satin handbag to the much lower sofa. "They may look good but they are hell to put on," she groused as Brian looked at her curiously.

She jammed the shoe on her foot and almost had the buckle fastened when Brian knelt in front of her. "Allow me, Cinderella." He brushed her hands away and expertly fastened the buckle on the right hole. He motioned for the other shoe and buckled it. "Now, does Madame have a wrap for tonight? It's cold out there."

"Madame does."

She rummaged in the tiny entry-hall closet a minute and unearthed a thirties-style coat with a faux fur collar. "Very nineteen-twenties," Brian said as he helped her into the coat.

"Madame does love her deco. And I get to indulge it every year when the Durango holds its big deco gala."

"The retro style becomes you."

She reached out and fingered the lapel of his uniform. "The hero style becomes you."

She wasn't talking about only his uniform. And they both knew it.

The convention center banquet hall was teeming with law enforcement from all over the county. SAPD, Bexar County Sheriff's Office, constables, and smaller suburban police departments, the park police, the airport police, and the school district police. There was a smattering of representatives from the various state and federal agencies that had offices in the city or county.

The law enforcement community was out in force, their smiles bright and their badges shining. Jessica had felt young and gauche when she'd attended with Robby. But tonight, with Brian by her side, she felt right at home. They made their way through the crowd to the tables marked SAPD. "The SWAT team likes to sit together. Is that okay?" He looked at her with concern. "Or would you feel more comfortable somewhere else?"

"Your SWAT team friends are fine. Pretty much everyone back to work?"

"All but one or two. Although some of them are still shaking it off. Mike's not doing too well."

"Maybe Mike's missing his wife and little girl," she said tartly. "He moved out last weekend."

"Shit. I'm sorry. I didn't know."

"I'm sorry too. That was the last thing Heather needed."

They found the tables designated for the SWAT team. Most of the chairs had wraps or purses staking a claim, but there was a pair of unclaimed seats next to an attractive older couple, faces weathered from the sun and bodies incredibly fit. Jessica's face split into a huge grin. "Mrs. Vance. Mr. Vance. How are you?"

Amanda Vance stood up and gave Jessica a huge hug. "We're doing well, dear. How's that beautiful baby of yours?"

"That beautiful baby's four years old."

"You feed them, they grow." Amanda winked.

Jessica turned to give Jack Vance a hug. "Are you still talking people out of doing things that aren't good for them?"

"Once in a while. When they think they need me."

"Which they usually do," his wife said. "Jessica, would you and your gentleman like to join us?"

"We'd love to." Brian extended his hand. "I'm Brian Howard. I've seen and heard your husband in action a few times. I promise you, we did need him." He shook hands with Mr. Vance. "It's good to see you without a phone in your hands."

"It's good to see you without a rifle in yours. So, Jessica, how are Jean and Eddie these days? I miss that son of a gun."

They all sat down and Jessica gave them a rundown on how her parents were doing. The Vances were practically legends in the police department. Amanda had headed up the CSU until her retirement a few years ago, and Jack, better known as "Silver Tongue Vance," was the best hostage negotiator in all of Texas, with an uncanny ability to get into the mind of a gunman and say the right thing to defuse a deadly situation. He'd retired from full-time work, but his cell phone was always close by and it rang often.

"So how are Blake and Johnny doing?" Jessica asked. "I see Blake on the news every month or so." Their oldest was a hotshot prosecutor in the district attorney's office.

"He's having the time of his life," Jack said.

"He's as persuasive as his father," Amanda added proudly. She lowered her voice. "He's considering a run for district attorney next year if the current DA decides to step down."

"If he doesn't get himself killed first," Jack said darkly.

Brian looked at him curiously. "Get himself killed? I thought he was a lawyer."

Amanda's lips twitched. "Blake got a bike. It's a big old Harley and probably safe enough, but Jack's fretting like a grandma." She turned to her husband. "Would you rather have him entering the amateur bull-riding contests or driving a race car like his dear old dad used to do?"

Jack gave Amanda a look and Jessica snickered. "He could get a couple of mountain bikes. Hell, I'd pay for them myself," Jack said. "You and I have plenty of fun on those without killing ourselves."

"So use some of that talent of yours and talk him into it," Amanda teased.

Jessica looked over at her dad's old friend. "I didn't realize Mr. Vance was into extreme sports when he was younger."

"No reason why you would. He gave them up not long after we married. He was taking too many chances. Both on and off the job. Like—" she hesitated.

"Like Robby. You can say it," Jessica said.

"I finally realized that it had to stop," Jack added. "If it didn't, I was going to end up dead. Amanda made it clear she wasn't sticking around to watch me die. It took a year of counseling, but I managed to give up the extreme sports. At the advice of the counselor, I asked to be moved off SWAT to hostage negotiations. And found my true calling." He took a sip of his water. "I've often thought it was a shame that Robby never had that kind of epiphany. If he had, he might be alive today."

Amanda made it clear she wasn't sticking around to watch me die. Jessica sucked in a breath. She'd made token protests when Robby did something dangerous. But she hadn't fought him all that hard. She'd never threatened to leave. She'd never made him choose between her and the danger. She'd admired that fearlessness in him a little too much. And hadn't really realized what it could cost them until it was too late.

Maybe if she'd taken the same stand Amanda Vance had, Robby would still be alive.

Or maybe they would have divorced and Robby would be just as dead.

Amanda asked Brian what he did off the clock and conversation turned to the prosthetic hands Brian made, and then to the Durango. But later, during a series of boring speeches, Jessica's thoughts returned to their conversation with the Vances. It was five years too late for her to do anything about Robby's risky behavior, but maybe it wasn't too late for Brian. Maybe he would be willing to take a less dangerous path. He didn't have to be on the SWAT team. He didn't even have to be a cop. He asked her earlier if he was worth the anxiety of worrying about him. Maybe the question she should be asking was what she was worth to him.

If they did fall in love, was she worth his giving up SWAT? Or even getting off the force?

Something to consider.

When they got back to Jessica's house, the streets were empty. Brian had been uncharacteristically quiet as the evening progressed. They'd made small talk on the way home, but Brian's mind was elsewhere. He followed her up the sidewalk and onto the front porch. "Am I invited in tonight? Or do we say goodnight out here?"

She turned to him and ran her hand down the side of his face. "You are most certainly invited in tonight. Mom is hosting a sleepover for both Bobby and Kinsey."

"Thank you. I've missed you so much."

"I've missed you too."

He followed her into the house. She hung her coat in the closet. They stared at one another for a minute, neither of them reaching for the other, until she took him by the hand and led him through the house to her bedroom.

"Feeling shy?" he asked.

"A little. It's silly. We've already done this."

"Maybe it's not so silly. We're at a different place tonight."

"But I do want you. A lot."

"I want you, too." He stepped to her back and slowly unzipped the dress, pushing it off her shoulders until it lay in a puddle at her feet. "Wow. Deco all the way," he said at the sight of her old-fashioned clingy full slip with it satin cups barely holding up her breasts.

She stepped out of the dress and sat down on the side of the bed. "Care to do the Prince Charming routine for me again?"

He sank to one knee and grasped her ankle. His fingers were deft as they unbuckled the straps and gently pulled the shoes from her feet. He ran his fingers up her leg, pushing the slip up as he went until he reached a pair of sheer tap pants. "That's the sexiest thing I think I've ever seen," he said as he pushed aside the flimsy material and buried his fingers in her warm folds.

Jessica gasped as his fingers found her sensitive nub. *He remembered*, she thought as he caressed her, careful not to put his fingers inside her. He teased and touched her, his gaze never leaving her face. When her sharp orgasm came out of nowhere, its throbbing convulsions leaving her gasping, he grinned at her wickedly. "Are we going for four again?"

"At least."

He sank his fingers into her elaborate hairstyle. "I promised myself I was going to have fun doing this." He removed the bobby pins one by one until her hair hung free around her shoulders. "You should wear it down more often. It's so beautiful." He pulled her up so that she stood next to him. "And I believe I promised to kiss off all the red lipstick."

"So you did."

He held her face between his hands. His lips were gentle as they caressed hers, tasting and teasing as they coaxed her response. She groaned and put her arms around his neck, holding him close. It felt so good to be back in his arms, she thought as she opened her lips and let his tongue invade her mouth. When they broke apart for breath, she made a production of eyeing him up and down. "You have on waaay too many clothes." He had yet to take off his dress coat.

"On it." When she went to take the slip off, he said, "No, leave that right where it is. That and those panties are hot."

Quickly, he shed his coat and tie and holstered pistol. The dress boots and socks were next. He held out his arms so Jessica could remove his gold cuff links. "Fancy," she said. She took off the chandelier earrings and put them all in the box on her dresser. "I've missed this." She ran her fingers through the red hair on his chest.

"So have I. I've missed a lot of things since I was in this bedroom." He touched her nipple through the satin with the tip of his finger, teasing it into a hard little knot.

"You still have on too many clothes," she murmured.

His pants and boxer briefs came off in one swift motion, leaving him bare. His body throbbed with tension and his hard cock rose from his groin. "Better?"

"Much." She held out her arms and he sank down beside her on the bed, bearing her down into the fluffy bedclothes.

His hands and lips skimmed her neck and shoulders, then he pushed down the satin straps and she pulled up her arms, allowing the bodice to fall free from her breasts. His breath was hot as he kissed her nipples into stiff peaks. His hands were strong as they caressed her. His fingers were sensuous as they found and tickled her stomach, stopping to pay special homage to her navel. He shimmied the slip down her body until she wore only her sheer tap pants. He nibbled his way down her body until his lips rested against her tender folds. But he didn't remove her underwear. Instead he worked his mouth over her tender flesh, taking advantage of the abrasion of the material as it moved under his tongue and sent her soaring. When she looked down her body, he was grinning as he pulled down the tap pants and flung them across the room. "Open up, honey. We're gonna keep those orgasms coming."

"What about you?" she breathed as she spread her legs.

"Ladies first. Then you can rock my world, I promise you."

He pushed her legs wide. Shivers ran down her back as once again his lips worked magic, finding the center of her pleasure and wrapping his tongue around it. She barely heard the moan that erupted from her throat as he brought her higher and higher to explode in a maelstrom of delight.

He gave her a moment to catch her breath before rolling over and opening her nightstand drawer. "Good lord, woman. How many condoms do you think we'll need tonight?" He looked again and his eyes narrowed. "Or do you keep this big of a stash in here all the time?"

She grinned a little wickedly. "Shame, shame. Your jealousy is showing." Her smile faded at the stricken look on his face. "I bought them this morning. They're all for you."

His face cleared. "I'd hate the thought of you with another man."

"If there was another man, you wouldn't be here tonight."

"Good. I don't share."

He rolled on the condom and slid into her in a single stroke. She gasped at the pleasure of having him fill her. "God, you feel good. So tight around me."

"So do you. So big."

He smirked. "And here you ladies love to say that size doesn't matter."

"I—I wouldn't know," she admitted, blushing furiously. "I have little basis for comparison."

He leaned down and kissed her lips. "And somehow that makes it even more beautiful."

He started thrusting into her slowly, and then when he found his rhythm, he moved faster and harder. She felt herself responding, her hips moving in counterpoint to his, her excitement level rising as they moved, their bodies in perfect harmony.

Brian's muscles strained as he moved faster, his tension level rising along with hers until they plunged together, his groans and her cries mingling in the dark of the night. She could feel his body spasming within her as his seed poured into the condom. Her orgasm went on and on, the powerful contractions slowly fading to soft tremors of pleasure. He rolled them to one side and slowly slid out of her. "Damn."

He caressed her backside. "You have the prettiest ass. Legs, too."

"I credit the dancing. My mom still dances some and she looks great."

"So does mine. You think they're gonna like each other? Both of them being dancers and all?"

Jessica stiffened. Keeping it light meant their mothers would have no reason to meet. "It…it would be interesting." She sat up and planted a big kiss on Brian's lips. "Are you hungry?"

If he noticed the change of subject, he gave no indication. He held her face between his hands and kissed her again, long and sweet, as his cock began to harden against her. He raised his head and looked at her with desire in his eyes. "Only for you," he said.

He went to the bathroom, came back right away, and rolled on another condom, then flipped onto his back and set her astride him. "Ride me, Jess. Ride me hard." They moved in tandem, once again scaling the heights and tumbling through space together as a million sparklers burned at once.

He decided he was hungry after all, so they raided the refrigerator and found an almost full carton of butter pecan ice cream, which they fed to one another right out of the carton. Then they crawled into bed together, curled around each other, and within minutes Brian's breathing eased into the even cadence of slumber.

Jessica stared into the darkness. This evening was great. All of it. Under other circumstances it would be the beginning of a wonderful relationship. But with Brian, this was as far as it went. The occasional date and booty call. She would take it no further, at least not at this point. Maybe later. Maybe if he ever got out of law enforcement, or left the SWAT team, they could move on to something more.

She hoped he was good with what she had to offer, because if he pushed for more, she was gone.

Chapter Fourteen

Brian blinked in the morning sunlight filtering through the bedroom blinds. It wasn't all that early, given the sun's brightness. He'd come awake earlier, his cock hard and ready to go, but Jessica was sleeping the sleep of the dead and he didn't have the heart to wake her. She was tired. They both were. And they had the infamous tech week to live through before the show opened on Friday night. He'd made a quick bathroom visit and crawled back into bed, dropping off almost immediately for a couple more hours of needed rest.

He yawned as a satisfied smile crept across his face. He didn't care how much sleep he'd lost, last night had been worth it. The woman he wanted so badly had let him back into her life. She'd overcome her fears and welcomed him into her bed and made love to him for all she was worth. She wanted to go forward with him.

The thought of where they might end up put a smile on his face.

He was about to wake her with kisses when she sat up and blinked. She'd washed off the makeup last night after the ice cream and her face was pale in the dim light. He sat up and ran his hand down the side of her face. "You're even more beautiful without all the war paint."

"You're prejudiced, but thanks." She hopped out of bed, unmindful of her nudity as she picked up her robe off the floor.

"You don't like being cold."

She smiled. "You remembered. So how about I make you a plate of toast and bacon before I have to get dressed."

Brian gave her a mock leer. "I was hoping we could have a bit of morning delight."

"I wish. Heather and I and the kids have a standing date with Mom and Dad for Sunday brunch."

"Mike, too?"

"He did until he moved out." Her lips tightened. "Asshole. But I'm not going to spoil my morning thinking about him."

Maybe Brian would be included in those brunches someday soon.

"Good choice." He reached for his boxers but she put out her arm.

"Would you be more comfortable taking a shower before going on the walk of shame?"

He laughed as he pulled her flush against his warm, hard body. "I'm not one damned bit ashamed of last night."

"I should hope not."

He gave her a long, lingering kiss that had his cock hard again. She giggled and pulled away. "Don't start something we can't finish." She pointed across the hall. "Bobby's bathroom is stocked for guests. There's even a rubber duckie to play with."

"What? I don't get to shower with you?"

"Tempting thought. But if we get in there together we'll be forever, and I really do have to meet my parents for brunch."

He put back on enough clothing to make a quick trip to the truck, where he had a duffel of clean clothes, packed in a hopeful moment yesterday afternoon. He found Bobby's bathroom, complete with plastic bath toys. He took a shower and found the shaving cream and a razor in his Dopp kit, which he used on his morning scruff before dressing in jeans and a long-sleeved tee. Jessica was already in the kitchen, dressed in fancy jeans and a blue pullover sweater that made her blue eyes pop and lovingly hugged every curve. He could hear bacon sizzling in the microwave. Buttered toast browned in the toaster oven. She handed him a cup of coffee. "Sugar's on the table, and creamer's in the fridge. I don't know how you like it. Sorry."

He opened the fridge and rummaged around until he unearthed a pint of creamer. "Cream, no sugar. You?"

"Cream and a bit of sugar." She took a second cup from the coffee machine and doctored it to her liking. "Sit down and I'll bring you a plate."

"I don't expect you to wait on me. Plates?"

She pointed to the end cabinet and then to the silverware drawer. He made his plate and they and sat across from one another. "So when can I see you again? Next Friday after the performance? Or maybe we can take Bobby for dinner Sunday evening. Someplace he likes."

A shadow crossed her face. "Maybe we need to talk about some ground rules before we start making plans."

His eyes narrowed. "Ground rules? Why do we need ground rules?"

She sighed and sipped her coffee. "Brian, what are you looking for from me?"

"The same thing I've wanted since I laid eyes on you. I want something real with you. I want to get to know everything about you. I want to get to know Bobby and spend time with him. I want to care about you, and for you to care about me. I want to see where this relationship might go. You know all that. Why do you ask?"

"I wanted to be sure before we have this talk." She wrung her hands and her eyes looked pained. "I don't want any of that."

"Then what do you want? And what the hell was last night all about?"

"Last night was a lovely date and a splendid night spent together, which I would like to repeat sometime soon. But I don't want anything else."

What the hell? "You don't want anything but the occasional dinner followed by a booty call?"

She had the grace to blush. "It sounds awful when you put it that way. But yes. That's all I want. Good conversation and great sex every so often. No getting closer. No caring. No relationship. No seeing where things are going, because they aren't going anywhere."

His eyes narrowed. "And why aren't they going anywhere?"

She raised her chin and looked him in the eye. "Because of what you do for a living. I don't want to fall in love with another cop. I sure as hell don't want a SWAT team member."

"So in essence you've decided I'm all right to fuck, but you won't let yourself care about me." He slammed his coffee cup down on the table, not trying to hide his anger. "How the hell do you think that makes me feel?"

"What man in his right mind would turn down what I offered?" she shot back. "Great sex and no involvement. What's not to like?"

"Maybe I want a little more out of life than great sex and no involvement. Maybe I want that involvement. Maybe I want to fall in love and get married. Maybe I want a family. Maybe I want all that with you." He stopped and ran his hands through his hair. "But all you want is a fuck."

"That's right. As long as you're carrying a rifle, rushing into houses, and getting shot at or gassed, I don't go past the booty call."

"So that's what this is all about. Hold out on Brian until he gives up the thing that makes him who he is. Damn, Jess. Did it ever occur to you I save lives? The other night when you got so freaked, all you thought about was the chlorine gas and the cops who got hurt."

"And died," she snapped.

"Yes, Pete died, and it hurts like a son of a bitch. But did you give a thought to the little kids in the back room or the mom the asshole had at gunpoint? We saved them, Jessica. That piece of shit was planning to shoot the woman and kill himself and the kids with the chlorine gas. We saved five people that night. That means nothing to you?"

Jessica sat quietly for a moment. "Am I glad they're safe? Of course. Am I glad there are cops and firefighters and soldiers who keep us all safe? Absolutely. But I am not willing to watch you walk out the door every morning with a gun on your hip, knowing you might not come home that evening and die a little more inside every time the SWAT team's called out. I'm not willing to take a chance on having to stand beside another casket someday."

"It's who I am and what I do."

"It was what Jack Vance did, too. Until his wife beat some sense into his head and then he didn't."

Brian glared at her across the table. "So I'm supposed to quit my job because you're too chickenshit to love me otherwise. I guess you've decided I'm not worth it after all."

"I see." She got up from an almost full plate of food and put another pod in the coffeemaker. "Maybe we're asking the wrong question. Jack Vance thought his marriage and his wife were worth making some changes. So maybe the question isn't whether you're worth it. Maybe it should be whether I'm worth it."

Brian pushed his plate away and stood up. "First off. We're not married. According to you, we're not even going to have a relationship. I'm just a fuck. Why in the hell would I want to give up a job that means the world to me for that? To hell with this shit."

"Suit yourself, amigo."

He swallowed the rest of his coffee and went in search of his duffel. He went back to the kitchen to grab a piece of toast off his plate to eat in the truck and found Jessica on the phone, her face white and her eyes frantic.

"Mom. Mom. Calm down. Did Daddy call nine-one-one? Mom. Get a grip. If Daddy's doing CPR, then hang up and dial nine-one-one. Okay, you've called already. You stay with Heather. I'll call Mike and then I'll come get the kids. Text me as soon as you know where they're taking her."

She ended the call and scrolled down to another number. "Mike? Get your ass out of bed. Heather tried to commit suicide. She left a note and took a whole bottle of sleeping pills. ... What do you mean she just wants attention? Jesus, Mike. Daddy's doing CPR on her right now. She doesn't want attention, she needs *help*." She paused a minute. "I'll text you when I know."

She ended the call with a vicious jab. "I need to get to Heather's. They went to pick her up and found her passed out from an overdose. Exactly what Bobby and Kinsey needed to see this morning. Go home. We can talk later."

She grabbed the satin evening purse off the sofa and ran for the door. He caught up with her on the front porch. "I'll go with you to pick up the kids."

"You don't have to go. It's okay."

"No, it isn't. You've got two scared children you don't need to cope with by yourself. We'll pick up the kids and get them squared away and go from there."

"I–"

"Don't argue. Get in the truck. Give me the keys."

She threw him the keys and got into her truck.

He jumped in behind the wheel and took off down the street.

***

Jessica steeled herself and walked down the long hall and past the nurses' station to the end of the hall. Heather had spent all day and all night in the ICU as medical professionals worked to flush the overdose of powerful sedatives out of her system. She had been judged medically stable this morning and had finally regained consciousness, hence the move to a regular hospital room. Jessica wondered if her sister would be better served on the psychiatric floor. That wasn't her call to make, but Heather needed more help than she was getting.

Her mother met her at the door. She was still dressed in yesterday's clothes and her eyes were bloodshot. "What's going on?" Jessica asked.

"They have a psychiatrist coming within the hour to do a consultation. She's in bad shape. Really bad shape. A lot worse than any of us imagined. They think it's a lot more than simple depression and that it has been for a long time." Tears welled in her mother's eyes. "They said her psychiatrist blew it, big time."

"Wonderful," Jessica murmured under her breath.

"I'm scared that if they send her home, she'll try it again when Kinsey's there. Did Kinsey say anything about what happened?"

"She can't understand why Mommy wouldn't wake up. She brought it up three or four times. I think it scared Bobby as much."

"He's older. He understands more. I'm sorry you had to deal with them all day by yourself."

"Actually, Brian was there for most of the day. He helped me distract them and kept them entertained."

He'd barely said two words to her, but he'd been wonderful with the children.

"Bless him. Your father's got them now."

"Did they say anything about what Heather's options are?"

"They can't hold her more than seventy-two hours against her will. Then they have to let her go unless she agrees to treatment or the psychiatrist gets a protective custody order, which I doubt will happen. Nothing your father or I say will be enough to convince her. And she's sure as hell not listening to Mike."

"Which is where I come in. I'll do my best, Mom."

"You always do. Since she's awake and you're here, I'll go help Eddie with the kids. The two of them together can be quite a handful."

Jean ducked in Heather's room and came out a moment later carrying her purse. "I told them you're here." She kissed Jessica on the cheek. "Thank you." She wiped tears from her eyes and took off down the hall.

Late morning sun poured through the windows of the hospital room. Heather was curled on her side facing away from the door. A bleary-eyed Mike sat in a recliner across the room. He was still in yesterday's clothes and sported a day's growth of beard. He eyed Jessica critically. "Took you long enough to get here."

She wanted to smack him. "Somebody had to take care of your daughter and my son," she said tartly. "Mom was here and Mrs. Borrego next door wasn't home. I had to take them with me to the theater last night." She had almost missed the Sunday tech week practice, which would have been bad, but Josh and Rachel had entertained the kids in their offices so she could rehearse. Still, it made her appreciate that much more her mother's involvement with her grandchildren.

"Heather asked for you when she woke up."

Jessica circled the bed to where she could see Heather face to face. Her sister was deathly pale, her face without expression and her eyes dull. She was hooked to a heart monitor and had an IV running into her arm. Her eyes blinked and she looked at Jessica. "You didn't have to come."

"Mike said you were asking for me."

"Mike can go to hell."

Jessica and Mike both flinched. Mike started to speak but Jessica caught his eye and shook her head. He sank back in the chair, defeat written all over him. Jessica pulled up a folding chair. At a complete loss for words, she took her sister's hand and sat down beside her. They were silent for a few minutes. "I botched it," Heather said finally. "I can't even manage to kill myself successfully."

Well, hell. She didn't know what to say to that. "I'm glad you botched it," she said finally. "I don't want to lose my sister, and I don't want Kinsey to lose her mother."

"She doesn't need me," Heather said bitterly. "Lothario over there would have me replaced before the funeral flowers wilted."

"That's a shitty thing to say." Mike's teeth ground together. "There are no other women. Never have been."

He opened his mouth to say more but closed it again after another laser look from Jessica. "We need to talk about how to make you better," she said soothingly.

"I'm not going to get better. I don't know why you want to bother. You'd all be better off without me. You and our folks wouldn't have to bother with me, and Mike could find Kinsey a decent mother who's not off her rocker."

"Kinsey needs you. You're her mommy. Nobody else is going to raise her the way you will. And think about this. Where am I gonna get another sister? Those can't be replaced. You go and I won't have a sister. I don't want that. Please."

Heather closed her eyes. Jessica and Mike looked at each other and then away, each lost in their own thoughts until a bespectacled young woman with a careless ponytail walked in carrying an iPad. She introduced herself as Dr. Chabra and asked to speak to Heather privately. "Do I get doctor-patient privilege or are you going to blab to them everything I say?" Heather demanded.

"I'll share only with your permission," Dr. Chabra assured her. She turned to Mike and Jessica. "I've already been apprised of the situation." She nodded her head toward the door. "Why don't you go downstairs for a cup of coffee?"

Mike and Jessica walked out of the room. "You want that coffee, or would you spit it on me?" he asked tiredly.

"Not funny." She started toward the elevator. "But coffee works."

They bypassed the cafeteria and instead visited the small food court that had been added to the hospital's first floor. Jessica got a latte and Mike ordered a couple of tacos. They commandeered a table at the back of the court. Mike unwrapped the taco and wolfed down half of it before looking up at her. "I didn't want to leave her. I had to."

"A meltdown at the hospital and a little unnecessary embarrassment enough to justify walking out on a sick woman?"

"It is when Lieutenant Perez calls me in and takes me to task for it," he snapped. "I got the ass-chewing of a lifetime. Was told I should have sent her home if she was going to act like that. Her behavior scared several of the other wives to death, and their husbands complained."

"Shitty on Lieutenant Perez's part."

"It wasn't like I could call him on it."

"Point taken."

"I know you think I'm a heartless bastard, but I was so freaked by what was going on, I misjudged a situation that afternoon and nearly got my head blown off. So yeah, I had to leave her. If I don't, I'm going to lose either my job or my life."

"I get it hasn't been easy, but it was wrong to leave. And it was even worse leaving Kinsey there with her. She and Bobby were both scared to death yesterday morning."

"I was afraid if I took Kinsey, Heather really would freak out and do something. What do you want me to do?"

"I want you to grow a pair of balls and go home and take care of your wife and child."

"I have to be able to keep my mind on the job. I can't live with her and do that."

"What about your daughter?"

"Depends on whether Heather gets effective treatment and can be trusted with her."

"Jesus, you're an ass."

"Tell you what, you think I'm an ass, you try living with her every day. Dealing with the mood swings and the meltdowns. Coming home to a refrigerator full of moldy takeout and her still in her pajamas. You and your parents have no right to judge me. You sweep in, hold her hand a bit and go back to your lives. *I'm* the one who had to deal with her every damned day."

Jessica opened her mouth and shut it. Mike was right.

They finished eating in silence. The psychiatrist was walking out of Heather's room when they came down the hall. "She's agreed to a thirty-day treatment at a psychiatric hospital. I'll start the process, and as soon as she's medically able, we'll move her over there." She turned to Jessica. "Are you the sister?" Jessica nodded. "Not to breach doctor-patient confidentiality, but she speaks highly of you."

"Thank you so much, Dr. Chabra." Jessica smiled at the doctor.

Dr. Chabra's eyes flickered toward Mike and away again. Mike grimaced. "I doubt she had much nice to say about me."

The doctor shrugged and walked off. "You'll need to make arrangements for Kinsey while you're working," Jessica told Mike.

"Both Jean and my mother have volunteered. Kinsey will be well cared for."

"Okay."

He hesitated a minute. "It's not what I wanted, you know."

"I doubt it's what she wanted, either."

Mike turned and walked toward the elevators. Jessica found Heather staring into space. "I'm glad you agreed to treatment."

Heather looked at her unsmilingly. "I can't leave Kinsey without a mom, can I?" Tears flooded Jessica's eyes. "I can't leave you without a sister."

"No, you can't." At least Jessica hoped Heather couldn't.

Jess stayed until Heather dropped off to sleep. It was a little early to report to the theater, but she had no reason to go home, so she picked up a hamburger and fries at Thirties and ate them at her desk. She dreaded tonight's rehearsal. Tonight being Monday, they would perform for the first time in their costumes and iron out any last-minute choreography issues. Which meant that she and Brian would be dancing together again. Dancing with him last night had been torture, acting like lovers when he was so angry with her. They had both hidden it well, but she could see glimpses of his anger, and his pain. She'd hurt him badly, and had miscalculated completely. He wanted no part of the occasional booty call. He was all in for the real thing. He wasn't interested in what she had to offer.

And she sure wasn't interested in what he wanted.

The whole thing made her want to cry.

Chapter Fifteen

Brian parked his pickup and ambled toward the back door of the Durango. Another night of rehearsal with Jessica pretending all was well when he wanted to strangle her. Or take her in his arms and kiss her until she changed her mind. But he didn't think all the kisses in the world were going to accomplish that. Her mind was made up. Casual booty calls or nothing.

He was about to vote for nothing.

A familiar F-150 pulled in next to his and Wade and Owen climbed out and made a beeline for him. "Any word on Jessica's sister?" Wade asked.

"You know as much as I do. I haven't heard anything since last night."

Owen looked puzzled. "She hasn't texted you an update? After you spent the day helping with the kids?"

Brian shook his head. "We were in the middle of a fight when her mother called about Heather. I stayed for the kids' sake. Not because of her."

Wade and Owen winced. "Sorry about that," Owen said. "I'll see what I can find out. Sounds like Heather's mental state's getting worse."

"She always had problems?" Brian asked.

"Yeah. It's gone on for years," Owen said. "Robby commented on it more than once. I was surprised when she married a cop. She didn't need that kind of pressure on top of everything else she had going on."

"Mike said something about Jessica trying to talk Heather out of the marriage," Brian said.

"Too bad she didn't listen," Wade muttered. "She should have kept it casual and not fallen for the guy."

Which was what Jessica was trying to do with him.

He had to admit she had her reasons, even if he didn't agree with them.

The three of them walked into the theater, Brian deep in thought. Maybe everything or nothing with her wasn't the right call. Sure, he was hurt by her proposal. He wanted so much more than that. But more and more he was starting to understand her reluctance to get seriously involved with him.

Booty calls would beat nothing, and nothing is what it would be, at least in the foreseeable future.

They could at least try going that route. At least at first. Maybe she would change her mind somewhere down the line.

And maybe he would find a couple of million dollars stacked in his bathtub.

He would talk to her about it tonight.

His costumes were hanging together on a rack in the dressing room. Wade and Owen were already in their underwear and getting their head mics on. He stripped down to his boxer briefs and got out his over the ear microphone, which he preferred to one that rested on his forehead. Eric Halabi, the newbie playing Ali Hakim, helped him secure the wire down his back to the box. He pulled the first costume, a kitschy cowboy outfit, off the hanger. The pants were a little loose. The better to dance in. The rest of the costume was fine, and his mother had sent him his specially designed dancing shoes that looked like boots but were so much more. He looked at Wade, spiffy in his Will Parker duds. "Lookin' good, cowboy."

"So are you, dudly studly." Wade winked and turned to Owen with a feigned sigh. "Such a waste."

"I doubt Jessica thinks so," Owen said dryly. He looked at his mangled face in the mirror. "I'm really gonna do this, aren't I? Show these to the world."

"Picture yourself in the scene with Laurey. The one where you threaten her. Say those lines in front of the mirror," Brian said. Owen stared into the mirror and delivered the lines. "Now picture yourself doing it with a beautiful face."

Owen repeated the lines. "The scars stay."

Letti called for the cast. They all sat down in the front rows. Brian sneaked a look at Jessica in her 1900 Laurey ruffled gingham dress and high-top shoes. She didn't have the makeup or hairstyle, they would add those tomorrow and Wednesday, but she already embodied the character of Laurey Williams.

Letti gave them a few instructions, and production manager Miranda Jenks was already making copious notes, which would be shared with the cast and crew after rehearsal. They took their places backstage, the curtain opened and for the first time he felt Curly McLain really come to life as he sang "Oh, What a Beautiful Mornin'."

There were the inevitable glitches. Jenna Salazar's costumes were already too tight and would have to be replaced in the morning with much larger ones. A couple of the newer ensemble members were off on their timing in the ballet sequence. But they had three more days to get it right.

He was waiting for Jessica when she came out of the ladies' dressing room. Her face looked tired and she seemed sad. "How's your sister?"

"She's agreed to a thirty-day inpatient treatment program. Everyone's relieved."

"Do you have time for a beer at Thirties?"

She looked at him doubtfully. "I thought you were mad at me."

He shrugged. "I'd like us to talk."

"Whatever."

The wind had picked up considerably, so they went in his truck. The bar was practically deserted and the waitress brought their beers quickly. He met her eyes across the table. "We'll do it your way," he blurted. "Keep it casual. The occasional date. Booty calls. No involvement, like you want."

"Do you mind if I ask why the change of heart?"

He shrugged. "You're not gonna change your mind. You're trying to protect yourself. Something Wade said this evening struck a chord. He said maybe your sister and Mike should have done that. Kept it casual and not tried to make a marriage work." He paused a minute. "I want you. I'll take you any way I can get you. Even if it's not the way I want it to be."

"Okay, then." She reached across the table and took him by the hand. "Thank you."

They made small talk while they finished their beers. Brian drove her back to the theater parking lot and parked beside her truck.

He opened the door for her. "Does this casual relationship include a good-night kiss?"

"Sure."

She was soft and willing as he took her in his arms. She met his lips, her touch igniting something within him as he kissed her with everything he had. Her arms crept around his neck and she moaned as she moved even closer to him.

He could feel her beautiful nipples harden into tight pebbles of need against his chest, and his swelling cock poked her in the stomach, letting her know how much she turned him on. They kissed for long minutes, breaking apart only when a police cruiser drove by slowly. She took a step back. "Looks like you're going to get a ribbing tomorrow," she said softly.

"You're probably right." He pulled in for one more short kiss. "See you tomorrow. Maybe we can have a beer or something after the show on Friday."

Something in your bed, preferably.

"Maybe. 'Night, Brian."

He waited until her truck was out of the parking lot before turning over his engine. He was making a mistake. He knew it down to his bones. There was no way in hell he could sleep with her and not fall in love with her. The arrangement he'd agreed to didn't make him happy.

She hadn't seemed all that happy about it either.

What the hell should he think about that?

***

Brian took Jessica by the hand and they ran onto the stage with huge smiles on their faces. The audience surged to their feet, clapping loudly in appreciation as she curtsied and he bowed low. It was gratifying the way the San Antonio audiences responded to the beloved old musical night after night. The newspaper critic had given them a hearty thumbs-up, and the theater had been sold out every night for the last four weeks. The acting had been superb, with Owen's portrayal of Jud Fry both sympathetic and terrifying, and the audience cheered at the end when Curly and Laurey and Will and Ado Annie got their much-deserved happily ever afters.

Too bad real life wasn't working that way.

They bowed and waved, and on Miranda's signal trooped up the side aisle and stood in the lobby to greet the audience. It was his understanding that their benefactors, the Navarros, were in attendance tonight and that he would get to meet them. He took his usual place beside Jessica. "Are you free tonight?" he asked under his breath.

"No. I have to pick Bobby up right after the performance."

"What about tomorrow after the matinee? We can take him to a cafeteria and let him pick what he wants for dinner."

"Uh, I don't think so. We're tied up tomorrow evening. Maybe next weekend."

He looked at her with exasperation. "You know good and well there's no earthly reason you and Bobby can't go with me to a damned cafeteria for a plate of food tomorrow evening."

Her face tightened. "We'll talk later." She smiled brightly and offered her hand to an elegantly dressed woman, greeting her by name.

Brian forced himself to smile. They shook hands with the audience for the next twenty minutes. Josh and developmental director Maggie Gutierrez made it a point to introduce each cast member to the Navarros. *El Jefe* did the intimidating thing, but Mrs. Navarro was the soul of gracious and charming, and Jessica seemed thrilled to hear that four of the Navarro grandchildren would be coming to the Academy theater camp this summer.

The line finally wound down and he fled to the men's dressing room, where he stripped out of his Curly costume. "Wade, can you get this mic off me?"

He turned his back to Wade and his friend started un-taping the mic cord. "What's your hurry? You got a hot date with Jessica or something?"

"I wish. I want to catch her in the parking lot before she drives off." He tried and failed to hide his irritation.

"Oops. Are things not going well in Jessica-and-Brian land?" Eric teased as he stripped off the gaudy plaid Ali Hakim jacket.

Brian stared at Eric. Owen quickly changed the subject and Wade got the mic un-taped. Brian changed his clothes, got his mic batteries replaced in record time, and was waiting beside Jessica's truck when she came out ten minutes later. She smiled weakly as she unlocked the door. "I thought for sure you'd go on to Thirties with the rest of the cast."

"I don't want to go to fucking Thirties with the rest of the cast. I want to spend a little time with you."

"We went out last weekend," she reminded him.

"So? That was last weekend. What about tonight? What about tomorrow?"

"I'm not lying about tonight or tomorrow. Mom's worn out from having to keep Kinsey as well as Bobby. I promised the kids I'd take them to a bounce house if they behaved for Mom."

"A what?"

"A bounce house. One of those places full of blow-up houses and slides and trampolines where they can jump and bounce and wear themselves out."

"Would you like me to go with you and help you watch them? You know I'm good with them."

"I—I no."

"Damn it to hell, Jessica. You're throwing up roadblocks."

"You're crowding me. You agreed to keep this casual. Which means we don't see one another all the time. You want too much."

"I want to see you one fucking time this weekend."

She stopped and took a deep breath. "All right. Give me an hour to pick up Bobby and get him to bed. We can sneak in a couple of hours together."

Was that all? He chided himself. At least it was something.

He appeared on her doorstep an hour later, freshly showered and shaved. She met him at the door in her fuzzy robe. Her stage makeup was gone and her hair was damp. "Come on in. I made us sandwiches."

They made quick work of the sandwiches and a couple of beers. He carried his plate to the sink and held out his arms. "Come here. I've missed you this week."

She melted into his arms. "You saw me last night and again tonight."

"But both nights we were Laurey and Curly. I want us to be Brian and Jessica." He picked her up and sat her on the kitchen counter. "This way I don't have to bend over quite so far."

She giggled as she looped her arms around his neck. "I thought we agreed kitchen counter sex was better on the pages of a romance novel."

"You said so. I don't remember agreeing."

She smiled.

"We can start here."

She nodded. "We can."

He cradled her head in his hands. Their lips came together slowly at first, as they gently explored one another. They deepened the kiss, their mouths opening as the passion ignited and the sparks flew. She felt so damned good in his arms. It was this way every time they kissed. It was this way every time they made love. They were made to be together, physically and in every other way. Why couldn't she understand that?

They kissed and caressed one another for long minutes. "Hook your legs around my waist," he said. "We'll finish this in your bed."

She obligingly slid her legs around his body. Without breaking hold, he hoisted her up and carried her to her bed, collapsing with her into the soft, thick comforter. He pulled open the lapels of her robe, baring her rosy nipples to his gaze. "You get more beautiful every time I look at you," he breathed. He dipped his head and gently sucked a nipple, feeling it pebble beneath his lips. She moaned softly as he caressed the other one.

She would be so beautiful with his child at her breast.

He pushed aside that thought and pulled the robe further open. Her body lay bare to his gaze, ripe for his feasting eyes and greedy hands. He sat up long enough to shuck his shirt and jeans. She ran her hand up his chest, ruffling his chest hair. "Don't ever wax this, please. It's one of the sexiest things about you. Along with this." She slid her hand down his stomach and buried her fingers in the thick red thatch surrounding his cock. "And this." She palmed his already hard cock, caressing it into a steel rod. "I'm ready whenever you are."

"We'll see about that." He slid his hand down her soft stomach and lower, finding her warm and already wet for him. She wanted a quick fuck, but he had other ideas. He was going to make tonight special. He was going to make every time they came together special. He was going to make her see that they belonged together for more than what she said she wanted.

They belonged together every damned night. His fingers found her nub and he stroked her, caressing her until soft cries came from between her lips and her body convulsed around his fingertips. He lowered his head to where his hand had been, his tongue replacing his fingers as he brought her to yet another peak. Only then did he don a condom and enter her welcoming warmth.

He could feel his own desperation as he pounded into her. He needed more than this. *They* needed more than this. He could feel her tremble beneath him as he brought her closer and closer, and when her body arched and she cried out he was right there with her, the two of them trembling together as they tumbled.

They held each other for long minutes, gasping as the shock waves faded into tremors before disappearing altogether. He slid out of her then rolled her over so that he was on his back with her straddling him, the robe still over her shoulders and covering her arms.

He took in her tousled hair, her sleepy eyes, and her satisfied expression. "You have to be the sexiest woman in the whole world."

"I doubt that." She leaned down and gave him a long, sweet kiss. "But I thank you for thinking so."

They stayed together for a few more minutes before she pulled off the condom. She disposed of it in the toilet and came back and snuggled down beside him. "I get that those things are necessary, but they're still a damned nuisance."

"You're preaching to the choir." He took a deep breath. "Have you considered that we could probably find another way to prevent babies?" She looked at him in surprise. "I mean, we're both clean and we're exclusive."

"We are?"

"We're what?" he asked more sharply than intended. "Clean, or exclusive?"

"Either. Both."

His eyes narrowed. "I'm clean and I'm pretty sure you are. So I guess you're asking about the other." He sat up crossed his legs in front of him. "Are we exclusive? Or are you keeping it casual to the point that there are other men?"

"I told you a month ago we were exclusive. At least I am. I didn't know if you still considered yourself to be." Her face turned pink.

"Hell, yes, I'm exclusive. What kind of an SOB do you think I am?" He got out of bed and started putting on his clothes. "I wouldn't cheat on you, and you know it. I care too damn much about you to do a thing like that." He jerked his jeans up his legs. "Don't you realize that?"

She pulled the robe around her body. "I'm beginning to. I thought we weren't going to do that. Start caring."

"Some of us don't have any control over that. I care about you. I like you. I want you. I'm falling head over heels in love with you. And you know what, sweetheart? You're doing the same damned thing. You're falling for me as hard as I'm falling for you."

"No. No, I'm not." Her jaw clenched and her hands fisted at her side.

"Oh, yes you are. You're falling for me. Why else would you keep pushing me away? Why else would you keep me away from Bobby? You're falling like a ton of bricks and you're too damned chickenshit to be with me for real. You don't want to let me in because it makes you realize how frigging shallow the booty calls are compared to what we could really have together."

"Arrogant and an ass. You can't stand admitting that I might not be falling for you."

"But you are. You couldn't make love the way we did if you weren't."

She sat up and leaned against the headboard and looked at him with eyes that were sad. "Why are you picking a fight? I hesitated because I wasn't sure if you wanted the freedom to go out with others. I wouldn't like it if you did, but I'm not offering you much. I'm not stupid. At some point you're going to want more."

Brian swallowed. She was right. He already wanted more. How long he was going to be content with what she had to offer was anybody's guess.

He put on the rest of his clothes. "We'll talk more about birth control later." He leaned down for a quick kiss and let himself out of the house.

How lovemaking so beautiful could leave such a bad taste in his mouth was beyond him.

***

Jessica took Bobby by the hand and led him through the restaurant where her parents had already commandeered a roomy booth. The family had four or five restaurants where they met for Sunday brunch, but this all-you-can-eat buffet was her favorite, mostly because they catered to children with Mickey Mouse pancakes and cardboard mouse ears for Bobby. She sat Bobby on the booster beside her mother and slid in beside him. "Kinsey didn't come this morning?"

"Mike picked her up to spend the day with his parents. His mother's keeping her most of next week. Thank God," Jean said tiredly. "They're taking a rain check on the bounce house this afternoon."

"Having both of them is wearing your mother out," Eddie added.

"Mom, I'm sorry. Do I need to put Bobby in afternoon daycare? That would relieve you some."

"No," Eddie said quickly. "Bobby by himself isn't a problem, never was. It's Kinsey. She misses her mother and acts out because of it. I hope Mike's mother's ready to handle her. She's a handful right now."

"Jo will do fine. She raised a houseful," Jean said. "And Heather will be released in a week or so."

"I went by yesterday afternoon. She seemed better."

"She does," Eddie said. "She told your mom and I that they've adjusted her meds so she's not so out of it all the time."

"There's also been counseling in regard to the separation," Jean said. "Some ideas on how to go forward."

"Do they have a snowball's chance in hell of getting back together?" Jessica asked.

Eddie and Jean shrugged and her mother changed the subject. Apparently neither of them was willing to speculate.

The waitress brought their drinks and they trooped to the buffet line to fill their plates. The next few minutes were quiet as they polished off big plates of eggs, bacon, and pancakes. Her father looked across the table at her. "Have you seen your young man recently?"

"Brian? Of course I've seen him. I'm costarring with him. He met the Navarros for the first time last night."

"Was he as gaga impressed with them as the rest of the theater people?" Jean asked dryly.

"He didn't say. You can think what you like about us all being gaga. Their generosity is paying my salary right now."

"Just asking." Her mother's eyes twinkled. "So, have you seen him other than at the theater?"

Jessica blushed. "He came over for a little after the show last night. We had a late supper together."

"Nice young man. You need to invite him to come with you to brunch next Sunday. I'd like to get to know him better," Eddie said.

Uh-oh. Her father was matchmaking again like he had with Robby.

Jessica sighed inwardly. She could handle this in either of two ways. She could hem and haw and promise an invitation that was never coming. Or she could be upfront with her father, knowing he wasn't going to like what she had to say.

She took a deep breath and went for Plan B. "Daddy, I don't think so. Brian and I aren't serious about one another. We're merely enjoying one another's company for a time. It's not going anywhere."

Her father's face fell. "I thought the young man liked you."

"He does. And I like him. But that's as far as it's ever going with him. As far as I'm concerned, he's not marriage material."

Eddie's eyes narrowed. "What's wrong? Is he married? Does he drink too much? Is he unkind to you or Bobby?"

"None of the above. He's a fine man, inside and out. But he's a cop. He's SWAT. It's who he is. And there is no way under the shining sun I'm getting seriously involved with another one of those."

"That's ridiculous," Dad snapped. "To turn away a man of his caliber because he's police. You ought to be thanking your lucky stars another fine man is interested in you."

"You mean a fine man like Robby? The one who did stupid things for fun and got himself killed? Tell me, Daddy, if Brian were exactly the same man he is now, except that he was a teacher or an accountant, or a pharmaceutical sales rep, would you be so interested in me dating him? Or would you be telling me to find somebody with bigger balls?"

"I wouldn't be nearly as pleased. Jesus, Jess. Brian and men like him are heroes. They save lives for a living. That makes them special. You ought to be honored that he's interested in you. It's time you sucked it up, little girl, and give that man a chance."

"Like hell I'm gonna suck it up again. I've already sucked it up. I've already had a hero. I've already paid the price for the safety of the public, and I'm not paying it again. I stood by Robby's grave while they put his casket in the ground. No way am I getting involved with another reckless fool."

"Jessica, you're being ridiculous. This man isn't like Robby," Dad said firmly. "I called Jack Vance and did some checking around with my old buddies. They can't say enough nice things about him. They say he doesn't take the kind of chances Robby did. For crying out loud, don't let a good one get away because of what happened in the past."

"It's not only the past. Look at Heather. I'm not blaming Mike or his job entirely for her problems, but being married to him didn't help her."

"You're not your sister. You're strong."

"Maybe she's tired of being strong," Mom said quietly. "Listen to yourself, Eddie. You're so damned eager to have another cop for a son-in-law you're completely disregarding your daughter's feelings. She spelled it out. She's unwilling to go there again. We all know sometimes it doesn't matter how careful a cop is, how hard he tries, sometimes shit happens. Sometimes cops die. He could get killed someday. Maybe she doesn't want to live her life worried every time he walks out the door. That's her decision."

"You did it," he reminded her.

"Yes. I did it. I also got shit-faced more often than not so I could get some sleep," she shot back. "She doesn't want that. And if she doesn't, it's her decision and you need to quit pushing. I for one would love to see her with a teacher, or a plumber, or an attorney."

Her father threw up his hands. "Whatever. It's a damn shame, though." He turned to Jessica. "Think long and hard, Jessica. Men like that are few and far between. You let him go, there may not be another one like him come along for years. If ever."

Jessica nodded. She knew that.

But she still didn't think she would be changing her mind any time soon.

Chapter Sixteen

Jessica parked behind Heather's crossover and carried the sack of submarine sandwiches to the front door. The door was open to the balmy April breeze and she could hear the television in the family room. She started to knock but Kinsey ran to the latched screen door. "Aunt Jessica! Is that something to eat?" She turned around. "Mommy! Aunt Jessica's here." She turned back around to Jessica. "Mommy's home. I missed her." The child's little eyes sparkled and she had a smile on her face.

Heather came to the door. Jessica hadn't seen Heather since the afternoon she came home a week ago and she'd wondered if Heather's improvement was permanent. One look at her sister had her breathing a sigh of relief. While Heather wasn't exactly smiling, her eyes were clear and she seemed more relaxed than she had in months. "Come in, bearer of my favorite deli sandwiches." She unlatched the screen door and motioned Jessica inside. "Thanks for bringing lunch. It will be our last chance to do this for a while."

Jessica felt herself smile. "So you got the job. That didn't take long."

"Helps to have a marketable skill." Heather was a trained veterinary technician and had worked for several veterinary practices before Kinsey was born. "Besides, I have a child to feed. I saw an attorney yesterday. Mike and I are definitely calling it quits."

Jessica followed Heather to the kitchen. "I'm not sure if I'm sorry for that or not. He was a real dick, leaving you at your lowest."

Heather shrugged. "If he cares that little about me, I'm better off without him." Her lip trembled. "Kinsey and I will be fine."

"Yes, you will. Kinsey sure seems happy you're home."

"I hope she still feels that way when I take her to daycare on Monday."

"Mom's not keeping her?"

Heather shook her head. "No. That's too much on Mom. With the odd hours you work and one salary, you don't have a choice. But I'll be working eight to five and I'm making Mike reimburse me for the childcare, plus I have his child support payments. It's the least the bastard can do."

Jessica set the table with paper plates and Heather made fresh iced tea. The three of them made quick work of the sandwiches and Heather put Kinsey down for a nap. Jessica had the table cleared by the time Heather returned. "So catch me up on what's going on in your life. The last time we talked, I told you to do the booty call thing with your cop sweetie, but not to get involved. Did you do that?"

"I'm trying to. He got mad at first. Then he agreed to give it a try. But it's not working." Tears flooded her eyes. "He says he cares about me. He keeps pushing for more. We've had three bad fights already and I'm afraid we're headed for another one tonight."

"What about?"

"His mom and dad are coming in to see the play. He wants to introduce me to them."

"Ouch. So how do you feel about him?"

"I'm trying not to fall for him, but that's a losing battle."

"If it's going like that, you're going to have to make a decision," Heather said quietly. "Unless he makes the decision for you. Like Mike did."

"I know. I keep thinking back to what Dad said. After he told me to suck it up and Mom and I told him to stuff it, he reminded me that men as good as Brian don't grow on trees and that it may be years before another one comes along. He's right. I may never meet another man as good as Brian."

"And he, of course, isn't willing to change jobs."

"Hell, no." She swiped angrily at the tears running down her cheeks.

Heather put her arms around Jessica and held her tight. "I am so damn sorry. I really am."

So was Jessica.

***

Brian swore as he inched down the expressway. *Damn fucking rubberneckers.* He could see the accident up ahead, but both lanes were clear, and the only thing impeding traffic was drivers slowing to get a closer look at the wrecked cars. He cursed the cars, the drivers, the road, and everything else he could think of. He'd been in a foul mood all week, ever since the blowup with Jessica last Sunday after his parents left town.

"Damn it, Jessica," he'd yelled. "How do you think I feel? I'd told them all about you and you wouldn't even meet them."

"Why in hell did you tell them all about me? For crying out loud, that implies something serious is going on. *And it's not.*"

She'd jumped in the truck and roared out of the Durango parking lot, leaving him literally in the dust. He'd not seen or heard from her since. And tonight they would have to get back up on that stage and play the parts of a couple falling in love.

Only he wouldn't be acting. He'd fallen in love with Jessica for real.

He could swear that she'd fallen for him, too. Not that she would admit it in a million years. She was bound and determined to keep him at arm's length and let fear rather than love rule. And he'd had enough of that. He'd texted her earlier in the day that they needed to talk tonight. He was going to put it to her in one-syllable words. Either they agree to move forward with a genuine relationship and a possible future together, or he was going to break it off. It'd hurt like a son of a bitch, but a swift clean break was infinitely preferable to the torment of seeing her, sleeping with her, and loving her with no hope of the future he wanted with her. He would find someone else. Sooner or later he would find a woman who wanted what he had to offer. But he feared it wouldn't be anytime soon.

It would be a long time before he was over her.

And he'd be damned if he did any more shows at the Durango. It would be less painful if he wasn't around her day in and day out. She could keep the theater crowd, and he'd hang out with his friends on the force.

He was almost to the exit that would take him to his condo when his phone dinged, followed immediately by the ringtone on his Bluetooth. SAPD was on the caller ID. He took a quick look at the message. ***Hostage situation. Report to command center.*** He swore and punched the steering wheel button to answer the phone. "Officer Howard." He put on the blinker to take the exit. "What's going on?"

For once Sugar Johnson did not sound cheerful. "Hostage crisis at a daycare. They need everyone ASAP."

"On my way." He took the exit and did a U-turn at the light. Deriding himself for distracted driving, he scrolled down and punched in Wade's number. "Wade, I need you to get Harry whoever to play Curly tonight. Hostage situation at a daycare and SWAT's being called in."

"Shit. That sucks."

"It does."

"No worries. Harry will do a good job as Curly." His friend paused a minute. "Be careful tonight."

"No worries. I'm always careful."

He got back on the expressway, which in this direction was flowing smoothly, and headed downtown. The department parking lot was nearly full, but he found a space in the last row. He ran into the building and was changing into his SWAT gear when Mike hustled in. "Are we ready for this?" Mike asked as he started stripping out of his street clothes.

"We better be. Is your mind off your situation with Heather?"

"It is." He raised his eyebrow. "Is yours off your situation with Jessica?"

"No, but it will be."

"Good. Now let's see what the hell's going on."

They finished getting into their gear and reported to the briefing room. As soon as the last man entered, a grim-faced Lieutenant Perez stepped to the podium.

"We know very little about what's going on inside the building. One of the workers sent a text that a disgruntled mom is holding a gun on everyone in the main playroom. Some of the workers in the side rooms have the doors locked and those children in lockdown. We've got Silver Tongue Vance on his way over now." He projected a roughly sketched diagram of the daycare's floor plan. "One of the parents outside the daycare drew this for us. According to the text, the woman's in here." He pointed to a central room. "As always, we'll try to talk her down. I have every hope and faith that we can do that. If not, we'll do what we have to do."

At the probable cost of children's lives.

Brian wasn't the only SWAT team member with swear words on his lips.

The ride to the daycare was silent. The streets around the building were clogged with police cars and crossovers. Barricades had been set up two blocks from the daycare. and nearby shops and businesses were being cleared. The distraught parents were being routed to a strip center parking lot one street over, and the mobile command unit was being wheeled into position.

Jack Vance drove up in a brand-new Mustang and disappeared into the unit along with Lieutenant Perez and other relevant personnel. The expanding side unit was folded out and the steps lowered for easier access. The SWAT team assembled behind the command center and memorized the hastily sketched floor plan.

Everyone settled in for what promised to be a long night.

There was no activity around the daycare. Whatever was happening inside remained a mystery. Nor was there any word out of the command post for a good two hours. Which meant either they couldn't get the perp to talk to Jack, or that he had the woman on the phone and was doing his best to wear her down. The sun went down and lights were set up around the perimeter of the building. The SWAT team waited patiently. Brian hoped they wouldn't be called on to use their skills tonight. He hoped the woman could be persuaded to let the children and the caregivers go.

It was well into the third hour before Lieutenant Perez came out of the command post. "We finally got the woman with the gun on the phone. She says the kids have been making fun of her daughter's prosthetic hand and they all need to die."

Oh. My. God. Brian sucked in a breath. Mike stumbled back and then surged forward. "Do you have a list of the daycare clients?" he demanded of the lieutenant. "That may be my wife in there. The little girl may be my daughter Kinsey."

"No, we don't." He motioned for Mike to come closer. "What does the hand look like? Maybe we can get the woman or one of the daycare workers to describe it. We can tell from that if it's her."

Mike motioned for Brian. "It's green and yellow and the fingers flex I made it for her," he added. Lieutenant Perez looked at him curiously.

The lieutenant disappeared and emerged five minutes later. "The daycare worker in lockdown texted us a description of the hand. It's yellow and green. She confirmed that the little girl's name is Kinsey."

Lieutenant Perez shot Mike a withering look. "Why didn't you tell us this is your daughter's daycare?"

"I didn't know," he said tightly. "We're separated, and this daycare is a new thing. What's going on now that she's on the phone?"

"Come with me. We're going to need you to tell us everything that's been going on with your wife. We need all the information we can get if we're going to convince her to give this up."

Mike disappeared into the unit. All was quiet for thirty minutes. Then a shot rang out. The window of the daycare exploded outward and a bullet slammed into a brick façade across the street. Everyone dove for cover and drew their weapons if they had one.

Brian's heart pounded in his throat as they waited five minutes, then ten, then thirty. Mike finally emerged looking shell-shocked. "She's off her rocker. She's absolutely, positively lost it. Silver Tongue can't get anywhere with her and I managed to piss her off good."

"So we all saw. Anybody know what kind of weapon she has?"

"It sounded like that little semiautomatic pistol I gave her a couple of years ago for Christmas. The pink one."

"Jesus, man. You didn't have enough sense to take it away from her when she went south?"

"I didn't think about it."

"Well, hell. What are they gonna do?"

"They're going to try other family members. I told them she was especially close to Jessica. They want you to get in touch with her at the theater and get her over here."

***

Earlier that evening, Jessica sat on a stool in the dressing room and stared down at Brian's text. He wanted to talk. She wasn't surprised. It had been almost a week since their fight in the Durango parking lot. He'd been angry then. Angry and hurt that she wouldn't meet his parents. But that implied a level of commitment she wasn't willing to make. He damned well knew it. But he was determined to take their relationship to the next level. She had a feeling she was going to get an ultimatum tonight. She could either have the genuine relationship he wanted so badly, or he was calling it quits. Heather had been right. Either Jess or Brian would be making a decision tonight. A painful decision. But it was the only choice she had. Giving Brian what he wanted would destroy her in the long run.

Maybe it would be better for them to call it quits. They wouldn't have to see one another anymore. This performance and two more, and *Oklahoma!* would be over. San Antonio was a big city. Their paths wouldn't cross.

Unless he wanted to do more shows at the Durango. The thought scared the hell out of her. Having to work with him again and see him with other women. Surely, there would be someone to take her place. A man like Brian had so much to offer. He'd find a woman who wasn't afraid of loving him, and he would have the life with her that he'd wanted with Jessica.

The thought made her want to cry.

Her heart heavy, she got out her mic. Jenna was in the corner stripping out of her street clothes. "Looking good, mama," Jessica teased. Jenna's middle was pleasantly rounded and the new costumes were getting tight.

"Thank goodness this is the last weekend. I plan to go out Monday afternoon and buy a batch of maternity clothes. You want help with the mic?"

"Thanks." She turned her back and Jenna had the mic taped halfway down her back when Wade came in the dressing room with Harry Bell wearing the first Curly costume. "Jessica, we thought we better let you know Harry will be playing Curly tonight. Brian got called into work." He started to say more but stopped.

Another SWAT incident. Cold tendrils of terror wrapped around Jessica. Once again, he was out there putting his life on the line.

Which was why she wasn't getting involved with him, she reminded herself. So she wouldn't have to worry about him. She wouldn't worry about him tonight. She had a performance to give.

She greeted Harry and thanked him for coming in. Jenna finished taping on the mic. She donned her first costume and did Laurey's fresh-faced makeup and took her place in the wings on the stage manager's five-minute mark. She thought again of Brian and again pushed away the thought. She *was not* going to worry about him.

But he was in the back of her mind the entire evening. Harry turned in a credible performance as Curly, especially considering the last-minute notice, but her performance was off, and the chemistry she had with Brian was sorely missing.

Wade and the others caught on quickly and put more into their roles. She hoped the audience wasn't cheated too badly. Nevertheless, she breathed a sigh of relief as she took her bows and walked up the aisle to shake hands with the audience. They were about halfway through greeting the crowd when Wade's phone buzzed. He spoke to his caller for a minute and leaned over and whispered to Owen. They both left their places and made their way through the crowded lobby to her. "Jessica, come with us. There's an emergency."

Oh, God. Something's happened to Brian. "What...what is it?"

Wade took her arm. "Come on."

They practically ran her down the aisle. "There's a situation at Kinsey's daycare," Owen said. "Heather's holding a roomful of kids and daycare workers hostage. They want you to try to talk her down. Get your clothes changed and don't worry about the makeup."

She stared at them in horror. "What...how...why?"

"That was Brian on the phone. They need you at the command post as fast as you can get there," Wade continued. "We'll take you."

They deposited her in the women's dressing room. Her hands shook and her lips trembled as she stripped out of her costume and threw on the jeans and tee she'd come in. *Her sister was holding a roomful of children hostage.* Unless she could talk Heather down, someone was going to die tonight.

The thought almost paralyzed her.

Wade and Owen were back in their street clothes by the time she was changed. Brian texted Wade the location and Owen put his old police driving skills to work getting them there. She tried to call her mom and dad, but she was shaking so badly Wade took her phone and explained the situation to her horrified parents. "Your mom will stay with Bobby. Your father's meeting us there."

"Not that she'll listen to him," she murmured.

He ran a comforting hand down her arm. "He's not going for her. He's going for you."

Owen got them to the neighborhood in record time. They made their way to the barricade and with a brief explanation the policeman waved them through. Owen parked behind the unit where the SWAT team was gathered. She looked around at the grim-faced men and pure terror had her shaking.

One of them might have to kill her sister tonight.

The thought made her teeth rattle.

Suddenly there was a familiar hand on her arm. "Come on up," Brian urged her. "I'll introduce you to Lieutenant Perez."

She stumbled on the steps and would have fallen but for his arm holding her steady. He threw open the door and they went inside the crowded trailer, chock full of consoles and electronic gear, as well as three workstations. Video feeds showed the daycare from four different angles. Mike and a man wearing lieutenant's bars sat at a small conference table. Jack Vance sat at one of the workstations with two other officers. All were wearing headphones, and Jack wore a face mic and a frustrated expression. "She hung up on me twenty minutes ago," he said. "She said to call her back when Jessica got here and not until."

"What's going on?" she asked through stiff lips.

"She's off her fucking rocker," Mike snapped.

A middle-aged man with startling green eyes gave him a blistering look before turning to Jessica. "I'm Lieutenant Perez."

"The one who chewed Mike out for Heather's meltdown?" she asked tartly.

The lieutenant's lips firmed. "We have a situation. Your sister refuses to talk to anyone but you. Please have a seat and we'll apprise you of the situation before you get on the phone."

She sat, not bothering to hide her trembling hands. Mike vacated his chair and Lieutenant Perez sat down. There was a commotion at the door and her father shouldered his way inside. "She's my daughter and I'll be here if I want to," he roared at the officer who tried to stop him.

Lieutenant Perez caught the eye of the officer and shook his head. "It's actually a good thing if Mr. Herrmann's here." He gestured to a seat. "Sir, Jessica, did either of you have any idea of her current mental state?"

"Do you think I'd have left my granddaughter with her if I had? No, we had no idea." Dad rubbed his hand down his face. "Her mother's been calling or going to the house every day. Last night she seemed fine."

"Dad's right. She gave no clue she was at the point of doing something like this. Or believe me, we would have done something." She graced Lieutenant Perez with a glare.

Jack took off the headset and squeezed in beside Jessica. "There's a kernel of rationality in there somewhere. We've talked about how sad it would be for the parents to lose their children. Maybe you could go with that." He summed up a few dos and don'ts when dealing with a hostage crisis.

They were already breaking protocol by letting Jessica talk to Heather. She was instructed to establish rapport and let Heather do most of the talking. "I know you're scared out of your mind. But try not to convey that to her. She needs to hear calm, soothing, and confident. Remind her that the hostages are human and that most of them are innocent children. Reach out to Heather's humanity. Find out what you can. See if she will tell you what weapons and how much ammo she brought. And be prepared for this to take a while. You may be hours on the phone. We need everyone who isn't absolutely essential to wait outside."

Brian squeezed her shoulder and took his leave. Mike stood. "I'll be right outside if you need me." Her heart pounding in her throat, Jessica, Jack, and an officer introduced as a secondary negotiator sat down at the workstation. "You do the talking, and if the conversation stalls we'll feed you ideas and topics to talk about," the other negotiator explained. "We also have a psychologist back at the station listening in remotely. She will monitor your sister's mental condition and advise us accordingly."

Jessica nodded. Jack helped her don the headset and he pushed a couple of buttons. At first there was no answer. They tried again and Heather came on the line. "I told you not to call back unless it was my sister."

"It's me, Heather. It's Jess. What's going on, hon?"

"I hate them. *I hate them all.* They're poking fun at Kinsey. They call her all kinds of mean things. They're terrible."

Jessica blinked at the venom in Heather's voice. "Let her rant," Jack said softly. "Don't argue with her. Mollify her."

Heather yelled and screamed for a good ten minutes. "I know, sweetie," Jessica said soothingly. "I know they were mean to her. Sometimes children can be so cruel. Remember how Doogie Markham used to pick on everybody?"

Heather seized on the memory and began to talk. Jack gave Jessica a thumbs-up. The minutes crept by as Jessica soothed and Heather ranted. One hour. Two. Jessica's shoulders and neck ached with tension as the night wore on.

Progress was slow as Jack and the secondary negotiator coached her from the sidelines and thought of things that might get through to Heather. But progress was made, and somewhere in the fourth hour, she agreed that the children taunting Kinsey were only children and didn't know any better, and that the parents would be so sad if anything happened to them. "So maybe could they go?" Jessica finally was allowed to ask. "Can they go home with their moms and dads tonight?"

"I—I guess. But nobody better try anything. My Glock's locked and loaded, and anybody messes with me, they'll be singing with the angels."

"Nobody's messing with you. I promise."

The line went dead. Jessica slumped with exhaustion as Jack and the secondary negotiator gave her two thumbs up. They waited a tense ten minutes until the front door of the daycare opened. They watched the video feed as the children emerged single file, escorted by the workers. They were quickly whisked into police cars and driven beyond the barricades to safety. "Lieutenant, I need to go get Kinsey," Mike said, his relief palpable.

"Absolutely. Go get your daughter."

Mike took off toward the parking lot, where the older children and the workers were being debriefed and the younger ones handed over to their parents. "Now what?" Dad demanded. "My daughter is still holed up in there with a gun."

"We try to talk her out."

But Heather wouldn't answer the phone. Tension mounted as the minutes ticked by. Ten minutes later, a white-faced Mike ran up the steps to the command post, followed by one of the policewomen conducting the interviews. "Kinsey's not with them," he gasped.

"The workers are all reporting that Mrs. Werner's wearing a vest they believe contains explosives," the policewoman said. "She took off her sweater and showed it to them. She told them as they left that she's going to heaven and taking Kinsey with her."

They all looked at one another, stunned. "Where in the hell would she get a vest with explosives?" Jessica asked.

"You get a vest with pockets and you stuff them with explosives and shrapnel. You hook up a detonating device and you're all set," Lieutenant Perez said. "It's not rocket science."

"A lot of the components are available on the Internet," Jack said softly.

"God almighty," Dad breathed. He put his head in his hands.

Jack and Lieutenant Perez looked at one another. "Try to get her on the phone. Stall her until we can come up with a plan."

"Do I try to talk her out of it?" Jessica asked.

"By all means, but *do not push* her, whatever you do. Encourage her to keep talking. Time is everything."

Jessica's hands were shaking so badly, Jack had to put the headset back on for her. It took her three tries, but Heather finally picked up. "What's happening, Heather?"

"What do you want? I let the kids go."

"Not all of them," she said as gently as she could. "What about Kinsey? We'll be sad like all the moms and dads if she doesn't come out."

"But you're not her mom. I am. And I don't care if Mike is sad. I'm taking her to heaven with me. She needs to go to heaven with me."

Crazy. Completely, totally crazy.

Mike uttered a sharp curse word and bolted from the room. Jessica turned to Jack, desperate for some guidance. "Keep her talking," he mouthed. The secondary negotiator shoved a list of possible topics to broach with her.

She nodded. Lieutenant Perez went outside and the door hung open. The SWAT team was clustered around him and they were talking in low voices.

Keep her on the phone. Keep her talking. Keep her occupied until they could get in there and stop her.

Little Kinsey's life depended on it.

Chapter Seventeen

Brian and the rest of the team waited patiently behind the command post as the drama continued to unfold. A parade of police cars had driven past them on their way to the parking lot a block over, and Mike had run in the same direction for a reunion with his daughter. It was too soon to breathe a sigh of relief. The situation wasn't resolved. Far from it.

Heather was still holed up in there with her pink Christmas pistol, and until she was disarmed and in custody anything could happen. But the children in the daycare were safe, including little Kinsey. He wondered what kind of emotional impact this incident would have on her and the other kids in the daycare. The kids would probably suffer less than the adults charged with their wellbeing. Those ladies were going to need at least a few months with a counselor to put this night behind them.

And Jessica. He shuddered when he thought about what this night had done and was continuing to do to her. It didn't matter how strong she was or how willing to do what needed to be done. This was going to take a toll. Selfishly he wondered what this would do to his cause. If seeing a crisis up close would lend to her more understanding of his world and why he did what he did, or if it would drive her even further away from him.

The answer probably hinged on tonight's outcome.

They had barely settled in for another round of wait-and-see when Mike sprinted up the block, followed by Sugar Johnson running almost as fast. "What?"

"It's bad," was all Sugar said as she blew past them and into the command post. The door closed behind her, only to burst open a minute later. Mike snatched his rifle from the back of the Tahoe. "Fuck that keep-her-on-the-phone shit," he snapped. "I'm getting my daughter."

"Mike," Brian called. "No. Wait."

Mike ignored Brian and the other team members. He ran full tilt toward the building, carrying his rifle with him. The minute he emerged from the shadows into the spotlights a shot rang out. He was knocked back a good three feet and lay supine on the sidewalk. "Oh, God, he made the situation much worse," Brian murmured to nods of agreement.

"Do you suppose she even knew it was him?" Tommy Sanchez asked.

There was murmured agreement that she couldn't have known for sure but probably guessed it was.

Lieutenant Perez threw open the door. "What the fuck happened?"

"Werner rushed the building and she shot him. No blood, so she must have hit the vest," Tommy said. They all looked at one another. There would be no retrieving Mike until the crisis was over. They couldn't risk her shooting someone else and maybe hitting them in an unprotected spot.

They could only hope Mike didn't get up and try to charge her again.

Lieutenant Perez spared a laid-out Mike another disgusted look before turning back to the team. "Gentlemen, she still has the daughter and she's wearing a vest full of explosives. Her stated intention is to kill herself and take the child with her."

Brian fought back the horror. The situation had become more dangerous for him and every other member of the team. If they stormed the daycare, she could detonate the explosives and kill them all. To save her, they would have to gain entrance without her knowledge and secure the detonator. It could be done, of course, if Jessica could keep her talking as a distraction. But it wouldn't be easy and the risk to the team was enormous.

But they had to do something. Kinsey didn't deserve to die.

"She's still talking to the sister," Lieutenant Perez continued. "We'll keep that up as long as we can." He handed out an updated layout of the center, and they spent the next few minutes developing a plan for sneaking into the daycare, and another plan for storming the daycare if the negotiators and the psychologist determined that continued negotiation was hopeless. Brian blocked out his fear and committed his part of the plans to memory. Even though his stomach burned, he helped himself to another cup of coffee from the urn someone from downtown set up. The sky was beginning to lighten, and if this dragged on much longer he was going to be ready for more than the energy bars he'd snacked on for most of the night.

The sun was peeking over the horizon when the door to the command center opened. "Officer Howard. In here."

Brian jumped up and trotted up the stairs. He peered around at the exhausted faces that were looking at him with a mixture of hope and fear. Jessica was still wearing the headset and her face was pale beneath the stage makeup she still wore. Sweat beaded on her brow and dampened the hair around her face and her tee shirt. Jack was still listening in as she continued to murmur into the mouthpiece. The lieutenant motioned Brian to the empty chair beside Jessica's father and sat down across from him.

"She's agreed to release her daughter. But the deal is that you and only you can come get the child. And you have to come unarmed and with your face showing so she knows it's you. No helmet cam and no earpiece. She said she'd recognize you by the hair."

Brian swallowed and nodded. "What about his body armor?" Eddie asked quietly.

"She didn't say anything about body armor, so that stays. Her instructions are that you are to go to the window facing us, the one she's shot out of twice. She'll break out the rest of the glass and hand the child over to you. You take the child and run like hell. We'll take it from there."

Jessica spoke into the mic. "Wait, Heather." She listened a minute before pulling off the headset. Jack was also in the process of removing his. "She says she's through talking." She rolled her wheeled chair across the floor and joined them at the table. "She said to go get Kinsey." Her eyes were swimming with tears as she looked around the table. "She's going to trigger the explosion. She really wants to die. It's been in every word she's said for the last hour."

"I concur. As does the psychologist," Jack said tiredly. "Get that baby out of there, first and foremost. Then do what you can, if you can, for the mother."

"What? And let my daughter die?" Eddie snapped. "Damn it, stop with the pussyfooting around and do your damn jobs. SWAT needs to go in there *now*. You need to save them both."

"No, Dad," Jessica said sharply. "They storm that building before he has Kinsey, she'll detonate and take Kinsey and half the SWAT team with her." She swiped at the tears coursing down her cheeks. "Brian needs to save Kinsey. Before Heather changes her mind. I'm sorry, Dad. I tried." She bent over the table as sobs wracked her body.

"You have to save Heather, too. That's my little girl," Eddie snapped. "You can do it. You can get in there and save them both. If you just will."

"You know better than that, Eddie," Jack said quietly. "Do you really want to risk Kinsey's life that way?"

"It would be reckless of us to storm the building with the little girl inside, Mr. Herrmann," Lieutenant Perez added. "You of all people should know that." He took a breath. "The SWAT team will be in position. If she doesn't detonate immediately, we'll go in. But we get the child out first."

Eddie's jaw clenched and he shook his head angrily. Brian and Lieutenant Perez looked at one another. Brian unstrapped his helmet with the cam and his earpiece and laid them on the table. He looked across the table at Jessica. There was pure, unmitigated terror oozing out of every pore in her body.

She met his eyes and he nodded once. He would do everything he could to save her beloved little niece.

The team's eyes widened at the sight of him coming down the steps without the helmet. Lieutenant Perez followed him down, snapped out a few terse orders, and within three minutes the rest of the team was in position around the building. The sun was up over the horizon now, its bright rays shining down on the unfolding drama.

Brian took a deep breath and started down the sidewalk. His heart pounded and he could feel his pulse in his throat. He had no guarantee Heather would hand over the child. She could just as easily shoot him in the head once he'd gotten close. She could wait until he was outside the window and set off the explosives. He and everybody else was taking it on faith that Heather would do what she'd said, that she'd hand her daughter over and let him take the child to safety.

He spared Mike a glance. The dumb shit had taken the shot in the vest. He had crawled ten feet or so and taken shelter behind a parked car. He watched Brian walk by, his eyes questioning as Brian passed him. At least the fucker was smart enough to stay put and not risk getting shot again.

His heart pounded even harder as he neared the window. The glass was partially blown out, with jagged edges that would have to be removed before Kinsey could be passed through safely. It was dark inside the building. There had been no talk of shutting off the power, so he assumed Heather had turned off the lights. If they did end up storming the building, he would need to somehow tell them it was dark inside.

He stopped about fifteen feet from the window and held his arms out to his sides. Suddenly a section of glass exploded forward, and then another, and then another, this time accompanied by a small children's chair with metal legs. Soon more glass flew forward, as Heather used another little chair to break out the remaining glass. Finally the window was mostly clear, with an opening large enough to pass the small child through. "Heather. Can I get her now?" he asked quietly.

"In a minute." Heather's voice was hoarse and rasping. It would be, if she'd spent the better part of the night ranting over the phone.

Sweat dripped down his back as he waited. Without his helmet cam or earpiece, he was completely on his own. No lieutenant monitoring his every move. No knowledgeable negotiator or psychologist coaching him through the upcoming encounter. He'd never felt so alone.

He'd never been so damned scared in all his life.

He waited for what seemed like an eternity. Finally Heather came to the window. Her eyes were blank, her expression detached. A hunting vest with stuffed and bulging pockets was strapped snugly to her upper body. What looked like a detonation device sat on a children's play table a couple of feet behind her. Cold chills ran down his back as he stared at her, willing some expression of emotion from her he knew was not forthcoming.

Heather Werner had already checked out.

He stepped closer. Wordlessly she handed a tired-looking Kinsey through the window. The little girl squirmed and reached for her mother with her prosthesis. "Mommy?" The child leaned toward her mother. "I want you, Mommy."

"Go with Brian," Heather said harshly.

He cradled Kinsey against his chest. "Heather, are you—"

She shook her head and glanced down at the detonator. *This was it*. She was going to detonate. He whirled and ran as fast as his long legs could carry him. One second, two, three…

He felt rather than heard the explosion. One minute he was running as fast as he could, the next he was flying through the air as a wave of heat and pressure lifted him off his feet and propelled him forward. He clutched Kinsey as they flew together. He stumbled, unable to regain his footing when a slab of something hard hit him in the back, sending him sprawling face-first on the concrete sidewalk, his forehead hitting the pavement as oblivion overtook him.

***

Jessica stared transfixed at the video feed of the daycare center as the back wall exploded outward, debris flying across the street and into the walls of the surrounding buildings. She watched in horror as Brian sailed through the air with Kinsey cradled in his arms. He stumbled and fell facedown on the sidewalk with the child beneath his body as debris rained down on them. *Oh, God. Please let them be all right.* Her sister was probably gone. She couldn't lose Brian and Kinsey too.

She left her father sitting in the corner and bolted from the command post and ran toward Brian and Kinsey. But she was blocked by a human chain of police officers, and not even the claim that she was Kinsey's aunt gained her admittance.

There was already a crowd of EMS responders around Brian and her niece, and the SWAT team and other first responders were running toward the blown-out back wall of the daycare center, ready to put out any fire and see to Heather. She watched, not that she could see all that much, as they examined Brian and turned him over, freeing Kinsey. He had a nasty gash on his forehead and appeared unresponsive. Kinsey was conscious but dazed. They strapped Mike onto a stretcher. She watched grimly as the crowd parted and the three stretchers were loaded onto three waiting ambulances and driven away, lights and sirens flashing.

He has to be all right. He had to be.

She couldn't imagine the world without him in it.

She looked at the fourth ambulance, now sitting alone in the street. Almost as one, the somber crowd turned its attention to the flurry of activity inside the daycare, waiting with macabre fascination until a SWAT team member came outside shaking his head. He signaled to the ambulance and the driver took out a stretcher and a body bag. What tendrils of hope Jessica might have had withered and died as she watched them carry the body bag into the daycare center. Heather was dead. The body bag was for her.

Jessica walked toward the command post in a daze. *Heather had done it.* Heather had blown herself up. Jess hadn't been able to save her sister. The special bond she and her sister shared hadn't been enough. She'd begged and she'd pleaded and Heather had died anyway. A crushing sense of failure swamped her as she sank down into a chair and put her head in her hands. "Damn it, Heather, why? Why did you have to do that? Why did you have to leave me?" Sobs wrenched from her throat as she poured out her pain.

The big sister she'd loved so much was gone.

She felt a gentle hand on her back. "You did what you could, hon," Jack said gently. He sat down beside her. "And you need to remember. She went in there planning to kill everyone in the building. Then she planned to kill herself and Kinsey. In the end she killed only herself. Think about that, Jessica. You did that. Think about all those little kids, safe at home with their moms and dads this morning. Think about your niece."

"That's right." Jessica raised her head to a grim-faced Lieutenant Perez. "You saved over thirty children and their caregivers tonight. And you and Officer Howard saved Kinsey. You and that young man are both to be commended."

"She could have saved one more, if your department hadn't been so chickenshit," Dad snapped from where he still sat in the corner. His face was red and he was practically vibrating with fury. "You blew it. Every damned one of you. Jessica blew it. Jack blew it. SWAT should have gone in there. Brian Howard should have done something to stop her. But no, you all had your thumbs up your asses and my little girl is dead. *I* would have gone in there. *I* would have sent in SWAT." He turned to Jessica. "Robby would have done something. He wouldn't have left her to die."

Jack and Lieutenant Perez looked at Dad like he'd grown two heads. Jessica stared at her father in horror. "How can you say a thing like that?" she whispered. "When we tried so hard?"

"Because it's true," he said bitterly. "They all played it safe and my daughter's dead."

"But everyone else made it out," Lieutenant Perez snapped. "Including a brave young man who risked his life this morning to save your granddaughter. Which makes it a good outcome from my point of view."

Jack looked at Dad grimly. "Ed, I'm going to excuse the comments you made because you lost your child this morning and I know you're grieving. But you owe everyone you insulted an apology. Your daughter did a magnificent job with her sister. Lieutenant Perez made the right call. So did Brian Howard. No, they didn't go rushing in. They didn't go the brave but reckless route. They acted with thought and discretion, and their cool-headed actions saved a daycare full of innocent children. And that young man exercised the utmost in bravery and discretion and *saved your grandchild.* I hate to think of the carnage we would have seen if that hot-headed fool Robby Clary had been here today." He looked at Jessica and his face turned red. "Sorry about that. But it's the truth."

Jessica nodded as she dashed more tears from her eyes. "I appreciate what everybody did, even if my dad can't." She reached out and squeezed Jack's hand. "Thank you, Mr. Vance. I couldn't have done it without you."

"You were wonderful, Jessica. And I'm so sorry about Heather."

"So am I." She turned to her father. "I'm going to the hospital to check on Brian and Kinsey. He was unconscious when they put him in the ambulance and she was dazed. Go home to Mom and try not to be an ass to her."

One of Robby's old friends on the force gave her a lift in his squad car to the theater parking lot. Rachel insisted on going with her to the hospital where they learned that Brian was going to be all right, but that he would spend most of the day in testing and examinations and that he was not to be disturbed.

Since she wasn't immediate family they refused to let her see him, and no amount of pleading changed their minds. She was permitted to see Kinsey for a couple of minutes. The little girl and Mike would be going home with Mike's mother later in the day.

When there was nothing left for her at the hospital, Jessica dropped off Rachel at the theater. Bobby was with Mrs. Borrego, who was willing to keep him for as long as necessary, so she went home to grab a few hours of sleep before heading over to her parents' house. The next few days would be a living nightmare. As selfish as it seemed, she needed to take care of herself at least for a little while.

She made a sandwich and sat at the kitchen table mulling over the events of the last twelve hours. Oddly, it wasn't the long conversations she'd had on the phone with her sister that kept replaying, or even the moment the back wall exploded out of the daycare and she knew her sister was dead. It was the sharp words exchanged between her father and Jack Vance that kept looping through her mind.

Her father thought they had all messed up. He thought they should have sent in SWAT, guns blazing so to speak, even though it was clear to everyone else that would have been counterproductive. He thought they should have taken the risk anyway. And was furious when calmer heads prevailed like Lieutenant Perez's, Jack Vance's, and Brian's.

She swallowed the last of the sandwich and chased it with a soda. There was the difference. Right there. They weren't the chickenshits her father had accused them of being. It had taken unbelievable courage for Brian to take off that helmet and go get Kinsey. But they weren't foolhardy either. They analyzed the situation and acted accordingly. Brian knew making a rash move would be reckless in the extreme and would get him and Kinsey killed, so he didn't do it.

He was brave, but he wasn't reckless.

He took chances, but only the ones that were necessary.

He would walk toward danger when he had to.

And if he didn't have to, he didn't.

Chapter Eighteen

Brian stood in front of the refrigerator in his underwear and surveyed the contents. His mother had finally gone back to Houston this morning, but she had left behind enough casseroles and fried chicken to feed him for a week. Which was a good thing, because as shitty as he felt, he'd be eating frozen dinners and pizza delivery otherwise.

The stitches in his forehead itched and his head still ached like a son of a bitch from the concussion. The body armor had spread out the impact of the chunk of whatever it was that had hit him in the back, and his entire back ached every time he moved. His arms and the back of his head were covered with bruises and tiny scabs where smaller debris hit, and his ears were still hinky from the pressure wave.

The department physician had taken one look at him and declared a medical leave of at least four weeks, minimum. "And no, you don't have any business up on a stage, either, as much as my wife and I enjoyed your performance in *Oklahoma!*. Give it a rest and heal." The department psychologist wasn't quite as adamant, but she was also on board with the leave, the better to schedule a few sessions with her.

Not that he would be going back to the Durango any time soon. Not while Jessica was there. No way would he willingly be anywhere near her. Not with the way she must feel about him. She hadn't wanted to get involved with him in the first place. She sure wouldn't want him now.

At this point, she most likely hated his guts.

He debated between his mother's famous spaghetti casserole and leftover beef roast. The casserole won out so he nuked a plate and sat down at the kitchen table. But the casserole was a mistake. The flavors reminded him so much of that second date with Jessica that he pushed it aside, virtually untouched. But then everything these days reminded him of her. The sunshine made him think of her smile. The moonlight made him think of how she looked in his arms as he made love to her. The printers reminded him of the joy on her face when he'd given Kinsey her little hand.

And the dirty, bloody uniform thrown in the trash reminded him of the night he'd failed to save her older sister. Every time he looked at the damned bin he was reminded of Heather's dead eyes as she handed Kinsey over, and of his decision to leave Heather to her fate and take the child and run.

Lieutenant Perez had informed him of Eddie Herrmann's tirade the morning of his daughter's death. "I doubt anything will come of it. But if he files a complaint with the department, Internal Affairs may have a few questions for you. Not that you have a thing to worry about. We did the right thing."

Brian sighed and carried his plate to the sink. It didn't matter if the department thought they did the right thing. Eddie didn't. Jessica probably agreed with him.

He had replayed the scene a hundred times in his mind. Had he been a coward for taking Kinsey and running? He'd asked himself over and over if there was anything he could have done differently. If there was, he didn't know what it might have been. Still, it pained him that he hadn't saved Heather.

Kinsey had lost her mother. Jessica had lost her only sister.

He'd lost Jessica.

And even if Jessica didn't agree with her father, she still had no business with Brian. He hadn't missed the look on her face that morning when he'd taken off his helmet and walked out of the command post. She had been truly terrified for him, as she had been that night at the hospital when she'd thrown up in the parking lot.

Maybe she did know best. Maybe living with him and worrying about him all the time wasn't the life she was meant to live.

Maybe she would be better off with Barry the Dentist.

He threw the soda can in the trash and was about to curl up on the sofa with a Netflix blow-em-up when his doorbell rang. He looked at his phone app and was shocked to see Jessica standing at his front door with an uncertain expression on her face. He hadn't seen her or heard from her since he'd left the command post to retrieve Kinsey. He didn't know what she was doing here now. Or why she would be here when she and her family were bound to despise him. He started to ignore her, but she rang the doorbell a second time and then knocked sharply. Fine. He would hear what she had to say and send her away.

He snatched a pair of sweatpants from the chair and pulled them on. His undershirt would have to do. He opened the door and looked down into her upturned face. Deep shadows rode beneath her eyes and her face was drawn and tired. He cursed the way his heart leapt at the sight of her.

"What do you want?" he asked curtly.

She took a step back. "May I come in?"

"Whatever."

She walked into his living room and he shut the door behind her. She looked around the room. "It's nice."

"That's right. You've never been over here."

She shook her head. "No, I guess I haven't." She stepped to the seating group facing the television and sat down in one of the chairs. "I'm sorry I haven't been over here until now to see how you're doing. We finally buried Heather yesterday." She paused a moment. "We had to do a cremation."

He flopped down in his usual spot on the sofa. "I didn't expect you to come at all."

"I went to the hospital that morning but they wouldn't let me see you. And then I had to take care of everything. The funeral home. The service. The reception afterward. Mom and Dad fell apart, and Mike had his hands full with Kinsey. She keeps asking for her Mommy."

"Damn. I'm sorry I didn't save Mommy."

Jessica's eyes grew round. "That's not what I meant. I know you couldn't save Heather. I was there, remember? I know damned well there was no saving her."

"That's not what your father thinks. Lieutenant Perez is afraid he's going to lodge a complaint with the department."

"Rash words spoken in the grief of the moment. After Mr. Vance got through with him, he regretted every one of them."

Brian shrugged. "Rash words but probably honest ones." He stared at her a minute. "What do you want?"

"I want to talk about us."

"Why? I know you want no part of me anymore. You could have sent me a text."

"Brian, *no*. I didn't come over to break up with you. I came over to tell you I'm ready for the real relationship you wanted."

He swallowed and looked her in the eye. "Not only no, but hell, no."

She looked at him in shock. "But you said that was what you wanted. You were ready to break up with me because I wouldn't go there. So now I do and you don't want it anymore?"

"You don't want it. You only think you do." He winced as he shifted on the sofa. "Look, I don't pretend to know what's going through your head. Maybe a weird sense of gratitude because I saved Kinsey, or guilt because I got hurt saving her, or maybe you're singing 'Holding out for a Hero' in your head. But that's gonna wear off before too long. And we'll be right back to square one.

"You'll be scared shitless every time I walk out the door. You'll be nagging me to change jobs or get off SWAT. You'll be puking in the hospital parking lot every time I have to go to the emergency room. I saw the terror on your face that morning when I took off my helmet and walked out of the command post." He raised his arms helplessly. "It wasn't the first time I've had to do something like that, and it won't be the last. That's who I am and that's the job I do, and it makes you crazy. It's not going to work."

Jessica's eyes flashed. "Of course there was terror on my face. You were facing off with my sister and trying to save my niece. I was frightened for you. How could I not be?"

"If it were that one time, I could understand. But it's a repeating pattern. Everything I do terrifies you. Remember? You were so scared you refused me over and over. Then you kept me at arm's length with the intention of taking what we had and making them meaningless fucks. And when you come to your senses that's all you'll want, if you'll want even that much. I've finally accepted it. I've finally gotten the message. I'm no good for you. At least, you don't think I am." He smiled sadly. "Go find that teacher or that plumber, or that engineer and have a happy life with him. Barry the Dentist would be a good choice."

"So you're giving up?"

"Yep. Tell your father I'm sorry I didn't live up to his standards."

"Is that why you're breaking up? Because of my asshole father?"

"No. But he doesn't help things much."

"I see." She looked at him sadly. "So that's that." She stood up. "Will I see you at the Durango?"

He shook his head. "That's your turf. I'll hang out elsewhere."

She walked to the door. "I guess today was too little, too late. I'm sorry, Brian."

"So am I."

The door shut quietly behind her. He cradled a throw pillow in his lap and stared into space as a single tear rolled down his cheek.

He would miss her. God, he would miss her so much.

But she was better off without him.

Chapter Nineteen

Brian pulled into the substation parking lot and found a spot close to the door. The bright May sunshine was somewhere between warm and hot in the middle of the day, but it would be cool when he got off work tonight at eleven. He was already on a late-to-bed, late-to-rise sleep schedule, having fallen into the pattern of sitting up half the night watching Netflix and sleeping in, courtesy of his enforced medical leave. Which, thankfully, ended yesterday when the department physician and the department psychologist pronounced him fit for duty. He was so stiff and sore the first couple of weeks after the explosion he wouldn't have wanted to work. But as his body healed, boredom set in, and by the last week he was spending hours out by the pool and climbing the walls looking for something to occupy his time.

Besides, if he were working he wouldn't have so much time to miss Jessica.

He passed both Sugar and Lydia going into the women's locker room. The men's locker room was filling up as the three-to-eleven shift drifted in. He took off his uniform shirt and was adjusting the fit of his new body armor when Mike came in with his uniform in a dry cleaner's bag. His face was drawn and tired and grief surrounded him like a shroud. His eyes widened when he spotted Brian. "Hey, man. Welcome back." To Brian's surprise Mike engulfed him in a bro hug. "Thanks for getting my little girl back to me." Mike's eyes were suspiciously moist.

Brian returned the hug. "I'm glad she's safe. I'm sorry about... I wish there was something more I could have done."

Mike shook his head. "That's not on you."

Brian shrugged. "Thanks. Not everybody feels that way."

Mike snorted. "You mean Eddie? They said he went off on everybody that morning. Even Jessica. He's known for running his mouth and eating his words."

Brian shrugged. "How's Kinsey?"

"I owe my mother and Jean Herrmann flowers every day for the rest of their lives. Heather's parents may still be pissed as hell at me, but they've been a godsend with Kinsey." He sat down and kicked off his tennis shoes. "Jessica's helped too. Even though most of the time she looks like she swallowed a pickle. That's what she gets, I guess. Dumping you after you saved her niece. Serves her right."

Brian looked at Mike. "Dumping me? Where'd you get an idea like that?"

"Well, she did. Didn't she? So damned determined not to fall for a first responder and all that. I figured after what she got a load of that morning, she couldn't run away fast enough."

"Well, you figured wrong. She didn't do the dumping. I did."

Mike looked at him disbelievingly. "*You* did the dumping? As long and as hard as you chased that woman? What the fuck?"

Brian lifted his chin. "I decided she was right. She's not cut out for the life. She doesn't want it and I told her so."

"You did, huh? When did you tell her that?"

"She came by the condo the day after the funeral. I sent her on her way."

"Why?"

"Because she was feeling grateful about Kinsey or guilty about me getting hurt, or something like that. She's probably over that by now." Tears stung his eyes.

Mike shook his head. "That explosion must have rattled your brain. You wouldn't have been that stupid otherwise." He stood up and shucked off his jeans.

"Stupid?"

Mike looked at him with exasperation. "Because Jess knows her own mind."

"Yes, she does. And she told me for four fucking months she wasn't getting involved with me. So forgive me if I don't believe her now."

"That's because you don't really know her that well yet. If you did know her better, you'd understand. She rarely changes her mind about anything. When she does change her mind, she's serious about it. If she says she's ready to put aside her doubts and proceed full speed ahead with you, she means it. She's not changing it back."

"And you would know this because?"

"I've known her for a long time. Years. Since she was married to Robby."

"Oh." He pulled on his uniform shirt.

"Look, man, I told you I'd stay out of your deal with Jessica and I meant it, but I'm gonna say one thing before I shut up. No, two things. No, make that three things you need to consider."

Brian rolled his eyes. "Whatever. Lay 'em on me."

"First, it probably took everything she had to come to you the way she did. Now that you've thrown it in her face, she won't be back. If you give a shit, the ball's in your court."

"The second?"

"If you do talk to her, you might want to find out what prompted the change of mind. I have an idea what it might be, but it would be better coming from her. At least ask."

"And if it's a bullshit reason?"

"Then you'll know."

"The third?" Brian prompted.

"This one's probably gonna piss you off."

"So? That's never bothered you before."

"Okay, then. If you do get back together, she's making a huge concession, agreeing to give you a chance, cop and SWAT team and all. Maybe she shouldn't have to be making all the concessions."

Brian nodded and buttoned his uniform shirt, ready to go out and do his job.

His shift kept him hopping, but he was deep in thought as he drove home that evening. He nuked some leftover pizza and drank a beer. Then he powered up his laptop, addressed an email, and began writing.

***

Jessica pulled into her parents' driveway and parked behind her father's pickup truck. She was later than usual, having taken advantage of a quiet hour after classes were finished to knock out some paperwork. Thanks to yet another grant from the Navarros, the summer theater camp was fully funded for four hundred children and teens from all over the city. Her staff positions were also filled with her regular instructors as well as several public-school drama teachers wanting summer work. Auditions for both the adult and

Academy casts for *The Little Mermaid* would be held next week, and rehearsals would begin soon afterwards. It was shaping up to be a busy summer.

Which was good. Maybe she would be too busy to miss Brian.

Or maybe she would find a fairy swimming in her coffee in the morning.

Neither was particularly likely.

She trudged up the sidewalk and knocked softly. Dad came to the door. "Come on in. We started to call you and tell you to go home. Bobby's asleep. He went to sleep when Kinsey did." He held the door so she could come inside.

"No, I need to take him home so Mom can sleep in tomorrow. Having the two of them here is wearing her out."

"It's also keeping her sane. With them to look after, she's too busy to brood. Come on back. Your mother made stew for dinner."

She followed her father through the family room into the kitchen. He motioned for her to sit down and took a plastic carton from the refrigerator. She looked at her father and mentally gave herself a shake. Both of her parents had aged ten years in the last month. The lines on her father's face were deeper and his eyes were sunken. His shoulders sagged and the spring in his step was gone. While he and her mother were doing better than they were the first few days after Heather's death, they still had a long way to go to recover from the devastating blow.

Admittedly, she wasn't anywhere near recovered herself. She'd already had a few talks with the therapist Maggie Gutierrez sent her to. There would be more visits in her future. Maybe someday they would all be able to come to terms with what had happened. But they would never put it behind them completely. They all were looking at a new norm, one without their beloved Heather in their lives.

Her dad spooned a generous portion into a bowl and held it out. "Is this about right?"

"It's more than enough."

He nuked the stew and set it in front of her with a glass of milk. He sat down across from her and folded his arms in front of him. "So have you forgiven me for those God-awful things I said the morning your sister died?" He'd come to house that evening, crying bitter tears and begging her forgiveness, and couldn't seem to believe that she'd forgiven him.

"Yes, I have. Did you ever make it right with Mr. Vance and Lieutenant Perez? The lieutenant was so concerned that you might file a complaint that he said something to Brian about it."

"I called them both the next morning. Jack was gracious, the lieutenant less so. But I did make the effort." He looked at her. "Do I need to apologize to Brian as well? Your mother sent him a letter thanking him for what he did that morning, but maybe that's not enough. Especially if you're still seeing him."

Jessica shrugged one shoulder. "I'm not. But thanks for the thought."

His eyes narrowed. "Don't tell me you broke up with him. Not after what he did for this family."

"I didn't break up with him, he broke up with me." She looked down at the stew, her appetite suddenly gone. "You want to hear the ultimate irony? I went by his house the day after the funeral to tell him I was ready to be his girlfriend for real. See where it took us. I was all in. And he showed me the door. Told me I didn't know my own mind, and that whenever I got over my guilt, gratitude or hero worship that I'd want out. He said he'd gotten the message and that I was right. I'm better off without him."

Her father whistled under his breath. "I can understand his reluctance. You'd been adamant for an awfully long time. And now you've changed your mind. I don't blame him for wondering."

"I thought he didn't want me anymore."

His eyes softened. "I doubt that. I saw the way he looked at you that night in the command post. He's either in love with you or damned close."

"Not close enough to want to try, or even ask why I'd changed my mind."

"You didn't tell him?"

"Dad, it was the day after we buried Heather. I was mentally and physically exhausted. It was all I could do to even go to his place and knock on his door. I didn't have the energy to argue or explain."

"And now?"

"He kicked me to the curb. I have my answer."

"No, you don't. You talked to him at the worst possible time for both of you. He was still injured and hurting from the explosion and in a world of guilt for not saving your sister. You were exhausted, and your emotions were raw from having to take care of everything for your mother and me. If you'd talked to him a week later, the outcome would probably have been much different."

"Maybe. Maybe not."

Her father looked at her thoughtfully. "If you don't mind my asking, why did you change your mind, especially after what you saw that night? That alone would have inspired most women to run the other direction."

"You sure you want to hear the answer?"

"No. But I probably need to."

"Because while Brian put his life on the line to save Kinsey, and he wasn't reckless about it. He did what he had to do, but he was careful. He didn't take any foolish chances. He didn't try to jump through the window and grab Heather or do anything stupid. He didn't go the brave but reckless route. He kept a cool head and did what he had to do as safely as he could. They all did."

"Unlike what Robby would have done."

"Exactly."

"Unlike what I would have done."

"That's right," she said evenly.

"Even though it made me mad."

"Even though."

"And you can live with that. Him doing a dangerous job, as long as he's careful."

"I can live with that."

"Then you need to put on your big-girl panties and go tell him so. Tell him what you told me."

"It won't make a bit of difference. His mind is made up."

"So was yours. But you changed it. And if you can change yours, you can change his."

She looked at him curiously. "Why do you even care?"

He leaned back and looked at her incredulously. "Because you're my little girl. The only one I have left. And I want you to be happy." His eyes filled with tears. "Your sister, she wasn't ever going to be happy. But you? You're meant to be happy. You're meant to have joy in your life. You've gone without it too long and it's time for that to change. And that young man, he can bring you joy, if you'll let him."

He stopped and cleared his throat. "It's getting late. Let me help you get Bobby in the truck. Then you go home and you figure out what you're going to say to Brian the next time you see him."

They stood and Dad pulled her into a hug. "I love you, Jessica. I know I was a shit that morning, but I'm proud of what you did that night with your sister. That young man you're going to get back, he's a hero. But in my eyes, you're as big a hero as he is."

"Thank you, Dad. That means a lot."

Her father scooped Bobby up off the bed and put him in his car seat. He gave Jessica another hug and stood in the driveway until she'd driven off.

Huh. Her father thought she and Brian still had a chance. She didn't think so. He'd been adamant that day about sending her away. But now she wondered if her father might have a point. They had both been in a bad place that afternoon. Now they'd both had a month to think and heal. Maybe if she talked to him again, explained that she still wanted to go forward with him, this time he would believe her.

She would take some time to think about it. She turned the corner leading to her house and her eyes widened.

Maybe she wouldn't be taking any time to think about it. Maybe she would be talking to him tonight.

She pulled into the driveway beside a familiar truck. Brian sat on the front step under the porch light, his hair shining like a beacon. Jessica's lips firmed. It was no coincidence, him coming over here not minutes after she talked to her father. She wondered what kind of incentive Dad had used to get Brian to come over tonight. She bit her lip as she turned off the engine. Her father had forced her hand. And she had no idea what to say to convince Brian to give them another chance.

He got up and met her at the passenger door next to Bobby's car seat. "Get him unbuckled and I'll carry him in."

She undid the buckles and Brian lifted Bobby from the car seat. He cradled the child to his chest, much the way he'd carried Kinsey that morning. Regret swamped her as she looked at Bobby in his arms. She should have let him get to know her son. She should have let Bobby get to know him. Unbidden, she imagined him holding the hand of a little redheaded girl with delicate features as she took her first dance steps.

He would be a wonderful father.

She unlocked the door and escorted them to Bobby's room. "As warm as it is, he can lay on the bedspread tonight."

"He's already in his pajamas. Does your mom give him his bath every night?"

"She does. Or sometimes Dad does."

They returned to the living room. She stared across the room. He was still in his uniform. The cuts and bruises had healed, but the gash on his forehead had left a long, red scar that would be a while fading. His freckles were darker, leading her to think he must have spent some time in the sun. But it was the uncertainness in his expression that caught her attention. Like her, he didn't seem to know what to say.

Maybe she should kiss him.

She finally broke the silence. "Have you had anything to eat? Or did you have to work straight through?"

"I caught a hamburger about six. Not one of those good ones like we ate that time."

"You're probably hungry again. I can make you a sandwich."

"I'd appreciate that. Thanks."

She piled on cold cuts and sliced cheese and got out her last beer. He wolfed down the sandwich and downed the beer. She sat down across the table from him. "Did Dad send you over here tonight?"

"Kind of. He got in touch with Mike, and Mike texted me. I was coming over to see you in a day or two anyway."

"You were?"

"Don't sound so skeptical. I was planning to come talk to you."

"I thought you pretty much said it all that afternoon at your place."

"I fucked up royally that afternoon. I was in a bad place and took it out on you. I'm better now. The department psychologist helped me see a few things more clearly. And Mike's kick in the seat of the pants didn't hurt."

"Mike? Mike spoke up for me?"

"He did. He said you rarely change your mind, and that when you do, you don't change it back." He stopped and took a breath. "He said I needed to ask you why you changed your mind." He looked at her quizzically. "So why the change of heart? I thought sure that after what you saw and went through that morning, you'd be more inclined than ever to run for the hills."

"Most people would probably react that way. But I saw something different. I guess you could say I had an epiphany of sorts."

"What kind of epiphany?"

"I finally understood what you've been trying to tell me all this time. I watched all of you that night. Mr. Vance, Lieutenant Perez, and you. Especially you. You were all calm, and you acted thoughtfully. You didn't rush in, and you didn't take unnecessary chances. You were brave, but you were smart at the same time. You went in there and you got Kinsey and you saved her. You knew you couldn't save Heather so you didn't endanger yourself or Kinsey any further by trying something rash or stupid."

She stopped and took a breath. "They had an argument about it afterwards. In the command post. Dad lost it. He thought they should have stormed the place. Gone in and done *something*. He said some shitty things about them not doing their jobs. He said you should have done more. He said he would have handled it differently, and that Robby would have handled it differently. Right there I saw the difference. Dad and Robby both would have taken a reckless chance that night. Maybe they would have saved her and maybe they would have died along with her. You did what you could, you weren't reckless or stupid, and you saved Kinsey. The world was a safer place for her that night because of you. The world's been a safer place a lot of times because of you." She felt tears stinging her eyes and she blinked them away. "I thought you were all like Robby. And Dad. But you're not. You do what you have to do, but you're as careful as you can be doing it. I can live with that. I couldn't live with the recklessness."

"What about all the worry? You said you didn't want that anymore."

"Sure, I'm gonna worry. But I'll worry a hell of a lot less knowing that you're not reckless. I can live with it."

"But what if you didn't have to?"

She shook her head. "Brian, I said I would. Please don't do this. At least give us a chance."

"That's not what I meant," he said quickly. "I meant what if you didn't have to worry about SWAT?"

"I thought SWAT was who you are."

"Maybe it's not." He reached across the table for her hand. "I did some watching of my own that night. What I could, with you and Vance inside and me waiting on the outside. And I decided that I wasn't the real hero that night. None of the guys on the SWAT team were. It was you, Jessica. You and Mr. Vance. You were the ones who saved a whole daycare center full of children and their caregivers. I saved one. You and Mr. Vance saved nearly forty."

"It wasn't me. I listened to her and said what Mr. Vance told me to say. It was him that night."

"I'm not sure I agree with that, but whatever. The point is that the negotiators were the real heroes that night. Not the guys holding the guns. I want to be that guy next time. I want to be the one on the phone, talking the perp down."

She looked at him thoughtfully. "I can see you doing that. I think you'd be good at it."

He smiled gently. "Thanks."

"Does that take a lot of additional training?"

"Sure it does. I might be a little scarce at the Durango for a few months. They'll have to do *The Little Mermaid* without me."

"Aw, and here I was looking forward to seeing you in a merman's tail."

He laughed. "I probably would have skipped that one anyway." His face sobered. "I applied for the change in position a few days ago. I haven't heard anything officially, but Mr. Vance dropped by yesterday morning. He said he's really getting tired of it, being on call like he is all the time at his age. He's willing to work with me and some others over and above the department training. I took it him up on it. All we're waiting for is the department go-ahead."

"Are you sure?"

"I'm sure. I want this for both of us. I want it for myself as much as I want it for you. I was going to come to you when it was official. But Mike called and relayed your father's instructions to 'Get my ass over here and make things right.'"

"Sounds like him." She sniffed back tears of joy as she looked across the table. "I love you, Brian. I know it's too soon."

"Damned if that's true. I love you, and have for a long time." He stood up and reached out for her. "I need a hug and a kiss about now."

194

"I thought you'd never ask."

She rose to her feet and melted into his arms. He wrapped his strong arms around her and held her close, his lips firm and gentle, his kiss holding a wealth of promise for the future. They clung together for long moments as they savored being in one another's arms again.

Finally he raised his head and looked down into her eyes. "So where do we go from here?" he asked, his face shining with love.

"We go into my bedroom and make love all night. I make pancakes in the morning while you and Bobby get to know one another a little better. We take it from there."

"Sounds like a winner." He kissed her again and scooped her up into his arms. "It's gonna be a lot of fun, you know." His eyes were shining and his smile was wide.

"It will be a lot of fun," she agreed. "I can hardly wait."

Epilogue

Letti stalked out of Jessica's office, trembling with fury. Jessica had to be out of her mind, casting Emma Ellis as Ariel in *The Little Mermaid*. Emma couldn't act her way out of a paper bag and was terrified of her own shadow. No way was the kid going to do Ariel justice, not like Sophie would have. And Jessica knew damned well Sophie needed the role on her résumé. Her daughter was applying to the top-name acting schools in the country and the competition would be stiff. Sophie needed every lead role she could get. Other considerations? The only other consideration Letti knew of was that every production at the Durango had to be quality. Or the Navarros would take their largesse and their big checks elsewhere. Sophie's performance would have been quality. Little Emma Ellis's? Not so much.

She heard footsteps behind her. "Mom, wait up."

Lettie kept walking. She had no desire to go a round with Sophie right now. They were almost to the lobby when her daughter caught up with her. "I can't believe you did that," Sophie hissed. "I have never been so embarrassed in all my *life*. You were so *pushy*. I am positively going to *die* of embarrassment."

Letti hid her smile. At seventeen, Sophia Carmen Aldrete was every inch the drama queen. She reached out and patted Sophie's arm. "I think you'll survive. Damn, you need that role. Sweetie, the competition to get into a top-notch acting school is fierce. You need the strongest résumé you can possibly build. You needed that role."

"Mom, you heard Jessica. I'll have other good roles."

"But how many before we start sending in applications? The window of opportunity here at the Durango is quickly closing. You'll have one more chance in the fall, and that's it."

"Mom, I have a list of credits as long as my arm," Sophie said quietly.

"So will every other kid's application. *The Little Mermaid* might have made the difference to an application committee." She looked at her beautiful daughter. "Sophie, I lost my chance for a career in Hollywood. I don't want that to happen to you. I want you to have the chance to do what I didn't. And if it means I have to be pushy on occasion, I'll push." She glanced down at her watch. "Your brother's soccer practice will be over in fifteen minutes. Aren't you supposed to pick him up on the way to your father's for dinner?"

Sophie nodded and ran through the lobby. Letti followed more slowly. It would be good to have a few hours by herself to grab some takeout and grade a few tests. She was halfway across the lobby when she noticed a familiar head of sun-streaked hair bending over to reach the under-the-counter refrigerator in the concession booth. "Those sodas are for sale," she said dryly. "We customarily bring our own."

Kevin straightened and grinned sardonically. "I know they're for sale. I plan to sell all I can Friday night. Gotta earn my money."

What the hell? Why would Kevin Summerset be selling sodas in the lobby? "Did Josh hire you?"

"Sure did."

Wonderful. She'd be tripping over him all the time now, constantly reminded of the night she'd been stupid in the extreme. "Why here? There are bound to be better jobs elsewhere. Or are you planning to be part of the theater?"

"Perfect part-time job. I can get involved with the theater and I can be here for Emma. Which appears to be necessary, given your performance in Jessica's office a few minutes ago."

"Tough. If Emma's going to do theater, she better get used to an honest assessment of her talent. Or lack of it, in her case."

"Jesus, you're hard."

"No, I'm honest. Sophie can act and sing circles around your niece. Sorry if the truth sucks." She looked him up and down taking in the sun-bleached hair, the dark tan, the muscular body showcased by his tight tee shirt and cargo shorts. Damn if she didn't feel a tingle of attraction, the same attraction she'd felt five years ago. "So you're back."

He nodded. "I'm back. Hollywood's not all it's cracked up to be." He looked her up and down much as she had him. "Damn. You're looking good, woman." He leaned forward, a wicked grin on his lips. "Care to take up where we left off? Go for a repeat or two? That was one hell of a night."

Cheeky asshole. The nerve of the little shit to bring up the most mortifying moment in her life. And the hell of it was that she felt the same pull toward him as she had five years ago. It was galling to have the hots for a young man fifteen years her junior. Hell, he was closer in age to Sophie than to Letti. He'd been in diapers when she'd been in high school.

If they'd been handing out a prize for audacity this afternoon, he'd won first place.

On the other hand, two could play at that game. She raised her eyebrow and looked him up and down for a second time before shaking her head. "I don't think so." She reached out and patted his arm. "The tutoring session with you was a fun departure, and I remember it fondly. But these days I've sworn off boys and I'm sticking to men who know what they're doing. But thanks for the offer. See you around, hon."

She winked and sailed out before he could reply.

ABOUT THE AUTHOR

The author of over thirty romance novels, Emily Mims combined her writing career with a career in public education until leaving the classroom to write full time. The mother of two sons, she and her husband split their time between central Texas, eastern Tennessee, and Georgia visiting their kids and grandchildren. For relaxation Emily plays the piano, organ, dulcimer, and ukulele for two different performing groups, and even sings a little. She says, "I love to write romances because I believe in them. Romance happened to me and it can happen to any woman—if she'll just let it."

Connect with Emily:
facebook.com/emily.mims.756
twitter.com/emilymimsauthor
instagram.com/mims_emily
website: emilymims.com

www.BOROUGHSPUBLISHINGGROUP.com

If you enjoyed this book, please write a review. Our authors appreciate the feedback, and it helps future readers find books they love. We welcome your comments and invite you to send them to info@boroughspublishinggroup.com. Follow us on Facebook, Twitter and Instagram, and be sure to sign up for our newsletter for surprises and new releases from your favorite authors.

Are you an aspiring writer? Check out www.boroughspublishinggroup.com/submit and see if we can help you make your dreams come true.

www.ingramcontent.com/pod-product-compliance
Lightning Source LLC
Chambersburg PA
CBHW030330180626
46810CB00003B/1299